I0686953

DICK BLOWHARD 2
BLOW HARDER

Also by T. M. Brenner

Luminaries

Sky Child

Sky Machine

Sky War

Clandestined

Clandestined: Dark Times

Clandestined: Oblivion

The Pan-Galactic Misadventures of Dick Blowhard

Why You Shouldn't Be an Author

Coming Soon: Murder at the Sylvia Beach Hotel

Dick Blowhard 3: With a Vengeance

DICK BLOWHARD
2
BLOW HARDER

For my friend Paul,

who supported and believed in me

even when I didn't.

1

Unicorns are still assholes. A dozen of them just showed up at Nunya's bar, looking for trouble. Apparently, they're upset that I killed a bunch of their friends a month ago, and they want payback. The good news is Nunya just gifted me two of the most fucking awesome space-blasters ever and I'm itching to use them. The bad news is she just reopened her bar after I accidentally destroyed it, and it looks like it's gonna get fucked up again.

Now, if you missed my earlier memoir, 'The Pan-Galactic Misadventures of Dick Blowhard', you may not know that these 'unicorns' aren't what you normally think of. They aren't whimsical creatures that inspire children and have their own cartoons. They're blood red, except for a single, demonic looking black horn on top of their head. They also wear leather head-to-toe like they're in a biker gang. Seriously though, if you haven't read 'The Pan-Galactic Misadventures of Dick Blowhard' yet you might want to, because this memoir will make a hell of a lot more sense.

I pull the space-blasters out of the gift box and start firing. Nunya bolts and hops over the bar like it isn't even there then dives into her stockroom. I try to distract the Unicorns so she doesn't get hurt. They seem to ignore her, either because they don't realize she's a threat or because they only care about killing me.

With my new blasters, named Nunya and Nunya, I start nailing the Unicorns. Black blood spurts out of their bodies, sending goo flying around like hot naked chicks wrestling in mud. Three of the Unicorns fall to the ground, making a huge oily mess on Nunya's brand-new wood floor. She's gonna be pissed.

Yup, she's pissed, because she pops her head over the bar and starts shooting at the Unicorns herself. The heads of the two Unicorns nearest the bar explode like melons, sending pieces of Unicorn brain splattering in all directions. A chunk of Unicorn brain makes its way into my mouth, and I start gagging. I've eaten a lot of nasty things in my time, and a lot of nasty women, but Unicorn brains have got to be the nastiest.

While I spew my breakfast onto the ground, the Unicorns light me up like a Christmas tree. Or a menorah. Or a kinara. Or an aluminum pole. Thankfully, the tux I'm wearing is blaster proof, as is the rest of me. Unfortunately, a lot of the blaster fire bounces off

1

and damages Nunya's brand-new bar. For some reason when she rebuilt it, she decided to make it look exactly as shitty as it originally looked. I tried to spruce the place up a little by hanging the most expensive piece of art in the galaxy on her wall: a velvet painting of yours truly, but she didn't appreciate it as much as she should have.

I take out a few more Unicorns with my blasters before the remaining five duck behind tables. The great thing about wooden tables is they make for shitty cover. Instead of waiting for them to pop their horned heads up I just shoot through the brown squares of wood, turning them into Swiss cheese. And yeah, like I mentioned before, Swiss cheese is definitely a thing here in the ass-end of space.

After a few seconds of firing wildly, Nunya and I both stop. I walk over to the tables the Unicorns are hiding behind and toss them out of the way. All but one of the Unicorns is dead, but the one that's still alive seems really fucked up. It looks up at me and starts firing right at my face. I just grab the blaster out of his hands and huck it behind me.

"How the fuck did you know to come here?" I ask.

"Go to hell," he says, spitting black blood into my face. I calmly wipe it away then stomp on his arm. The Unicorn screams out in pain.

"I asked, how the fuck did you know to come here?"

It takes him a moment of groaning to finally respond. "One of the guys that came here a month ago, Carl, has a cousin named Larry. Larry's the dead one over there," he says, nodding toward one of the Unicorns who's missing their brains. "Carl told Larry he was supposed to meet up with you to steal your malorian ore, only he never came back. After a while Larry grew suspicious, so he asked the rest of us to come along to see what happened."

"Shit, you guys have names? That's weird. And I didn't think you were intelligent enough to hold a conversation. I thought you just grunted at each other like cavemen."

"Yeah, well, fuck you. I could say the same about you humans. We're higher up on the food chain, which is why our skin is so tough, and why we have these stabby things on the top of our heads," he says, pointing to his horn. "You humans are all pink and squishy and stupid looking. I could eat a dozen of you in a day if I wanted."

"Wait, you eat people?" asks Nunya, who appears next to me suddenly.

"I wouldn't call you 'humans' people, but yeah, sure, we eat people. You aren't too bad with enough barbeque sauce."

"That's fucking gross," I say.

"Have you ever tried eating humans?" asks the Unicorn.

"Well, I've eaten a lot of women out, but I don't think that counts," I say.

"So have I, and it doesn't," says Nunya.

I glance over at her, and she has the biggest smirk. Rolling my eyes, I turn back to the Unicorn. "So, tell me..."

"Ted."

"So, tell me, Ted, are there going to be more of you coming to kill us now? Because if I have to deal with this a third time, I'm gonna hunt down your friends and family and kill them too. I really don't want to do that because I'm trying to be a better person now. From what stupid movies tell me, vengeance is wrong. I don't really believe that, but it fucking shows up in so many TV shows that it may as well be true. And honestly, if I want a chance at having sex with God, I figure I better be as good as I can be. She seems like the type who'd have standards, unlike the chicks I'm used to."

"Wait, what? Having sex with God? And you think there's something wrong with me?" says Ted.

"Well, yeah, you're a Unicorn. That automatically makes you an asshole," I say.

"Yeah, well we feel the same way about humans. And to answer your question, I have no idea if anyone that you just murdered had told their family or friends about coming here. So, I have no idea. So, fuck you and all that."

"Okay, I hear what you're saying, and I don't really like it. But since I'm trying to be a better person, I'm going to take your weapons and let you go. You've been a big help, Ted. Now, you go back to whatever shithole you came from and tell the other toilet cloggers not to come back. I'll leave you alone if you leave me alone. Understood?"

"Yeah, sure, understood. The only thing is you shot me up pretty bad and I'm feeling a little woozy. Can you at least get me a Band-Aid, or gauze or some shit?" asks Ted.

"I'll do you one better," I say.

I place my hands on his arm and start to heal him. It takes a few minutes, and he writhes around in pain for most of it, but eventually he's back to his normal, asshole self.

"Uh, wow man, thanks," says Ted.

I help him get to his feet then walk next to him to keep him from doing anything stupid. We go outside together, with Nunya trailing behind. Parked in front of the bar are a bunch of space-

3

cycles, but their owners won't be returning to them. He hops on the third one, slowly pulls out (heh), and flies up into the sky.

"Well, that sucked," I say.

"At least the bar's still standing. We'll need a fuck-ton of new wood to repair everything, but I can still serve drinks in the meantime," says Nunya.

As we're talking, two large, green laser blasts hit the bar, sending wood and glass flying everywhere. Instinctively, I holster my new blasters and turn to cover Nunya with my body. She would have been fine on her own if she was wearing her magical armor and robes. Without them, she's just as soft and squishy as the Unicorn said.

"Nooooooo!" she screams.

I can tell she's pissed as she struggles to get out of my arms, but I don't let go of her until I'm sure everything is still, and that nothing can hurt her. Once I've moved us out of harm's way I let her go.

"Are you okay?" I ask.

"No, I'm not fucking okay! That fucker, Ted, just blew up my bar again!" says Nunya.

"I meant, are you hurt?"

"No, I'm fine."

I think for a moment. "Oh fuck!" I yell. Pushing my way through the debris, I wade over to the wall where my priceless velvet painting of me was hanging. Sifting through the rubble, I finally find it, but it's been torn to shreds. My priceless, one-of-a-kind, irreplaceable portrait! I turn from being angry to going absolutely ballistic.

Flying into the air I hear Nunya yell 'go kill that fucker'. You're goddamn right I'm gonna do that. Using my super-vision, I scan the sky for Ted, that evil vindictive fucker. He betrayed our trust and just when I was beginning to not hate him. Soaring higher, I finally see something that surprises me. Yes, Ted is in the sky, and yes, Ted is firing the blasters on his space-cycle, but when they fire, they aren't green, they're orange. Someone else is there, on their own space-cycle, firing at him. I watch as a bright green blast of laser fire hits Ted's ride, annihilating him in the process. Poor bastard.

Moving as swiftly as I can toward the person who just killed Ted, I see something I'm not expecting: a man about my age, with roughly my massive build, blue eyes and blond hair. He looks like he'd fit on the cover of some trashy romance novel, and he's wearing a full black leather biker outfit. What he does next surprises

4

the hell out of me: he waves. I point my blasters at him.

"Hi!" he yells, and he seems super proud of himself. "I killed the last one for you!"

"We just let him go so he could tell the other Unicorns not to fuck with us, so thanks for nothing. And who the fuck are you?" I yell back.

"Why don't we fly down to the ground where it's easier to talk?" yells the guy.

"Or I could kick your ass right now for destroying my friend's bar, and my priceless velvet portrait," I say.

"Oh, did I? That's a shame," he says, seeming not to care. He flies his space-cycle down toward where Nunya is.

"One false move and I swear to God I will tear you into pieces," I yell at him.

"Don't worry, I'm just here to talk," he says, as we both land on the ground.

Nunya comes running up. "Are you the asshole that just destroyed my bar?"

"That sort of thing happens when you're in my line of work," says the mysterious stranger.

"Well, you owe me a new bar, motherfucker," says Nunya.

"I'm sure the government will take care of the tab," he replies. "You must be Nunya, and you're Private Detective Dick Blowhard, right?"

"Yeah, that's right. Who the fuck are you?" I ask.

"I'm Knob Johnson, Space Investigator!"

"Aw, fuck," I say.

2

"Wait, you know this guy?" asks Nunya.

"No, not personally. He's just some asshole that's been trying to steal my business for the last few years. I want to punch his fucking face in," I reply.

"I'm standing right here," says Knob.

"Don't fucking care," I say. "You're just another asshole in a long line of assholes that are number two or lower."

"So, you think you're the best there is?" asks Knob.

"I don't 'think it', I know it," I say.

"Well, we'll see if that's true or not, because we've been tasked with a mission by Bob, President of the Pan-Galactic Space Federation. And we're supposed to work together," says Knob.

"Bullshit. Bob knows I work alone."

"Not this time. He says it's too important. Someone's kidnapped one of his daughters, and he wants everyone he can get to find her."

"Fuck. Which one?" I ask, as I finally holster my blasters.

"Beg pardon?"

"Which daughter?"

"Oh. Tiffany," says Knob.

I start thinking back to all the times I've banged Tiffany. She's a real minx in the bedroom, super creative and up for anything. There are things she's done with pastries that would make Satan blush. If Satan were real, that is. I really should have asked God if Satan was real when I talked with her.

"Alright, let's say I do try to work with you. How do I know you won't steal all the glory?" I ask.

"I'm sure there will be plenty to go around," says Knob.

"Yeah, we'll see," I say. "I have no reason to trust you, and I hate your fucking guts. So why should we work with you?"

"Wait, what do you mean 'we'?" asks Nunya.

"I just figured…" I start to say.

"Well, you figured fucking wrong," says Nunya. "I just finished getting my life back to normal and now my bar is blown up again. Why would I want to go on another adventure?"

"The President asked for you personally," says Knob.

"I don't care if God herself asked for me personally," says

6

Nunya. "I just want to be left alone."

"You'll be rich," says Knob. "You could buy yourself a hundred bars with the reward money."

"I'm already that rich."

"Oh, really? How did you get that rich? Looking at your bar, I wouldn't have guessed that."

"I came into some money," says Nunya, trying not to give too much away.

"And how much in taxes did you end up paying on it?" asks Knob.

"Wait, what?"

"When you received the money. How much in taxes did you pay?"

Nunya is silent.

"Exactly," says Knob. "But if you were to lend a hand with this case, I'm sure that Bob would be happy to turn a blind eye to your... financial situation. And double whatever you already have, from the sounds of it."

"So, you're trying to blackmail me? You son of a bitch," says Nunya, who starts running at Knob.

I grab her and hold her back as she lets loose a barrage of expletives and insults. Once she finally wears herself out, Knob speaks again.

"I wouldn't call it blackmail. I think extortion has a nicer ring to it. But whatever you call it, your President needs your help. I have no idea why, because you don't seem like you'd be able to find your way out of a wet paper bag."

Nunya turns to me. "Keep him busy while I go grab my armor."

"Wait, Nunya," I say. "I think maybe we should take him up on his 'offer', no matter what bullshit he's trying to sell us. The President's daughter is in trouble, and we're the only ones who can save her. I think that's enough reason to help. Remember, we're the good guys."

"You're not that good. Tax evasion and all that," says Knob.

"Just do yourself a favor and shut the fuck up," I say. "Otherwise, I'll not only let Nunya get her armor, but I'll help her kick your ass. And we'll both be giggling while we do it."

"You can certainly try," replies Knob.

We stand there for a moment, waiting to see who will attack first. After a few seconds, Nunya finally breaks the silence.

"Okay, let's say we agree to help find her. What assurances do we have that you won't double cross us?"

"Oh, I have no assurances to offer. In fact, it's possible that at some point in the future, maybe during the climax of our mission, I'll suddenly turn on you and reveal myself to be the bad guy all along. Maybe I'm the one who kidnapped the President's daughter in the first place, just to get close to you and Dick so that I can figure out your weaknesses and kill you. Wouldn't that be surprising?" asks Knob.

"Well, not now, since you did all that foreshadowing bullshit," says Nunya.

"Yeah, that's kind of dumb, giving the entire plot away this early," I say.

"Yes, but why would I tell you my master plan ahead of time? Wouldn't that make you distrust me and try to stop me?" asks Knob.

"Unless your machinations are already so well planned that you think we have no chance of stopping you," says Nunya. "You seem like the kind of egotistical bad guy that thinks he's always a step ahead of the good guy. So, is this all really an elaborate ruse just to kill us? Did you just give away your master plan?"

"No, it was merely an exercise of hypotheticals to gauge your intelligence. And you passed. Congratulations," says Knob, smirking.

Nunya turns to me. "I hate this guy."

"Yeah, me too," I reply. "You want me to kill him, just in case?"

"I won't stop you," says Nunya.

I start moving closer to Knob.

"Wait," he says. "I tell you what, if you do this, and we rescue the President's daughter together, I'll even make sure that your portrait is replaced. I know how much you love your portrait."

"And you'll have one made for Nunya too?" I ask.

"Why yes, of course," he says.

"I don't want a velvet painting of myself," says Nunya.

"It's not for you. I'm going to hang it up in my house, so I can look at you whenever I want," I say.

"Oh. Actually, that's kind of nice," says Nunya.

"And you'll be nude in the painting," I say.

"I take the 'nice' thing back then," replies Nunya.

"Okay, so now that we have everything ironed out, we should probably go check out the crime scene," says Knob.

"Where's the crime scene?" asks Nunya.

"The Blue House," replies Knob.

"Damn," says Nunya.

3

"Are we really going to the Blue House?" asks Nunya.

"Yeah," I reply.

"And that's no big deal to you?"

"Not really. I've been there a thousand times. Remember, I used to bang the President's wife and daughters, and this isn't the first time the President has sent me on a mission."

"Wait, you banged the First Lady and their daughters?" says Knob.

"Yeah, what's it to you?" I ask.

"Oh, no reason. I mean, I'd be impressed if I hadn't done it myself," says Knob.

"You really desperately want me to kick your ass, don't you?"

"I think I'll pass for now."

"Then keep your mouth shut. Before we go, Nunya's gonna need to get some equipment from her place. Shouldn't take us too long."

"That's fine, but hurry," says Knob. "Meet me back here in thirty minutes."

"How about we just meet up with you at the Blue House instead?" says Nunya.

"No can do. We're supposed to be working together, and it's difficult to work together if we take separate ships. We'll go in mine," says Knob.

"Why don't we all go in my ship, instead," asks Nunya.

"I've seen your ship before, and it looks… quaint. Besides, my sidekick is back at my ship waiting for us, and we already have the mission information uploaded to it. So, there's no reason to take your form of conveyance," says Knob.

"Fine. We'll see you back in thirty," I say.

To save some time I wrap my arms around Nunya's waist and fly us back to her house. When we get there, she doesn't go to the house itself, but instead heads to the barn. Moving an old bucket out of the way she reveals a touch pad. Tapping away at it, the ground eventually starts to rumble, and the barn's floor splits in half. A platform rises from below the ground revealing an entire room of weapons, as well as Nunya's ship, the Illenium Falcon.

The newest addition, however, is super cool. In a round glass chamber are Nunya's helmet, shield, armor and robes. It looks like something out of Batman, the way he stores his cape and cowl. It's fucking badass.

"Wait, I thought your shield was destroyed and you lost your helmet back when we battled the Mega-Sloth," I say.

"I did, but I figured out that if you're wearing the armor you can just kind of will them back to you," says Nunya.

"So, your shield wasn't disintegrated?"

"Oh, no, it was. I just basically made a new one magically, I guess."

"That's kinda cool," I say.

"Fuckin' A it is," says Nunya. "Do you think Knob really was just testing us when he laid out his 'fake' master plan?"

"No, I think he really is going to do all that stuff, and probably worse."

"So, why did he tell us all of that?"

"Because I think you're right, he has such a huge ego that he thinks he's smarter than us. He may be as smart as me," I admit, "but I don't think he's smarter than you. I think you'll figure out a way to fix his wagon."

"You're goddamn right I will," says Nunya.

She goes over to the chamber that contains her armor and waves her hand in front of the glass. The cylinder whirrs as it twists, granting Nunya access to the goods inside. I turn away and give her a little privacy as she changes out of her clothes and into her battle gear.

"Okay, you can look now," says Nunya.

I turn and look and she's still naked. "What the fuck?"

"I'm just fucking with you," she says, putting on her tactical outfit, then armor, robes, helmet, and shield.

"Not fucking cool, Nunya. Since you won't sleep with me you shouldn't tease me like that."

"I'm not teasing you. I'm harassing you. There's a difference."

"Great, glad we have that cleared up," I mumble. "Are you gonna bring your magic wand?"

"Don't you think I should? It's pretty powerful," she says.

"Yeah, but you've already accidentally used it on me once. Not looking forward to reliving that."

"Are you worried that I'll make the same mistake again and be tricked by cute, murderous kittens?"

"No, I don't think you'll do that exact thing, but I think it's possible in the middle of a fight you'll accidentally hit me with it. Or drop it, and then some bad guy will use it against me. Things like that."

"It's really because my ability to hurt you intimidates you, isn't it? That you can't stand being partnered with a strong woman who's even stronger than you?" says Nunya.

"Nope, that's not it at all. I just don't want to die," I say.

"Then I'll be extra careful with it," she says, pocketing the wand.

"Fine. Here, let me bring along my device that creates a vacuum and sucks all the air out of a room, just in case," I say.

"Wait, you don't really have a device like that, do you?" asks Nunya.

"No, but now that I think about it, it could come in handy. You know what we really need is someone that makes super cool and dangerous gadgets for us. Things that could get us out of a pinch if we're in trouble."

"Kind of like 'Q' from James Bond?"

"Yeah, exactly like 'Q'!"

"Well, we have the Wise Old Wizard, Steve, don't we?" asks Nunya.

"Sure, but he just gives us magical stuff and points us in the direction of information that we still have to get for ourselves. He isn't like the creative type that puts forth a gadgety effort. I want a laser watch, or bazooka-boots, or explosive bubblegum. Although I will say, I could totally go for a Six Demon Bag, which Steve could probably get for us. Anyway, I want some gadgets, goddamn it!"

"I bet Blhack Glass might know someone," says Nunya.

"I bet they know a lot of 'someones'. The question is whether they know a gadgeteer," I reply.

"Gadgeteer?"

"I dunno. What would you call one?"

"I mean..."

"Yeah, so anyway, why don't you give them a call and see?"

"Sure."

Nunya goes over to her ship, opens the cargo ramp, and we climb inside. After a few seconds, she's got the ship powered up and she's placing an encrypted call to Blhack Glass.

"This is Blhack Glass, for all your hacking needs. Please press one and you will be connected directly to one of our representatives," says a muffled voice.

"Ha-ha," says Nunya. "Seriously, we just want to talk to someone about a little information we need."

No response.

"Come on guys, are you really gonna make me do this?" asks Nunya.

11

Nothing.

"Fine, whatever." Nunya taps on her touchscreen a few times and a holographic phone keypad comes up. She presses the number one on it and holds it for three or four seconds, just to show how annoyed she is.

"Thank you," says the voice. "Hello, this is M-Ray, what can I assist you with?"

"Hi, it's N and D, hoping to get in touch with a gadgeteer," says Nunya.

"Not sure who N and D are. We know a lot of 'N's and a lot of 'D's."

"You know, we met at a concert a few weeks ago. You helped us get into the Chateau Marmot Hotel and Casino."

"Oh, yes. We definitely remember you. And you're asking for a 'gadgeteer'?"

"Yes, someone that builds elaborate devices used for spycraft. Things like laser tag watches, moon boots, pop rocks, and shit like that," says Nunya.

I look over at her like she's lost her mind. "Moon boots?" I silently mouth. She just shrugs.

"I think we can accommodate you. You'll want to ask around for someone named Nord, on the planet Veepee Enn. They should be able to help you out," says M-Ray.

"Okay, thanks!" says Nunya.

"And remember, you still owe us one," they say.

"We do remember. See ya!" she says, dropping the connection. She turns to me. "They're so helpful!"

"Yeah, they're pretty great for being computer nerds," I say, rolling my eyes.

"Hey, why'd you do that? There's nothing wrong with computer nerds," says Nunya.

"You're a computer nerd, right?"

"Yeah?"

"Exactly. Do you ever get invited to parties because you're a computer nerd?"

"Well, no."

"And when you've told people you're a computer nerd, are they really impressed?" I ask.

"Actually, no, they tend to tune me out," says Nunya.

"Exactly. Let's just say it's not that sexy and leave it at that."

"But what about the movie 'Hackers'?"

"What about it?"

"The main character Dade ends up with Angelina fucking Jolie!

She was like one of the biggest names of her era, and super fucking hot," says Nunya.

"Yeah, but that's fiction," I reply.

"Actually, she got married in real life to the guy who played Dade, Jonny Lee Miller."

"Seriously? Still, in real life he was an actor, not an awkward computer super-nerd. And wasn't he British?"

"What does that have to do with anything?" asks Nunya.

"You know that women love men with accents. They'll take a weird looking man with an accent over most good-looking men that don't have accents any day of the week. I'm not saying Jonny Lee Miller was weird looking, because he wasn't. But the accent definitely helped his cause."

"Fine, whatever. At least the few hackers that we actually know are in a band. Bands are cool."

"Only sort of. They wrote a program that writes their music for them. How nerdy is that? I'm sure when they tell women their music was written by a computer and not by them it makes them really wet," I say.

"GRRRRRR!" says Nunya, punching me in the arm.

"Ow! What the fuck! You know your magic strength can hurt me, right?"

"Yeah, I do know. So just leave me alone already."

"Hey, I didn't want to get into an argument with you. And you don't have to be so damn sensitive about the whole computer nerd thing. I'm mostly just trying to fuck with you since you fucked with me while you were changing," I say.

"It's not the same," says Nunya. "I just showed you my naked body, which you should be on your knees thanking me for. But what did you do? You tore apart a huge chunk of my existence, making me feel uncool. So, fuck you, Dick. Haven't you learned anything?"

"I've been trying to, but it's hard when I'm constantly being insulted. And honestly, having to work with Knob is pissing me off so much it's probably making things worse. Sorry, Nunya."

"Damn right you're sorry. Seriously, if we're gonna do this mission, we need to communicate better. I can't have you backsliding just because you're irritated at the competition. And this isn't even a competition; we're trying to save the President's daughter."

"Nunya, if there's one thing that I've learned in all of my galaxy hopping, it's that everything is a competition. If you aren't winning, you're losing. Second place is just as bad as last place. There's only one first place, and I plan to be the guy wearing the gold medal at the end of the race. So, fuck Knob Johnson for trying to steal my crown. If anyone's gonna be the biggest asshole in the galaxy, it's me."

"The way you're acting now, I think you're already there. Just shut up and let's get going."

"Yeah, fuck you too and all that," I say.

As we leave the spaceship, Nunya turns to me and asks, "Did you need to borrow any of my weapons? Last time you didn't take anything with you, and the one weapon you had exploded in your hands."

"Nah, I should be good with my two Nunya-blasters."

"Okay, suit yourself."

We leave the barn, and Nunya uses the touchpad beneath the bucket to lower the ship and armaments back underground.

"So, what should we do first? Head to the Blue House or go meet up with Nord?" asks Nunya.

"How the fuck should I know? Do I look like Edward Packard?"

"Who the fuck is Edward Packard?"

"He's the guy who invented 'Choose Your Own Adventures'," I say.

"Sure, whatever. Just make a choice already," replies Nunya.

"I dunno, I guess it depends partly on what Knob 'lets' us do, since it's his ship. But my guess is it'd probably be better to go to the Blue House first, so we know what we're up against. That way when we visit the gadgeteer, we'll have a better idea of what we might need."

"Makes sense. Now was that so hard?"

"It was hard enough. Are you ready to meet back up with Knob?" I ask.

"No, but we should anyway," says Nunya.

She turns around and flies up into the air, and I follow her back to the remnants of her shitty, blown-up bar.

4

We're a few minutes early arriving back at the bar. There's not much of it left, but what does remain is burning. I feel bad for Nunya losing her bar again because it's basically my fault. I mean, I wasn't the one who literally destroyed it, but if I hadn't gotten duped into fucking with the Unicorns in the first place, they wouldn't have sent a second group to try and kill me.

"Hey, Nunya," I say, as we slowly reach the ground.

"Yeah?"

"I'm really sorry about your bar. I'm gonna pay for the repairs again. This is my fault."

"Yup, it's definitely your fault, but you don't need to worry. I insured the place, figuring it was only a matter of time before this would happen again. I mean, not a lot of people come here, and those that do are usually looking for trouble. Lower traffic usually means rougher clientele. Could be because they've been kicked out of all the good places," says Nunya. "My bar is kind of their last resort."

"That's what you should name it: 'The Last Resort'," I say.

"Actually, that's not bad. Maybe I'll put that on the sign when they rebuild. Anyway, I've been thinking. You know how Knob told us about trying to figure out our weaknesses? We should do the same for him and his sidekick. Size them up, so if they do double-cross us, or I guess when they do double-cross us, we'll be ready to take them out. Be proactive and shit."

"Yeah, that sounds like a really smart idea," I say.

Suddenly, as if on cue, Knob shows up. He hovers down to the ground on his space-cycle. I take a good look at it and realize it's the exact same model as Bessie was.

"Are you two ready?" he asks.

"First, let me ask you this: why did you buy this particular space-cycle?" I ask.

"What do you mean?"

"I mean, why did you pick this particular make and model? It's a Saturn-Davidson Space King, right?"

"Yeah, it sure is."

"That's the same make and model as the one I used to have. It looks like it's even in the same color, and it's the same year," I say.

"What a strange coincidence," says Knob.

15

"Look, if you're trying to become me, or replace me, I'll just let you know up front it's not possible. There can be only one and all that shit. I'm an original, and no matter how many wannabes try to copy me, they ain't me. Got it?"

"I seriously don't know what you're talking about. The Saturn-Davidson whatever-it-is is the most commonly sold space-cycle in the galaxy. The guy at the dealership even told me so. There's a reason it's so popular, and that's because it's the best. That's all. Just a coincidence."

"Then why are you dressed like me?" I ask.

"I'm not dressed like you, Dick. I'm wearing a black leather jacket, black leather pants, black leather belt, and black leather boots. You're wearing a tux," replies Knob.

"Yeah, but what you're wearing is what I used to wear when I was riding around on my space-cycle. Sometimes I'd change it up and wear a suit, but a lot of times I'd wear exactly what you're wearing."

"Seriously, you're just being paranoid. Most people who ride wear leathers. That's a totally common thing."

"Actually, that is true," mumbles Nunya.

"Hey, whose side are you on?" I ask.

"My side. I'm on my own side and nobody else's," says Nunya.

"Great, I have my very own dorkelganger here, and a turncoat sidekick. That's just fuckin' wonderful," I say.

"You're the sidekick," says Nunya.

"You're also delusional," says Knob.

"Fine, if you're both gonna treat me like shit then fuck you. I'm outta here." I start to fly up into the air when I hear Knob say, "What about Tiffany." I stop dead in my tracks, if you could leave tracks in the air. Goddamn it.

I fly back down. "Fine, I'll help you assholes, but both of you need to fuck off. Knob, quit copying me..."

"I'm not!"

"Seriously, shut your mouth and stop doing it. And Nunya, at least be on my side a little. Even Batman helped Robin and took his side occasionally. If I'm your sidekick, I need you to have my six, okay?"

"Yeah, sure, whatever," says Nunya.

"Okay. Now let's go save Tiffany. I'm guessing she'll have sex with me once I rescue her. Totally worth it," I say.

"I know, she's amazing!" says Knob.

"I'm gonna murder you now," I say matter-of-factly. I start to lunge for him when I hear a large spaceship approach. It hovers directly above us, casting a brilliant beam of multicolor light onto the ground.

"This is our ride, ladies and... I guess ladies," says Knob.

"Hey, women are awesome, so I'll take that as a compliment. And fuck you at the same time for using the word 'ladies' in a derogatory fashion," I say.

"Wow, that's real fucking progressive of you, Dick," says Knob.

"I'm trying."

"It wasn't meant as a compliment," says Knob.

"I really don't care. So, is this beam of light a tractor beam or teleporter?" I ask.

"Nope, just a beam of light. I'll fly up in my space-cycle, you two can fly up with your superpowers."

We let Knob go ahead, mostly because we just didn't want to get caught in his space-cycle's jet wash. That's how Gooses die.

It doesn't take very long to float up into Knob's spaceship. It's actually much bigger than it looks from the ground. I'd say it's roughly ten times the size of Nunya's ship. Not that Nunya's is that large, but we were able to fit nearly two hundred Reginalds inside of it, uncomfortably.

"Looks like he may be overcompensating for something," says Nunya.

"Probably. Thankfully, I don't have that problem," I say, winking at her. She just rolls her eyes.

As the ship gets closer, I can make out that it's a dark gray color. There's not really a whole lot to look at because we can only see the underside of the ship. Since no one tends to look at the underside of a ship when they're parked, they don't spend a lot of time making them look great.

The light beam seems to be coming from a large hole at the center of the ship. I look up and watch as Knob floats up into the large opening. Nunya looks over at me and I nod, letting her know to go first, and I follow behind her through the hole.

We make our way inside, and the appearance of the ship is disorienting. It's both brightly colored and sterile looking at the same time, as if a clown built a hospital and it had little mutant babies with a space cruiser. Once Nunya and I both reach the floor, the hole we just flew through closes.

"Welcome to the coolest ship in the galaxy," says Knob.

Standing next to him is what looks to be a twenty-five-year-old human, dressed very stylishly in light gray slacks, matching gray suit vest, white dress shirt and black and bright red striped tie. I notice him noticing me as I float down to the ground inside the ship.

17

"My God, I can see why you're so into him," says the man to Knob.

"I'm not into him, Whip!" yells Knob. "And I'm not copying him, either!"

"Hi, I'm Whip, Whip Noodbottom," says the well-dressed man, coming over and shaking our hands.

"Dick," I say, smiling at him.

"Yes please," he says.

"I'm Nunya," says Nunya.

"I know! You are one powerful bitch! I love you!" says Whip.

"Thanks! Now I feel bad that I don't already know who you are," says Nunya. "And actually, how do you know who I am?"

"Oh, that's easy. Knob spends all his time watching videos of you two. Mostly of Dick, but lately there's been a lot of videos of the two of you battling things. And don't worry, I've only caught him masturbating to the videos once," says Whip.

"I've NEVER masturbated while watching those videos!" says Knob.

"Then explain how I walked in on you naked, rubbing yourself."

"I'd just gotten out of the shower, and I had an itch!"

"If that's what you want to believe then you go ahead and believe it," says Whip. "Anyway, welcome to our home. Cozy, isn't it?"

"Yeah, very... cozy," I say.

"Oh, I know it's a little dramatic, but it helps keep Knob in a good mood. He likes bright and shiny things. He's a bit of a labrador in that way. So, would either of you like something to drink? We have a full bar," says Whip.

"How about a double of bourbon," says Nunya.

"Done," replies Whip. "And for you... Dick?"

"Uh, Dirty Shirley, extra dirty," I say.

"Wow, I would have thought a man like you would be drinking something like gasoline or napalm. Nice to see you have a softer side. Would you like a little pink umbrella with it?" asks Whip.

I laugh. "No, I'm good."

"Yes, yes you are. Anyway, I'll go fix you those drinks," says Whip, walking away.

Me, Nunya and Knob just stand around, waiting. The silence is super uncomfortable, when Knob finally says something.

"I swear, I wasn't masturbating while watching videos of you two fighting."

"Uh-huh, sure," I say. I just shake my head.

"You know, one thing that bothers me is how you got footage of us fighting things in the first place," says Nunya.

"Oh, well, uh... they're publicly accessible videos. Yeah, that's it, they're just on the news," says Knob.

"I don't believe that bullshit for a second," says Nunya. "We've taken precautions to avoid that sort of thing. Have you been spying on us?"

"No! I mean, define 'spying'."

"It means that you're watching us without our knowledge."

"Well then, 'yes', I have been doing that," says Knob.

"Okay, this is some bullshit! Do you have any video of us naked?"

"Nooooo..." says Knob.

"Double bullshit. If you don't go delete all the videos of us naked right now, I'm going to tear your spaceship apart," yells Nunya.

"Fine, just give me a minute," says Knob. He pushes a button on his watch and says, "Initiate program: Dirty Sweep."

A voice, seemingly from nowhere, says, "Program: Dirty Sweep initiated."

We sit in uncomfortable silence for what feels like a few minutes. Eventually, the voice returns. "Program: Dirty Sweep completed."

"What the fuck!" says Nunya. "Just how many nude videos of us did you have? You could have deleted all of the galactic government's databases in the same amount of time!"

"No, there wasn't that many. Really," says Knob.

"You lying sack of shit!" says Nunya.

We are interrupted when Whip comes back with our drinks.

"Are you three getting along okay?" asks Whip. "You aren't being your normal, inhospitable self, are you Knob?"

"No, he's just been deleting his nude videos of us," I say.

"Oh, that's a shame," says Whip, handing us our drinks.

I take a sip of the Dirty Shirley, and it's easily the best I've ever had.

"This is amazing!" I say.

"Glad you like it," says Whip.

"And this bourbon, it's also amazing. What is it?" asks Nunya.

"Four Roses Small Batch, 2,000th Anniversary Edition," replies Whip.

"My God it's good," says Nunya. "Thank you!"

"My pleasure. Anyway, let's all go sit down and talk about what the plan is," says Whip. He gestures to have us follow him. We walk

19

down a hallway, take a few turns, and end up in what looks like a conference room. The crazy thing is that the table is identical to the one in Nunya's spaceship.

"I can't even..." mumbles Nunya.

"Yeah, it's getting to the point of being ridiculous," I say.

"What? What's ridiculous?" asks Knob.

"The fact you've tried to copy every aspect of our lives but still try to deny it," I say.

"What? What do you think I copied this time?" asks Knob, seemingly offended.

"The table. It's the same one that Nunya has in her ship," I reply.

"No, it's not! Nunya's ship has a Guttenberg table, while this is a Hasselhoff," says Knob.

"They look identical," says Nunya.

"Well, they're not. This one is one inch in diameter larger than yours."

"The fact that you know that makes you seem like a psychopath," I say. "Seriously, you need a hobby."

"Whatever. Can we just get on with the planning?" says Knob.

We all sit down.

"So, what's the plan?" I ask.

"Well, I guess we go to the Blue House, search for clues, and then try to find Tiffany," says Knob.

"Okay, good meeting," I say, standing back up.

"Wait, we still need to go over the details," says Knob.

"Like what details?" I ask.

"Like, who will be lead investigator? Who is going to interview witnesses? Things like that," says Knob.

"I nominate Nunya for all of that," I say.

"Wait, why me?" asks Nunya.

"Because you're smarter than everyone else, that's why," I say.

"Oh, that's true," she says.

"I don't know about that. I'm pretty smart, too," says Knob.

"Could you hack into the government's security systems with a calculator watch, a roll of duct tape, and some WD-40?" I ask.

"Well, no," says Knob.

"She can. So, unless you can come up with a compelling reason why you should be in charge, I think we should all take our cues from Nunya."

"How about I get to be in charge because I put our team together," says Knob.

"I thought you were sent here by the President. So, the President put the team together."

"Well, that's not entirely true. He couldn't get a hold of you to send you on this mission, so he asked me to handle it instead. I told him I might know where to find you, and that I'd do the mission if I was able to work with you. So, technically, it's my group," says Knob.

"Wait, if that's true, then did the President actually ask for me to help out specifically?" asks Nunya.

"Uhhh…"

"Wait, are you saying that I'm here because you lied to me?" asks Nunya.

Knob doesn't respond.

"Okay, you're gonna turn this Willy Wonka looking spaceship back around and drop me off on planet Houston. Now!" yells Nunya.

"Sorry, no can do," says Knob. "The President has given orders to put together a team and find his daughter as soon as possible. We can't spend the time taking you back."

"Fine, then I'll just punch my way out of here," says Nunya. She pulls her arm back and brings it down on the table, shattering it into tiny pieces.

"What the fuck?" says Knob. "That cost a lot of money!"

"Not as much as your medical bills are gonna cost," says Nunya, moving toward Knob.

"Now hold on. There's still a girl out there who needs our help. A person. She's been kidnapped. I admit, I may have gotten you to come along under false pretenses, but she really does need to be saved. So please, stop destroying my shit and help me save Tiffany," says Knob.

Nunya looks like she wants to kill Knob right now. I kind of hope she does. But instead of beating the shit out of him, she calms down.

"Okay, so here's the deal. If I'm staying on, you will do anything and everything I say. That means if I tell you to shut up, you shut up. If I tell you to get me a fucking cup of coffee, you get me a fucking cup of coffee, and it better be the fanciest, tastiest fucking coffee in the universe. No questioning things. No whining. No 'I'm too good for this' bullshit. You take your orders from me or I kick your ass. Is that understood? Because if you're not okay with that, I'm going to find the flight controls and crash land us on planet Houston. Then you're stuck there. Do you understand?" asks Nunya.

"Yeah, that's fine," says Knob, sounding dejected.

"You're like an Amazonian warrior princess!" says Whip to Nunya. "I'd follow you to the ends of the galaxy, so count me in."

"You know I'm down," I say.

"Okay, good. So, the plan is there is no plan. We go to the Blue House and we investigate and go from there. Meeting fucking adjourned," says Nunya. She walks through the remains of the table, goes down the hall we came through, and disappears.

"I think that went well," says Whip.

5

I decide to follow Nunya, as much to see if she's okay as to get away from Knob. God, I hate that guy.

"Nunya?" I say.

"What, Dick? What do you want? And it better be good."

"I just wanted to make sure you were okay."

"No, I'm not fucking okay. Some jackass secretly videotaped us naked, masturbated to it, and now we're being forced to work with the same fucker at the request of the President? I feel violated, I feel lied to, and I feel like killing someone right now. Just promise me something, that once this is all over, we kill this guy," says Nunya.

"I won't promise you that, but I promise you I'll try to ruin him. Maybe get rid of his powers somehow. Or prove publicly that he's a piece of shit and not worth trusting. I'll make sure he's taken his last case. Is that good enough for you?" I ask.

"Not really, but it'll have to do," says Nunya. "In the meantime, do you have any guesses as to who might have kidnapped Tiffany?"

"Sure, I have a lot of guesses. I mean, every President has their enemies. It seems like Knob's at the top of the list though, based on the comments he made. But it would be rather obvious if he was the kidnapper. Still, we should try to figure out if he's behind this first. Can you hack into his onboard computer and see if there are any clues that might point to him being the kidnapper?" I ask.

"Yeah, I can do that. I don't think we have a lot of time though, because we should reach the Blue House soon, I would think. We had to have passed through a space gateway already."

"You mean 'space-asshole'?"

"Yeah, fine, we should have passed through a space-asshole already, and we should be getting close to the Blue House. Maybe if you created some sort of distraction or something, I could find a computer and hack in," says Nunya.

"I think I can do that," I say. "How much time do you need?"

"About ten minutes."

"On it."

I make my way back down the winding hallway and into the conference room. Knob is trying to fit some of the table pieces back together, but as soon as he gets a few assembled they fall apart.

23

Whip on the other hand is sweeping pieces into a dustpan and dumping them into a large bucket.

"Hey, so uh, Nunya's taking a shit right now, so we won't see her for a while. She likes some time and privacy. Could be ten or twenty minutes," I say.

"That's a bit too much information," replies Knob. "Wait, we didn't even show her where the restrooms are."

"Oh, don't worry about that, she'll just shit wherever. She once shit on a tree and didn't even have any toilet paper. I started calling her 'poo-fingers' after that," I say.

"That's disgusting. I'll go find her and show her where the restrooms are. She does know how to use a toilet, doesn't she?" asks Knob.

"Yeah, she knows how to use a toilet. And I was just messing with you about the 'shitting in random places' thing. I'm sure she'll find the restroom on her own. Remember, she's the smartest one here," I say.

"I'm still not convinced," says Knob.

"Well, thankfully no one really cares whether you're convinced or not. Am I right, Whip?"

"Yes, I definitely don't care," says Whip.

"And I can tell you for sure that I don't care. Nunya doesn't either. And even if you were smarter, which you're not, she's still in charge," I say.

"For now," says Knob, ominously.

"So, in the meantime, uh... let's get to know each other. Like, are you two a couple?" I ask.

"Hahahahahaha!" laughs Whip.

"Oh, sorry, did I say something funny?" I ask.

"Yes, yes you did. First, Knob isn't my type. And second, he's so fixated on you that I doubt he'd be able to look at anyone else," says Whip.

"That's not true! And I'm not into guys, okay!" says Knob. "I bang hot chicks all the time, like the First Lady and her daughters, which we already established."

"Well, you said that you did, but you don't really have any proof," I say.

"I don't need to give you proof of anything," says Knob. "I had sexual intercourse with them, end of story."

"It seems like I've hit a sore subject, and it sounds like you're hiding something. And who calls fucking 'sexual intercourse'? Wait, Knob... are you a virgin?" I ask.

24

"No, of fucking course I'm not a virgin! I've banged literally thousands of chicks across the galaxy," says Knob.

"Whip, is that true?" I ask.

"I wouldn't really know. It's possible, but he hasn't banged any chicks that I know of since I've been working with him," says Whip.

"Yeah, but you've only worked for me for three months now," says Knob.

"Wait, so you haven't had sex in three months? Seriously, I can't imagine going that long without fucking someone. You're practically a virgin now anyway," I say.

"I'm no goddamn virgin! So shut your hole about it!" yells Knob.

"Wow, you don't have to be so sensitive about it. I was just fucking with you. If you say you've banged a thousand chicks, I believe you, Knob."

"I really don't care if you believe me or not," says Knob, but I can tell that he does. Even if he isn't sexually fixated on me, which he probably is, he still cares about whether I believe him. I dunno if I should be honored or not because he's still a huge fucking asshole. I'll probably still harass him about it whenever he's being a dick.

"So, Knob, where are you from?" I ask.

"Like you give a shit," he says.

"No, seriously, where are you from?"

"I'm from the planet Deeznutz, in the Caramel cluster," says Knob.

I laugh. "Wait, seriously?"

"Yes, seriously. Why is that funny?"

"Because 'Deez Nuts' means 'my balls', and you have nuts in a caramel cluster, which is kind of like a cookie. So, it's like saying 'my balls are delicious'! That's fucking hysterical!" I say.

"See, this is exactly why I don't tell anyone anything about myself!" says Knob, looking quite angry.

"Hey, I can't help it if you're accidentally funny. I tell you what, I just asked you a question, now you can ask me one. What do you want to know?" I say.

"Oh, uhhh... well, what was it like meeting God?" asks Knob.

"Wait, how the fuck did you know that I met God? Oh, right, constantly spying on me. Well, Knob, it was fucking amazing. Hottest chick I've ever run into. And between you and me, I'm trying to clean up my act so that I have a chance with her."

"Hold on, you're trying to get with God? Have actual sexual inter... I mean fuck her?" asks Knob.

"Yeah! She's so goddamn hot!" I say.

"Huh. That's crazy. Why would she be super hot? I would have thought she'd just be plain looking or something. Or maybe even a dude."

"Well, she did say she looks different to every person she meets. Whatever fits that person best. So, for me, she's super fucking hot!"

"Huh, I wonder if she'd look the same to me," says Knob.

"Doubt it," says Whip. "I'm sure to you she looks like Detective Blowhard."

"Whip, I swear, knock it the fuck off," says Knob.

"Not likely. I can say what I want, when I want," says Whip.

"Fine. Whatever. Just quit harassing me, okay?"

Whip decides not to say anything.

"How about you, Whip, where are you from?" I ask.

"I'm from Macho Centauri," says Whip.

"Wait, seriously? I own that planet! That's where my mega-mansion is!" I say.

"I know," says Whip.

"Wait, who's your mom?" I ask, starting to get worried.

"Ember. Ember Noodbottom."

"Oh my God! She's one of the best lays I've ever had! I mean, sorry, she's a very respectable woman, and she's, uh, great! Great person, your mom," I say.

It gets kind of quiet, and the gears in my head start turning. I look at his face, his hair color, his chin, his chiseled jaw. Oh, fuck.

Whip notices the look on my face. "Don't worry, Detective Blowhard, you aren't my father. My father passed away when I was a teenager. He was an intergalactic truck driver. Took shipments from place-to-place. Didn't see him much. There weren't many other jobs on Macho Centauri that didn't require you to be named Ember, so he did what he had to."

"Oh, hey, I'm sorry. I didn't realize it was that rough for him, or for you. Just know that your mom has a job for life with me. She'll be taken care of," I say.

"Thanks," mumbles Whip.

"Well, that was fucking awkward," says Knob.

"Just like your face," I say.

Whip snorts while trying to stifle a laugh. Knob just continues to look pissed.

"So how did you two meet?" I ask.

"Actually, we didn't. I was hired through a temp agency," starts Whip. "It was the promise of intergalactic travel that caught my eye. He was looking for someone who was either LGBTQ+, or a minority, or both. I think since Nunya is Black and a lesbian, he wanted to get a similarly diverse sidekick for his adventures. I'm gay, if you couldn't tell, and I'm half Latinx, half Polish."

"How very progressive of you, Knob," I say.

"Shut up," he replies.

"No, seriously, I think it's great. I'm not mocking you for once."

"Oh."

"So how are you liking your job, Whip?" I ask.

"It's alright. I mean, I have to keep Knob in line, call him out when he's being an asshole, which is pretty much always. It's like babysitting a professional wrestler, is what it is."

"I'm sure Nunya would say the same thing about me."

"I dunno, you don't seem so bad," says Whip.

"Meh. So, what skills do you bring to the table? Do you have any superpowers?"

"I don't have any superpowers, but I'm a good cook with a creative flair. Also, I'm a master of seven different martial arts."

"No fucking shit?" I say.

"No fucking shit. I can kill almost anyone with my bare hands. Every part of me is a deadly weapon," says Whip.

"Wow, that's a pretty fucking cool. How did you become a master of seven different martial arts? You seem young to be that skilled."

"Oh, I was part of an assassins' guild. They taught me."

"But you aren't part of it now?"

He laughs. "Do you think I'd be temping for a superhero if I was?"

"No, probably not. Growing up, I always wanted to pick up martial arts. Once I was old enough, though, I got my superpowers. Never really needed martial arts after that. Still, knowing a few moves could come in handy," I say.

"Well, if you ever want to learn, you let me know," says Whip, winking at me.

"Sure, I'll let you know."

I look over at Knob and his mouth is hanging open.

"Uh, Knob, you trying to catch flies?" I ask.

"No. Just didn't realize that Whip was a killing machine," says Knob.

"That'll teach you not to judge a book by its cover," says Whip.

"Seriously, I just hired him because he was a good cook. I'm a shit cook," mumbles Knob.

"Yes, you definitely are," replies Whip.

Right at that moment, Nunya returns from hacking Knob's computer system.

"Hey Nunya, how was your shit?" I ask.

"My shit?" she repeats, puzzled.

"Yeah, the big shit you just took. It always takes you a long time to take a shit," I say.

"Oh, right, the big shit. Yeah, I took a big old dump. It was great. Probably lost three pounds in the process," says Nunya.

"You didn't shit on the ground, did you?" asks Knob.

"Uh, no. Should I have?"

"No. And you did use a toilet, flush, then wash your hands afterward?" asks Knob.

"Yeah, isn't that what normal people do?" asks Nunya.

"Yes. Sorry, Dick just made it seem like you weren't potty trained yet," says Knob.

"Well Dick can be an asshole. He likes to fuck with people sometimes. But yes, I shit in a toilet, flushed, washed my hands then dried them off. And I feel much better now, thanks for not asking."

"Anyway, I should probably go check and see where we're at. We should be nearly there," says Knob.

"Hey, I was wondering, how'd we cross through one of the space-assholes without having to talk to security?" I ask.

"What's a space-asshole?" asks Knob.

"You know, one of those gateways that everyone uses to get from system to system," I say.

"Space-asshole is just his nickname for them," says Nunya.

"Oh, we have an IRFID device onboard that automatically identifies us and sends it to the security team. That way we can put the ship on autopilot and go wherever," says Knob.

"That must be nice, not having to deal with racist security people who want to board your ship for no reason," says Nunya.

"Uh, yeah, sure is," says Knob, walking down the corridor and out of sight.

"I guess I'll need to get another bucket," says Whip, looking unhappily at the remains of the table.

"Sorry about that," says Nunya. "Here, I'll clean up the rest."

Whip hands her the dustpan and broom and carries the bucket off with him.

"So, were you able to find any clues?" I whisper.

"Not really. I was able to hack into their system but couldn't find any information that would make me believe Knob was behind the kidnapping. I will say that although it seems like he did delete most of the nude videos of us, there were a couple still in a folder marked

'Spank Bank'. I would have deleted them, but if I did, he might figure out I'd hacked into his on-board computer," whispers Nunya.

"Well, that doesn't really clear his name since he still could be behind the whole thing and be smart enough to not leave evidence in the computer system. Either way, he's holding onto some of our videos, he's still an asshole, and I think we should take him down,"

"Glad we're on the same page," says Nunya.

"But let's do it after we rescue Tiffany. If it turns out he's behind the kidnapping, and we get him thrown in jail or banished or whatever too soon, we may never find her. My guess is if he's kidnapped her, that he'll try and make it seem like he was the one who found her. That way he shows me up, and at the same time looks like the hero."

"Wow, that's really smart," says Nunya.

"Seriously, quit being so goddamn condescending every time I have a good idea," I say.

"Let me think… nope."

6

I decide to head to the bridge of the ship to see if we're close to the Blue House yet. It takes me a little while to find it, winding my way down brightly painted hallways, past dozens of portraits of Knob. Thank God none of them are Vivantes, but it's still annoying seeing that he loves his own appearance so much. At least I'm less of an asshole than this guy. I mean, I do admit to keeping an autographed picture of myself on my desk back home, but Knob's taking it way too far.

Eventually, I reach the bridge, which has a nice wide view of everything. Instead of being a small viewport you can barely see out of, it's like a large half-sphere made of glass. I mean, I'm sure it's made of something stronger than glass, but you get the idea. Knob is standing in the middle of it with his back to me. I can see on the other side of him that we're finally approaching the Blue House.

So, the Blue House isn't just a house, it's actually a very large mobile space station, designed with the latest security, and protected by a series of shields of increasing size. It's kind of like a Russian doll, where there's a smaller one inside each shell.

Also, the reason it's called the Blue House is that several thousand years ago one of the leaders on Earth Uno lived in a place called the White House. To be more inclusive, when the Blue House was constructed, they picked the color blue, because at the time there were no known sentient species that had blue skin. Now that there are so many space-assholes, there have been several species that have been discovered who have blue skin, or hair, or fur. They just haven't gotten around to picking a new color, since pretty much every color is represented in the known galaxy now.

"Knob?" I say.

He turns around and looks at me. "Yeah Dick, did you come to ridicule me more?"

"Well, that's not why I'm here, but I can if you like," I say.

"Have you ever met someone that you look up to, that you respect, and they treat you like shit?" asks Knob.

"Nope, can't say that I have."

"Well, it sucks, Dick. It sucks a lot. I was really looking forward to working with you on this mission. Do you know what it's like to have someone constantly berating you while you're trying to do the right thing?"

"Actually, yes, I do. As you already know, Nunya gives me shit all the time. But honestly, I'm glad I have someone like that around. She's helped me be a better person," I say.

"Oh, so is that what you're doing by insulting me? You're trying to make me a better person?"

"No, I just think you're an asshole. Especially because of the nude video shit. That's so not cool on so many levels. And remember, this is coming from a guy that fucks anything that moves. But only stuff that moves, regardless of what Nunya says."

"Well, I just hope you never meet your hero," says Knob.

"Man, I am my own hero. Everyone should be their own hero. Isn't that the whole point?"

Knob doesn't respond.

"Seriously, just be yourself. Unless yourself is a giant douche bag, then be someone else. Or is that what you're doing? You don't want to be yourself?" I ask.

"I do want to be me. 'Me' just happens to be very similar to you. You have superpowers, I have superpowers. You bang hot chicks; I bang hot chicks."

"Yeah, but I don't manipulate and extort people into coming on missions against their will. You've made an enemy for life with Nunya. And she really is smarter than you, so I'd work real hard to get on her good side if I were you. That, and if your powers are anything like mine, you're susceptible to magical damage. Oh shit, I didn't mean to say that," I say.

"I already knew. It was very obvious from watching videos that your weakness is magic. You stood in the center of an explosion and walked away without a scratch, but when you got hit with magic, it did the same amount of damage it would normally do to someone. But to answer your question, no, my weakness isn't magic," says Knob.

"But you do have a weakness?"

"Yes, tall leggy blondes."

"Cute. I'm serious, do you have a weakness? Something that bypasses your superpowers?"

"If I did, I definitely wouldn't tell anyone. Do you think I'm stupid?" asks Knob.

"Do you actually want me to answer that question?" I reply.

Knob just ignores me. Or tries to, anyway.

I notice a cup of coffee sitting on a small round table next to where Knob is standing. As quickly and quietly as I can, I creep over, grab the mug, and dump its contents onto Knob's head. In a flash he turns to me.

"What the hell, Dick? Why did you dump coffee all over me?" asks Knob.

"Oh, sorry, I thought you might be like the Wicked Witch of the West, who melted when she got water tossed on her," I say.

"Dick, if I had a hot cup of coffee and I was drinking it, don't you think that would have already killed me if that was my weakness? Not only that, but do you think I'd keep the one thing that can kill me in a mug a few feet away from me?"

"Maybe you were trying to throw me off your scent. Be all sneaky like."

"No, Dick. Now I understand why Nunya's the brains of your operation. I'm going to go get cleaned up. I don't want to see President Bob with coffee all over my super-suit."

"That's fine. I'll just start pushing buttons at random to see what they do," I say.

"Haven't you had enough fun pushing buttons? You've certainly pushed mine enough," says Knob.

"I'll let you know if I ever reach my limit, but I doubt I have one."

"Seriously, don't touch anything," says Knob.

I don't respond, just to fuck with him.

"Just stay here," says Knob, leaving the bridge.

I stand there alone for a while, looking at the Blue House as the ship floats silently toward it. My eyes barely make out each energy shield that winks out of existence just before we pass through them, as we creep ever closer. The Blue House itself is massive, about the size of a small planet, with many weapons systems littered throughout its light-blue surface. It makes my planet look tiny in comparison. But it's not the size of your planet that matters; it's how you use it.

After a few minutes, we reach our destination. The ship's autopilot drifts us down and into a hangar. The Blue House thankfully has its own atmosphere, so breathing isn't a concern. No need for oxygen tanks or anything for the others. Since the ship has finally arrived, I make my way back to the conference room.

Nunya and Whip have finished cleaning up the pieces of the table, so the room only has a dozen or so chairs in it now. I notice that Knob hasn't come back yet.

"I noticed that Knob hasn't come back yet," I say.

"Did he go somewhere?" asks Whip.

"Yeah, I think he was changing, or cleaning himself up or something," I say.

32

"Why? He looked fine before," says Whip.

"I poured coffee on him."

"Why'd you do that?"

"I thought it might make him melt. You know, like in the Wizard of Oz."

Both Nunya and Whip start laughing at me.

"You seriously thought that would work?" asks Nunya.

"I was just trying to figure out his weakness. He already knew that my weakness is magic, and I was trying to turn the tables. Hey Whip, do you know his weakness?" I ask.

"Well, I haven't seen one yet. I don't think magic hurts him any worse than anything else. But honestly, if he did have one, I don't know that I'd feel comfortable about telling you. He is still my employer."

"I could be your employer," I say. "You may have to change your name to Ember, but I could always use a sidekick. Nunya, are sidekicks allowed to have sidekicks?"

"Sure, why not. At least it's not a common trope or anything," says Nunya.

"See? It's not a trope, Whip. The three of us could be a team!" I say.

"Well, I think two Embers in one family is at least one too many," says Whip. "Also, I think that loyalty is important, even if it's to someone like Knob. If I were to jump ship at every better offer, I got I'd be constantly jumping ship. But I appreciate the thought."

"Hey, I completely understand. If you do ever find yourself looking for a new job, though, at least let me know," I say.

"I mostly definitely will," replies Whip, winking at me.

"So, how do we get out of this thing? 'This thing' meaning this spaceship?" I ask.

"Oh, follow me," says Whip.

We follow him out of the conference room and back to the room we first came in with the giant hole in the floor. Whip goes over to the wall, presses a few buttons, and a large hole opens on the side of the ship, just as large as the hole we flew up into.

"Wait, so if you have the same hole you can go through on the side of the ship, why do you need a big hole on the bottom?" asks Nunya.

"Just for dramatic effect, I guess," says Whip. "And like I say, you can never have too many holes!"

"Wait, do you really say that?" I ask.

"No, but it sounded funny," says Whip.

"That's fair," I reply.

That's when Knob reappears. He's changed outfits and washed his hair and face. He still looks pissed, but I don't really care, because he's still 'Knob'. Instead of the brightly colored super-suit he was wearing before, he's now wearing a tuxedo like me. Only instead of it being dark black like mine, his tuxedo is mostly white with black collar and accents.

I turn and look at Knob and say, "Really?"

"What? Are you insinuating I'm copying you just because I'm wearing a tux? I just wanted to look formal while we're here at the Blue House. And if you'll notice, my tux looks nothing like yours. And I'd be wearing my normal superhero outfit right now if you hadn't spilled coffee on me," says Knob.

"You're blaming me for you wearing that monstrosity?" I say.

"It's not a monstrosity. It was designed by Pierre LaFleur himself."

"Wait, Pierre made clothes for you? That son-of-a-bitch!"

"Who is Pierre?" asks Nunya.

"He's my personal tailor. I buy like fifty suits from him a year because I go through them so quickly. He told me he wouldn't work for anyone else!" I say.

"Yes, well, he said that you haven't been into his shop in a few months and wondered what had happened to you. Everyone needs to make a living," says Knob.

"You asshole! You stole my tailor! Now I'm definitely going to kick your ass!" I say, as I start to pull back my fist.

That's when a deep, masculine voice resonates into the ship. "Thank you both for coming. Please follow us inside where it's more secure."

Looking out through the hole, I see that the voice came from a very rugged looking soldier. He's got close-cropped black hair, dark skin, a broad chest, and a chin that looks like it could withstand getting hit by a Mack truck. His dark gray fatigues make him look like a G.I. Joe action figure. I wonder if he has a kung-fu grip, or some equally cool accessories.

"I'm General Admission. Welcome to The Blue House," he says.

7

As we exit the ship and follow General Admission down a long red carpet, I turn to Nunya and do my best to not laugh at his name.

"What? Why are you giggling?" asks Nunya.

"Because of his name!"

"At least his name isn't Seaman Samples," says Nunya.

That's when I actually snort out loud. General Admission stops walking, turns around, and eyes me warily.

"Are you okay back there?" he asks.

"Oh, uh, yes sir. We're all fine here now, thank you. How are you?" I reply.

He just ignores me and turns around, continuing to lead us down the red carpet and toward an entryway.

"You're quoting Han Solo?" whispers Nunya.

"Hey, I thought it would make you happy," I whisper back.

"Not when we're in the most secure place in the galaxy. Maybe we should start acting more serious."

"Sure, I can act serious," I say, trying hard to stifle a laugh. "Sorry, I was just wondering what he was like when he was only 'Private Admission'."

Nunya snorts loudly, but this time General Admission doesn't turn around. I'm sure he's had people make fun of his name before. I start to feel a little bad, but his name is just too damn silly. Of course, it's not like Nunya and I have normal names, and growing up I was definitely laughed at. I dunno, maybe it isn't so funny when I think about it.

At the entryway sits a young female Kielbasean, also wearing fatigues, looking at us expectantly from across a large rectangular table. Kielbaseans are known for their dark orange skin, slightly spicy personalities, and pleasant snap when you bite into them. Just kidding about that last part. Or am I? The last name 'Kabanos' is embroidered on her outfit.

She puts her hands out, waiting for us to give her something. "Your weapons," she says.

"That might be difficult, because three of us are living weapons," I say. "The fourth one is Knob."

Both Nunya and Whip snicker. I turn and see Knob rolling his eyes.

"Your weapons," repeats Kabanos, clearly unimpressed.

35

"Fine," I say, placing my blasters down on the table.

"I don't have any," says Whip.

"Nor do I," says Knob.

Nunya walks over and starts pulling weapon after weapon out of her outfit. There's about a dozen knives and guns from various secret pockets and pouches that she empties onto the table. The only thing I notice her not handing over is her wand.

Knob is the first to walk through the weapon detector, which doesn't go off.

"See, I told you he's not dangerous," I say.

Next is Whip. He goes through no problem too. Then I go through. Again, no problem. But as soon as Nunya tries to go through, the detector goes off. She walks back over to Kabanos and pulls her wand out, handing it over. This time Nunya passes through with no problem.

We follow General Admission down a long hallway, past doors that lead to small offices. Everything looks very official; dark brown wood trim, white walls, dark blue carpets and ornate art deco sconces illuminate the hall. It feels like something from long ago, yet still clean and new. After a few hundred feet, General Admission turns right and heads down a short flight of stairs that leads to a subway platform. Parked in front of us is a brushed-silver subway train that reminds me of an Airstream space-trailer, with rounded corners, and a few insignias of the office of the President of the Pan-galactic Space Federation. We all hop on board, and unfortunately Knob chooses to sit next to me, while Nunya is across from me on the other side.

The train ride doesn't last very long but it does take us deep underground. I watch through the windows as the dark gray tunnel walls pass by. Knob seems to want to say something, but I keep my head turned away from him so he doesn't have the chance. Once we reach the other end of the tunnel we arrive at another security station.

Stepping out onto the platform, a small group of soldiers who were waiting for us are keeping their rifles lowered. I can tell if any one of us makes a sudden move they'll shoot us. Not that it's likely to do any good, unless they have magic imbued weapons, but I guess they figure it's better than nothing.

I follow behind the line of people through the security checkpoint as we all get scanned again. This time no one has a problem passing through. I do my best to catch up to Nunya, who looks like she has something to say.

She whispers to me, "How the hell was the First Daughter kidnapped if there are so many security checkpoints that someone would have to go through to get her out?"

36

I whisper back, "I have no idea. Maybe there will be some clues that will tell us. Are you thinking it was an inside job?"

"Maybe. It would make sense. I can't imagine it'd be easy to pull off. The kidnappers would probably need help."

"I will say that some places are meant to keep people out, like this one, and not keep people in."

Nunya nods at me.

"Anything you want to share with the class?" asks Knob.

"Nope," I say. "But if it makes you feel better, we weren't talking about you behind your back this time."

"I really wouldn't care if you did," says Knob.

"You say that..." I reply.

The hallway we're walking down looks a lot like the one upstairs. However, I happen to know that this hallway has a bunch of security systems built into it. Lasers, tasers, phasers; you name it. I think it's meant to be a gauntlet in case someone was able to make it this far without being stopped. Again, unless they have magic weapons, the security systems won't do much to me, but it still gives me an uneasy feeling. It's the one thing I don't like about coming here.

After walking several hundred feet, we finally reach a giant round logo of the Presidential Seal. And no, as hysterical as it might be, it's not a drawing of the animal named a seal, it's just the emblem they use on all the official Presidential stuff. Although now that I look closely at the fifteen feet across wooden emblem, someone has added a tiny seal drawing to the bottom. My God, those clever bastards did it.

General Admission walks up to the logo and a familiar green laser beam scans his entire body, making sure he is who he says he is. A dull thud comes from inside the door, and the massive logo swings open, letting us inside. I follow the rest of the group through, making sure no one stays behind.

Finally, we reach an actual room meant for people to use. It's a large reception area, like what you'd see in a schmancy hotel, with a long wooden counter. Three different people stand behind the counter waiting to see if we need help. After they've each noticed General Admission, they relax and go about their business as if we aren't even here.

Flanking the two sides of the counter are two hallways, each considerably nicer looking than the previous hallways we've come down. The walls and floors are wood, and the ceilings are white and recessed. General Admission takes us down the hallway to the left, and after passing a few entry ways to some very beautiful rooms we reach our destination. We're inside the Rhombus Office.

Now I know what you're thinking, didn't they used to have a thing called the Oval Office? Yeah, they sure did. But what they eventually realized is that it's super hard to hang a fucking flat painting on a curved wall. So, to make it easier to hang stuff, one of the Presidents several hundred years ago had it rebuilt into a rhombus. Personally, I think that was just a smokescreen because the President at the time, President Feelmore, had a sense of humor. My guess is he liked how silly the name Rhombus Office sounded.

Sitting down at his desk is Bob, the President of the Pangalactic Space Federation. Normally he has a smile on his face, but I can tell that his missing daughter has him worried. When I usually visit, I get a firm handshake, a pat on the back, a glass of Scotch, and a fine cigar. This time I'm met with sadness.

Bob waves us toward the two sofas in the middle of the room. Nunya and I sit on one while Knob and Whip sit on the other. General Admission and a group of accompanying soldiers stand behind us.

"So, Dick, has Knob briefed you on what's happened?" asks President Bob.

"All I've been told is that Tiffany has been kidnapped. Have there been any ransom demands?" I ask.

"Actually, yes. We received a letter from the kidnappers several hours ago. They're asking for fifty million burgmorps for her return," says Bob.

"What else did the note say?"

"It set a time and place for where the money should be dropped off. They also said no police are allowed to be at the dropoff. That's why I asked the four of you for help, since you aren't police. Is it a loophole? Yes, and it's one I'm willing to exploit. I want you all to take the money, make the drop-off, secure Tiffany, and get her home. Do you think you're up for that?"

"I can't speak for anyone else, but I'm in," I say.

"I'll help," says Nunya.

"Me too," says Whip.

"I've been onboard from the start," says Knob.

"Good," says President Bob, nodding his head.

"So, when and where is the drop-off?" I ask.

"The 'when' is two days from now. The 'where' is The Outback," says Bob.

"Wait, the steakhouse restaurant?" I ask.

"No, the planet Outback," says Bob.

"But that's where…" I start to reply. "Are the kidnappers crazy?"

"Apparently they are," replies Bob.

"What? What's so dangerous about planet Outback?" asks Whip.

"Quokkans," says Nunya.

"What the fuck are Quokkans?" asks Whip.

"They're these fuzzy, cute creatures that always smile. But the smile is just to lure you into thinking they're friendly, which they're not. You've heard stories about gremlins before, right?" asks Nunya.

"Yeah, they're those creatures that sneak onto ships, tear them apart, and knock them out of the sky," says Whip.

"Yes. That's what Quokkans are. They're extremely intelligent, incredibly deadly, and sickeningly adorable. If you thought Meows were bad and Sloths were worse, these guys will take apart an armada of ships in minutes. We are so fucked," says Nunya. "The craziest thing about them is if they feel threatened, which admittedly is rare, they will throw their babies at you. They're fucking psychopaths."

The mood in the room has shifted from one of sadness to one of fear. Even Knob, who thinks he's the shit, seems a bit scared. Admittedly, even I'm scared. The last thing I want to see when I die is a cute furry creature tearing my insides out. It's like something out of a deeply disturbing horror movie. I mean Sloths were one thing, but Quokkans? Honestly, I'd rather die at the hands of a Unicorn than by a Quokkan.

"So, were there any clues left behind when your daughter was taken?" asks Nunya.

"Not really. There were no signs of struggle in her room. Our security system didn't record any footage of her leaving, either. They show her going to bed, and then she's not in her room the next morning," says Bob.

"You, uh, don't have security cameras in her bedroom?" I ask.

"No. That would be inappropriate. But we have them positioned at every door she could have left from, or been kidnapped from," says Bob.

"Honestly, it wouldn't be that hard to hack into the security system and alter the footage," says Nunya.

"But my people have assured me our security is top-of-the-line," says Bob.

"If it's a government system, it's easy to get into. Sorry to burst your bubble, but going with the lowest bidder on a security system usually gets you the least amount of security," says Nunya.

Bob looks upset but not surprised.

"Can we see her bedroom?" I ask.

"Of course. You have access to anything you need for your investigation," says Bob.

39

"I've already seen it and I didn't find anything," says Knob. "I doubt you'll find anything, so why waste your time?"

"Because I can see the unseen. Know the unknown. Detect the undetectable," I say.

"Whatever you say, Sherlock," says Knob.

"You're welcome to stay here," I reply.

"Thanks. Whip and I actually will wait here. And in the meantime, Bob, can we have some of that Scotch you keep around?" asks Knob.

While they continue talking, Nunya and I stand up and follow General Admission to Tiffany's room. We walk back out to the reception area and follow the hallway on the right side of the desk to get there. Her room is very far down the hallway, and it takes us a few minutes of walking to reach it. Her ornately carved wood door has been painted over in pink, which is a bit of a travesty.

The general opens the door and Nunya and I both step inside. Before Nunya takes another step, I turn to her and say, "Be very careful not to step on anything. In fact, can you give me a quick moment to use my super-vision on everything?"

"Yeah, sure, go nuts," she replies.

Tiffany is in her twenties but for some reason still acts like a teenager, so everything is designed like a rich teenager's room. Pink carpet, pink drapes, a pink four poster bed; it's like a nightmare of pink. At least the walls are white. She has a large collection of stuffed dolls and knick-knacks lining her pink-shelved walls. I always feel a wave of vertigo when I step into this room.

I scan over her things using my super-vision. The first thing that stands out to me is the vibrator she hides under her mattress is still there.

"She was definitely abducted," I say.

"You only started scanning the room. How can you know that?" asks Nunya.

"Her dildo's still here. She wouldn't go anywhere without it."

"Seriously, you're basing it off that?"

"If you knew Tiffany, and you knew how much she loved that dildo, you'd know she would never leave without it. She'd let the whole rest of her stuff burn, but that dildo is like the center of her lifeforce," I explain.

"Dude, not only is that too much information, why would she be that attached to it?"

"I could pull it out and show you. That would explain it for sure."

"Yeah, no thanks," says Nunya.

"Let's just say it's fancier than probably anything you've ever seen. Not only is it top-of-the-line, but it's also a one-of-a-kind device created to fit her body perfectly. It stimulates... everything. Simultaneously. And it never relents."

"Wow, where would you even get something like that?"

"SpaceMall."

"Wait, the company that advertises on intergalactic commercial flights?" asks Nunya.

"Yup. They have everything," I reply.

"Anyway, do you see any other evidence of her kidnapping? Or who might have taken her?"

I continue scanning the room. It takes a while because she has a few piles of dirty laundry piled up on the floor, and it's difficult to determine whether there was any evidence left behind on all the pairs of panties she'd worn. I mean, there's a lot of evidence left on them, just not necessarily evidence of her kidnapping.

One thing I've never noticed before is that under her bed is a trap door leading to an underground tunnel. That's probably where the kidnappers came from. Now in my defense, I'd never noticed it before because my ability to see through things is something I have to actively concentrate on. And you don't want to use your x-rays on a person, because you don't want to see their last meal digesting. It's disgusting. Total mood ruiner. The only times I've been in here were when Tiffany wanted some Dick, and I wanted some Tiffany, so you do the math.

"There's a trap door under the bed," I say.

"Where does it go?" she asks.

"A tunnel, but I didn't look down it very far. I need to keep scanning, though, before we check it out. There has to be some clue, something the kidnappers left behind."

Finally, I notice a few particles of something that could be mistaken for normal dust right next to the trap door. I keep checking the rest of the room just to be cautious, but I don't see anything else out of place.

"Okay, so there's a few particles of powder near the trap door. We'll need to be careful checking it out. General Admission, do you have any evidence bags I could use?" I ask.

"Yes, I'll have them bring you one," he says, hurrying down the hallway.

We wait a few moments for General Admission to return with what looks like an Intergalactic Intelligence Agent in tow. She's about half my size and muscular, wearing a dark black suit and tie. She also wears sunglasses, even though we're a few hundred feet below the surface of what's effectively a Presidential Death Star. I admire her style. She obviously stole it from me.

"This is Secret Agent Mann, and she should be able to help you gather whatever clues you've found," says General Admission.

"Thanks," I say.

"Here's the evidence bag you asked for," says Secret Agent Mann. "Is there anything else you need?"

"Tweezers, if you have them," I reply.

"Here," she says, pulling a pair out of her pocket. I also notice that she's wearing black nitrile gloves, so I can tell she's taking the evidence thing seriously.

I walk over to the bed, pick it up, and set it out of the way. Whoever designed the trap door did an amazing job with it because you can't see any weird carpet lines that would give it away. To someone with normal vision it'd be completely invisible.

I lay down on the carpet and make sure not to breathe while I carefully tweeze up some of the dust and place it into the evidence bag. There isn't much, but it should be enough to analyze. It's kind of a weird reddish orange color I could only describe as reddish orange.

"Do you have a lab?" I ask, as I hand Secret Agent Mann back her tweezers.

"Of course. I can analyze what you found if you'd like," she replies.

"That would rock. I don't know if the contractors have finished renovating the Dick Cave, so I don't have a place to test it myself," I say, handing her the evidence bag.

"Wait, Dick Cave?" repeats Nunya.

"Yeah, you know how Batman has a Bat Cave? I have a Dick Cave. It's where I do all my analyzing and strategery," I say.

"Analyzing?"

"Yeah, analyzing. I have a lab, deep underground, where I can perform experiments. You do know that I'm a famous detective, right? What kind of detective would I be without a lab?" I ask.

"A normal one," says Nunya. "Most private detectives don't have their own forensics labs."

"Well, that's because they're private detectives, not a 'privates' detective like I am. Also, even though I kind of have powers like Superman, Batman is way cooler. He's the best detective there ever was. He doesn't really get enough credit for his detective skills, and they never really show it in the movies," I say.

"I thought Sherlock Holmes was the greatest detective," says Nunya.

"Oh, don't get me wrong, Sherlock Holmes was definitely a great detective. But Batman is just as good of a detective, and he can also fight, has a cooler outfit, and has a whole bunch of gadgets at his disposal. Sherlock just had a pipe, a deerstalker cap, and a violin."

"Well, what about Jim Rockford? Or Magnum P.I.?" asks Secret Agent Mann.

"What about them?" I reply.

"They were both great detectives."

"Were they? Neither of them did much actual investigating, and neither really went up against a similarly brilliant arch-nemesis. Hell, even Detective Grover was a better detective," I say.

"Okay, there's no reason to be hating on any of them. And don't ever refer to Grover in a negative way. I'll cut you down where you stand," says Nunya. "Not only is he a detective, like you, he's also a superhero, like you. In fact, you owe everything you are to Grover. He's the fucking monster at the end of the book! The OG of superhero detectives. And you can't tell me that Batman counts as a superhero, because he has no powers."

"Personally, I think Mabel and Dipper Pines were the greatest detectives of all time," says Secret Agent Mann.

"Okay, now you're just being silly," I reply.

"I dunno, they were pretty great," says Nunya.

"Oh, I don't disagree, but still, comparing them to Batman is just ridiculous," I say.

"This whole conversation is ridiculous. Can we just get on with the investigation, please?" says Nunya.

"Fine. I'm just glad you didn't bring up Scooby Doo," I say.

"Yeah, no. Although that Velma is kinda hot," says Secret Agent Mann.

Nunya's mouth opens in surprise. She turns to Secret Agent Mann, who winks at her. They both smile and blush. Using my heightened senses, I can tell they're both quickly becoming sexually aroused.

"Okay, so do you two think you can keep it in your pants long enough to finish this investigation? If not, there's a really nice bathroom down the hallway. Just keep it to under twenty minutes, we're on a tight schedule," I say.

"Only twenty minutes?" asks Secret Agent Mann.

"That's barely enough time for foreplay," says Nunya. "Although that's twenty times longer than Dick needs."

"Hey, I'll have you know that I'm a machine in the bedroom. I can go and go and go," I say.

"Sure, Dick. Sure," replies Nunya.

"Just go do what you're gonna do and hurry back," I reply.

Secret Agent Mann hands me back the evidence bag. "I don't want to lose it," she says.

"Oh, when you see Nunya naked, you'll definitely lose it," I say. She just laughs.

43

The two women walk off in search of the bathroom. I turn and notice General Admission just staring at me.

"What?" I ask.

"Is it common for you two to have sex in the middle of a mission?" he asks.

"I'm always on a mission, so I have to have sex whenever I can. As for Nunya, this is the first time since I've known her that she's had sex. But honestly, we've really only known each other for less than a month."

"Well, I'd recommend you keep your 'weapon' holstered for the remainder of this mission. Finding Tiffany is the only thing that matters right now."

"That's why I'm still working on the case instead of trying to join in. Anyway, are you up for seeing where this tunnel goes?" I ask.

"Lead on," he says, all serious-like.

8

I walk back to the patch of carpet over the trap door and plunge my fingers into it. Man, if that doesn't sound like a euphemism, I don't know what does. Anyway, I grasp the metal and yank it free. Setting the large square down next to the hole, I find a concrete staircase. Thankfully, the tunnel is illuminated, because otherwise the General would have to carry a flashlight while we walk along it.

The first thing I notice is the smell. The air is super stale, and I actually catch a whiff of Tiffany's deodorant that remains from when she was abducted.

"It smells like Teen Spirit," I say.

"What do you mean?" asks General Admission.

"Tiffany's deodorant. She wears Teen Spirit deodorant. Plus, I like the song, and I've always wanted to say that."

"Maybe just focus on finding Tiffany."

"Sure."

As we make our way down the long sloping tunnel, I notice the lack of cobwebs. I also realize that this must have been part of the original design plans because it's obvious this tunnel was designed by an architect, and not a group of people trying to get in and get out. There are handrails, plenty of lights overhead, and it goes perfectly straight for quite a distance.

"So, do you think this was built as a way for the First Family to escape if there was ever an attack on the Blue House?" I ask.

"That would be my guess, but I can't imagine that too many people know about it. There's always rumors of hidden tunnels, secret passages and that sort of thing, but I've never actually seen one," says General Admission.

"We can probably pick up the pace since it just goes in a straight line."

"What if it's booby-trapped?"

"I tell you what, I'll run ahead and try to set off any booby traps. If I do and get injured, run back and get help."

"I thought you were indestructible," says General Admission.

"I'm only mostly indestructible. There are a few things that can still kill me."

"What are your weaknesses?"

"I'm not gonna tell you. Are you crazy? The last thing I need is the military trying to kill or enslave me," I say.

45

"No one's out to kill you, especially since the President thinks so highly of you. But even so, I'm sure if we wanted to capture and dissect you, we would have figured out a way to do so already."

"Unless my powers were given to me by the government as part of a super soldier project, and they already know everything about me. If so, I want a super-shield I can throw at people."

"I haven't heard of any super soldier projects, and if I had, I doubt they'd be giving away… super-shields," says General Admission. "Now can you hurry up and run down the hall?"

"Yeah, sure, I'm on it," I say.

I take off running down the long tunnel that looks like it's probably a half mile long, but I don't run anywhere near my top speed because I don't want to destroy the tunnel in the process. Once I get to the end of the tunnel I reach a door. It looks like your standard metal door, only I can't see a way to unlock it. When I pull on the handle it won't budge. Just as I'm about to rip the door off its hinges, General Admission finally catches up to me.

"How come you haven't opened the door?" he asks, sounding a little out of breath.

"Just wanted to see if there was a way to unlock it without destroying it. I should probably check for clues first anyway."

I spend a few minutes looking all over the door, looking through the walls, and trying to see what's on the other side of the door. It doesn't seem booby trapped, which is good. I also don't notice anything that stands out as a clue. Looking on the other side of the door is a large room with a ship inside of it. Ripping the door off its hinges, I drop it with a loud clang. General Admission looks pissed.

"Sorry," I say.

"What?" he yells.

"I said I'm sorry!" I yell back.

"Dammit, I'm not really deaf, that just hurt my ears. Could you not do something like that again?"

"I didn't realize it'd be so loud."

He just shakes his head at me.

We walk through the end of the tunnel and into a large round room. Parked near us is a medium-sized ship, emblazoned with the Presidential Seal, and painted blue to match the outside of the Blue House. It looks practically brand new.

"Must be an escape ship in the event of an emergency," says General Admission.

"You think so?" I say sarcastically.

"Why do you think they left it?" he asks.

"Because they probably came in their own ship," I say.

46

I look up and notice that the room doesn't have a ceiling. We're at the bottom of what feels like a well, and I can see outer space directly above me.

"So, you think the kidnappers flew down here, abducted Tiffany, then flew off?" asks General Admission.

"Yeah, Captain Obvious. Wow, you military guys sure are sharp."

"That's General Obvious to you. It's a wonder that the President likes you so much."

"Well, I've done him a lot of favors in the past. That, and we have the same taste in Scotch, cigars, and women. Give me a minute, I'm gonna need to use my super-vision to see if they left any other clues," I say.

It takes me a few moments to scan everything. I walk around the large round room, looking at the ground and the walls. I even take a quick look at the escape ship, but I don't see anything out of the ordinary. In fact, it's crazy just how clean everything is. I guess it could just be that people don't use this escape route very often, but if I were to guess I'd say that whoever abducted Tiffany knew what they were doing and knew how to avoid detection.

"I'm starting to think the dust may be a red herring," I say.

"What do you mean?" asks General Admission.

"I mean I haven't seen a crime scene this clean before, and it's odd that whoever took Tiffany left the reddish orange dust behind. It's almost as if they wanted us to find it."

"So, you think it was left deliberately?" he asks.

"Dude, seriously, you make the worst backup sidekick. Yes, I just said that. I think they wanted us to find the dust. We may have a problem, because I think I know what we're up against."

"And what's that?"

"A criminal mastermind," I say.

9

"Well, that was dramatic," says General Admission.

"I gotta keep things exciting. Detective work is usually pretty boring. Look at this, analyze that. Stick some weird goo in a container, add a liquid and shake it up. Maybe stare at some things under a microscope. It's all fairly technical. But yeah, I think whoever did this not only had help from the inside, but they were intelligent, methodical, and precise."

"Any guesses on who it might be specifically?" asks General Admission.

"No, not yet. When we analyze the powder, we'll know more. But even then, I don't know if I'll trust what it tells me. Either someone planted the dust to throw us off their scent, or they left it as a calling card. Calling cards let you know your enemy has an ego. Either they want to be caught, or they want you to find them so they can trap you."

"Wow, that's pretty smart."

"What the fuck? Does everyone just automatically assume I'm dumb or something?" I ask.

"I think so, but I don't know everyone, so I can't say so for sure."

"Look, I already have a full-time sidekick that gives me shit, I don't need another one."

"Hey, you were giving me shit for asking what you thought were obvious questions," says General Admission. "You deserved it."

"Whatever. Anyway, we should head back. There's nothing more to see here.

I walk past him and head down the tunnel. The General follows behind me, close enough that if I came to a quick stop he'd run right into the back of me. I don't get why people do annoying shit like that.

Walking up the steps I end up in Tiffany's room again. Nothing's been moved since we went down the tunnel. I also notice that Nunya and Secret Agent Mann haven't returned.

I decide to head back to the Rhombus Office, and of course General Admission follows right behind me. When we get there, Knob and Bob are smoking cigars and drinking Scotch while Whip just looks at them as if he's mildly annoyed. Soldiers still line the walls, making sure the President is protected at all times.

"Did you find anything?" asks Bob.

"Yes, we did. I found some powder that Secret Agent Mann is going to analyze for me, but she's preoccupied at the moment," I reply.

"Preoccupied?" repeats Bob.

"Yeah. I think she was in the middle of someone. I mean, 'something'."

"Oh, I see. Well then where's Ms. Business?" asks Bob.

"I think she's in the bathroom. Should be back shortly," I say.

"She has been known to take exceedingly long dumps," says Knob.

I nod. "If it's okay with you, Bob, I'd like to wait before I explain what I found so that she can hear it too."

"Of course."

We wait a few minutes, and then a few more. I look at the grandfather clock in the corner and realize we've already waited at least thirty minutes. I figure it took us about fifteen to twenty for me and General Admission to check things out, so they've been doing their thing for almost an hour. Eventually, they both show back up at the same time. Nunya has a dumb grin on her face and a little moisture, while Secret Agent Mann's legs seem wobbly, and she looks slightly embarrassed. Good for them.

"So how was your poo?" I ask Nunya.

"My poo? Oh, it was the dumpiest. Yup, really gave birth to a big one. Probably at least seven pounds," she replies.

Bob spits out some of his Scotch accidentally.

"Sorry about that," I say. "My sidekick is a little rough around the edges."

"You keep forgetting that you're my sidekick," says Nunya.

"Anyway, now that everyone's here in the room, I found a tunnel that runs underneath Tiffany's bed. Did anyone here know about it?" I ask.

I look around the room, trying to use my keen powers of observation to see if anyone reacts to the question. Almost everyone shifts their weight, as if they all knew about it.

"It's well known that there are secret passages throughout the Blue House in case of emergencies. It's the best way to protect people on the inside. So yes, everyone pretty much is familiar with what you're saying," says Bob.

"Good. Well, this secret tunnel leads out to an escape ship. I'm fairly certain that whoever kidnapped her came down into the hangar that connects to the other side of the tunnel, broke in, and left some powder that I don't recognize next to the trap door," I say.

"For what reason?" asks Bob.

"To either throw us off their scent, or to lure us into a trap. Either way, I believe it was left behind deliberately. The rest of the tunnel and launch room don't have any other clues that I could find. I should also mention that I can say with one hundred percent certainty that she was abducted and didn't leave on her own."

"Oh, how do you know that?" asks Bob.

"She left something incredibly important to her in her room. Something she would never leave without," I say.

"Which is?" asks Bob.

I start to panic and look over at Nunya.

"It was a photograph of your family," says Nunya.

"Yeah, a photograph!" I repeat.

"Oh, well that I can understand. Is there anything else you need to investigate?" asks Bob.

"Not here, not as far as I know. We'll just have to see what we learn from the powder," I say, handing the evidence bag back to Secret Agent Mann. She takes it and carefully places it in her pocket then leaves. Before she goes though, I notice her wink at Nunya. Now it's Nunya's turn to blush.

"I do have a question," says Bob. "How come you were able to find the powder when Knob was unable to?"

"Because I don't have Dick's super-vision. Not all of us superhero types have the same powers," says Knob.

"Oh, okay," says Bob, seemingly happy with the response. "Anyway, what do you plan to do while the powder is being analyzed? Basically, what's your next step in the investigation?"

"Well, we have a line on a gadgeteer. Might be able to get a few gadgets that could help us out if I'm right and this whole thing is some elaborate trap," I say.

"That's assuming I'm willing to fly you there," says Knob.

"If you're not, I would be very happy to find my own spaceship somewhere and fly there on my own," I say.

"I would prefer it if you two both worked together on this," says President Bob. "I'm sorry, I just don't know who to trust right now, and I figure if either of you was behind this, the other would discover it and alert me."

"But wait, what if we're both behind the kidnapping?" I ask.

"Are you?" asks The President.

"Noooooo," I reply.

50

"Then everything should be fine. But Knob, I do need you to transport Dick and Nunya wherever they need to go, without restrictions. I've known Dick for many years, and I trust him more than most. And he's the best detective in the galaxy," says President Bob.

"Not for long," mumbles Knob, under his breath.

"I'm sorry, did you say something?" asks The President.

"Nope, I'm good," replies Knob.

"Okay, well if you've concluded your investigation here, General Admission will see you out safely. Find Tiffany. Please."

Knob throws back the rest of his Scotch but brings his cigar with him, as well as a large duffle bag that I can only assume is the ransom money. Whip follows right behind him, and he doesn't seem very happy about the smoke wafting into his face. Nunya falls in behind Whip and I bring up the rear. The soldiers that were in the Rhombus Office follow us, making sure we don't get 'lost'.

As we make our way back through the lobby and down the long hallway we came in, (heh, 'came in'), I turn to Nunya and whisper, "So how was it?"

"How was what?" she whispers back.

"How was it with Secret Agent Mann?" I ask.

"You mean Vanessa?"

"I guess, if that's her name."

"It is," she says smiling.

"So, are you gonna answer me?"

She thinks for a moment. "Nope."

"Come on, I want details!"

"Not happening. You'll just have to imagine it."

"You know, I could have watched the whole time if I wanted to with my super-vision, but I respect you enough to not use it. That and I didn't want to see your last meal," I say.

"Uh, sure. And thanks for that, I guess. Still, I don't lick and tell," says Nunya.

"Ah-ha! I knew it! That's why your face is still moist!"

"Shhhh, shut up, Dick!" she says, trying not to laugh.

"I'm just glad you finally got yours," I say.

"Yeah, me too," she replies. "About damn time."

Eventually, while we talk about nothing in particular, we reach the table where they took all of our weapons. I grab my blasters while Nunya spends the next couple of minutes putting her various knives and guns back into their holsters and pockets. Once we're all loaded back up with our armaments, we walk back to Knob's spaceship.

"So, where are we headed?" asks Knob.

"We're supposed to meet someone named Nord on the planet Veepee Enn. Do you know how to get there?" asks Nunya.

"Never been, but I'm sure the ship's onboard IPS can find it," replies Knob.

We all climb aboard and make our way to the conference room, except for Knob who goes to the bridge to program in our next destination. Whip, Nunya and I sit down, staring at the place where a very nice conference table used to be. I glance over at Nunya who looks a bit sheepish, realizing we're just sitting uncomfortably now, with nowhere to place our drinks. Not that we have any drinks at the moment, but the struggle is still real.

"Maybe we should go to the table store first," says Nunya.

"I'm sure we can make do without a table," says Whip.

"I just feel bad about it," says Nunya. "Not because I broke something of Knob's, but because it really tied the room together."

"It does feel more like a chair room than a conference room now," admits Whip. "Maybe instead of having one large table, everyone can have their own smaller table."

"That could be cool," says Nunya.

"That way if you go ballistic again, we only have to replace one small table instead of one giant table," replies Whip.

Nunya looks sheepish again. It's definitely not something I'm used to. Normally she's more balls-out than even I am, but I guess she has a conscience when it comes to breaking people's things.

"So, have you two ever been to planet VeePee Enn?" asks Whip.

"No, why, have you heard something about it?" I ask.

"Just that it's filled with hostile puppies with grenade launchers attached to their backs," says Whip.

"Wait, seriously?" I ask.

"No, but after hearing about your adventures, it sounds like you're constantly battling cute things. Is there a reason for that? Do you just hate 'cute'?" asks Whip.

"I don't have any real problem with cute. Do you, Nunya?"

"No. That's how I got attacked by the Meows. I let my guard down because I love cute things. But now I can't even trust myself around them. I mean, eventually we're gonna have to deal with some killer Quokkas. How fucked up is that?" says Nunya.

"Pretty fucked up," says Whip. "Would either of you like a drink?"

"No thanks," I say. "Nowhere to set it."

Nunya gives me a look.

"What?"

"You don't need to rub it in," says Nunya.

"No, I'm pretty sure 'Vanessa' already took care of that," I reply.

"Har-har," says Nunya. "And yes."

"Oh, so Is that what you were doing instead of shitting?" asks Whip.

"Maybe..." says Nunya.

"Good for you," says Whip. "Hopefully I get some man trim on this adventure. I usually do." Whip winks at me and I just smile and shrug.

10

Eventually, Knob comes sauntering back in and sits down. "It shouldn't be too long before we reach planet Veepee Enn. Computer estimates it at about twenty minutes."

"So, what should we do in the meantime?" I ask.

"Well, we could brainstorm who we think kidnapped her," says Nunya.

"Sure. Do you already have some ideas?" asks Knob.

"No, not really. Do you?"

"Actually, no. The President has too many enemies for too many different reasons. It could be a lot of people," says Knob.

"Well wait, what if it really isn't an enemy of the President, what if it's one of our enemies trying to lure us into a trap?" suggests Whip.

"That's also possible. But Dick and I both have substantial enough rogues galleries of villains that it wouldn't help to guess," says Knob.

"Yeah, I mean there's Dr. Footlong, Professor Nippletwist, Fanny Flamebutt, La Cabeza De Los Pantalones, Mai Cherona, Mr. Meatwhistle..." I say.

They all just stare at me.

"Well, what about an enemy of mine, or maybe Nunya's?" says Whip.

"You have enemies?" I ask.

"No, not really. I have a couple of exes I don't get along with, but nobody who would be capable of something like this," explains Whip.

"How about you, Nunya?" asks Knob.

"Nah. I mean, I have one, but he's in prison, and will be for the next four hundred and seventy years," says Nunya.

"So, we're back to square one," says Knob.

"I dunno, I still think it's you," I say.

"Well, it isn't. Besides, how do we know it isn't you?" asks Knob.

"Really?"

"Sure. What, is it really that far-fetched?" asks Knob.

"Yeah. Why the fuck would I kidnap a chick I like, from her dad who I like, forcing him to hire some douche nozzle I hate to come harass me, destroying my friend's bar in the process, and stopping me from getting the fucking unicorns off my back? I'm totally that kind of mastermind. I'm just so clever, I decided I wanted to fuck myself over for the fun of it. Yeah, let's go with that theory, genius," I say.

"It does sound unlikely, now that you've said it out loud," says Knob.

"You think?"

"Okay, guys, c'mon, if we're going to figure this out, we need to stop accusing each other," says Nunya.

"I'm just waiting on the lab results before I jump to conclusions," I say. "Just need those lab results."

Just then a voice comes over the loudspeakers, "the lab results are complete."

No, not really, that didn't happen, because that would be too damn big of a coincidence, and real life doesn't work like that. If your life is that easy, then you can suck it.

"Yeah, bickering is obviously getting us nowhere," says Whip. "We could talk about what the plan is if we do find out who's behind this."

"We kill them," I say.

"Yeah, we kill them," says Knob.

"That's not really a plan. That's barely a step in a plan," says Nunya.

"Well, since we don't know who it is, and we don't know what it'll take to actually rescue Tiffany and get her back, it's kind of hard to plan past that one simple step," I say.

"Fine, let's just sit here in uncomfortable, unproductive silence for the next fifteen minutes until we make it to planet Veepee Enn," says Nunya.

"Sounds good to me," I say.

"I'm good with that," replies Knob.

Whip just gives a half-hearted shrug.

Nunya, on the other hand, looks frustrated. She crosses her arms and spins her chair so she's facing the wall instead of facing us.

So, we sit there for fifteen minutes, not saying a word. I figure if I speak up it will only piss off Nunya, and I really don't have anything productive to say. We literally have no idea what we're up against, and guessing is just as useful as what newscasters do when they speculate on a situation that they have no information on just to fill airtime. I can only guess that neither Whip nor Knob had anything useful to say as they don't speak up either.

After fifteen minutes the ship's automated systems speak out: "Now arriving at your destination, planet Veepee Enn. Please wait until the ship has made a complete stop before disembarking. Thank you."

"That female voice was oddly soothing," I say.

"That's because it's my mom's," replies Knob.

"Seriously? Because I was just about to say it was also super sexy. She can totally ASMR my boner any day," I say.

"C'mon, man, that's not cool," says Knob.

"Well, you're the guy who was weird enough to make his ship sound like his mom. It's a little Norman Bates, isn't it?"

"I have no idea what you mean,"

"I mean that I don't think a normal, well-adjusted person would have his mom's sexy voice talking to him all the time when she wasn't there. It's not a good look."

"Hey, just because I have a special relationship with my mom doesn't mean you get to mock it!" says Knob.

"What do you mean 'special relationship'?" I ask.

"It just means we're close, and nothing more," says Knob.

"Nothing more?" I repeat.

"Nothing more."

"Fine, if you tell me that you aren't a serial killer who's fixated on his dead mother that you like to dress up as then I believe you, Knob."

"Good, thank you."

"It's still weird," I reply.

Knob looks over at Whip who nods that he agrees with me. Nunya has turned back around at this point and nods too.

"Whatever," says Knob.

Nunya gets up out of her seat and starts walking down the hall toward the ship's large opening. I decide to follow her because I want out of the ship too. Whip follows closely behind me, and as we stand there a few seconds I realize Knob hasn't come out of the conference room. Maybe he's just sulking.

After a minute of waiting for the ship to finally dock, Knob shows up. He won't look me in the eye, but I really don't care. He's an asshole, and I can't stand him, and he's probably behind this whole mess, so why should I be nice to him? Even if he does seem sensitive and a bit pathetic.

The side of the ship opens and fresh air rushes in. By fresh air I actually mean the smell of garbage, and it's bad enough it makes me gag. It doesn't help that I have an unnaturally strong sense of smell. But yeah, the smell is nasty. Even the others look at me in disgust, as if I let loose one of my famous pewtonium bombs. Which I didn't. I swear.

"What is that smell?" asks Nunya.

"It's the smell of success!" comes a voice just outside of the ship.

I follow behind everyone else as we cover our faces, doing our best to not breathe in the noxious fumes. Standing about fifteen feet from Knob's ship is a young female Effbee. Her species have been named Effbees because of their resemblance to Frigatebirds. You know, the initials F. B. for Frigatebird. Anyway, a Frigatebird is this weird bird on Earth Uno where the male's chest is red and puffed out. Only with female Effbees, it's their breasts that are huge and red, and they sparkle like someone spilled glitter all over them.

This particular Effbee is no exception. She has those massive trademark boobs, and she's displaying her cleavage to full effect in a pair of overalls, clearly proud of the reaction they produce. Other than having large red knockers, she also has twinkling eyes covered by a pair of goggles and long flowing blonde hair. I try briefly to hide my boner, but then I just give up and let it fly free.

"Welcome. You must be Dick and Nunya," says the woman. "M-Ray said you'd be stopping by. I'm Nord. May I ask who these other two people are?"

She has got the damned sexiest southern voice I've ever heard. I can just imagine her calling me 'sugar'. Yup, this boner isn't going to calm itself any time soon.

"Uh, yeah, this is Knob Johnson and Whip Noodbottom," says Nunya.

"Charmed, I'm sure," says Nord. Both Knob and Whip just slowly nod their heads.

"Do you have a place that's less... odorous?" I ask. "Sorry, but my super-sniffer can't handle the fumes."

"Oh, of course, follow me. I know the smell can take getting used to by outsiders. I've been around it all my life, so it makes no never-mind to me," says Nord.

We follow her through some stacks of garbage piled thirty feet high and across several plank walkways that just barely keep our feet from dipping into some very foul-smelling liquid. The dingy color of the stacks plus the toxic looking runoff give the whole place a swampy feel.

Eventually, we make our way to a large, nondescript-looking building. It's painted dark flat brown, and its tiny windows don't let you see through them into what's waiting inside for us. I could use my super-vision to see through the walls, but again, I'd have to see people's guts, and with the smell around here I'd be risking throwing up all over everyone.

Nord opens the door and waves us inside. As we step in, I'm floored by how regal the place looks. It's actually quite similar to my place, only more so. Very elegant, but not overstated. You can tell

57

whoever decorated it knew how to use restraint. It's breathtaking without being gaudy.

The walls are nearly white, with just the slightest hint of lavender to them. Grand white marble staircases curve upward on both sides, eventually reaching the second floor. On the first floor is an entryway that leads into a massive living room, also with white marble floors, and although it is common to see gold trim pieces offsetting the white marble in homes like this, she's chosen not to use any gold anywhere. I'm not sure if I agree with that philosophy, but I gotta admit, it makes it feel more serene, like it's not trying too hard to be fancy.

One thing I realize is that once we passed through the threshold it no longer smells like rotting death. Instead, the air is a mix of vanilla and lavender. I breathe in deeply and feel a sense of calm I haven't felt in forever. I start to wish that maybe my home was more like this one.

Nord has us follow her into the living room and waves us to sit down on some very beautiful white sofas. I'm a little surprised at just how comfortable yet stylish they are.

"So, M-Ray was a little vague with the details, which is kind of her style. I'm assuming you're here because you're interested in acquiring some items that might help you on some sort of mission," says Nord.

"Yes, we're trying to rescue someone who's been kidnapped, and we're fairly sure we're up against a criminal mastermind. We aren't sure who, and we aren't sure where, and we aren't sure how. So, I guess we're looking for things that could be useful in a lot of scenarios," says Nunya.

"Ah, I see. You need multi-purpose items, devices that can be discreetly concealed on your person and overlooked in the event that you're captured as well," says Nord. "Have you considered cybernetic implants?"

Nunya, Knob, Whip and I look at each other, not sure how to answer.

"Honestly, I don't think any of us had considered that option," replies Nunya. "Usually, devices like that are for people who are missing limbs or paralyzed in some way."

"Usually," repeats Nord. "But these are unusual times that sometimes require unusual solutions. I can replace any body part from any known species and make it work far, far better than what they were born with. Bionic arms that can crush tanks, bionic legs that can let you outrun a hover cycle. I can even replace your eyes with a full heads-up-display targeting system. And each replacement is designed to otherwise look and act exactly how your original appendage did. You wouldn't be able to tell the difference, other than the enhanced abilities. They will also pass for real under close scrutiny. But if you're squeamish about body modification, I understand."

"I'm not totally squeamish about it," I say, "but my near-invulnerable skin would make bionic devices tough to implant, and my accelerated healing ability would likely reject whatever you'd implanted in me."

"Same for me," says Knob.

"I appreciate the offer, but I think I'll pass as well. My body is perfection, and I wouldn't dare do anything to alter it," says Nunya.

Nord smiles and nods at her.

"Huh, well, I think I might like some modifications," says Whip.

"Wait, Whip, are you really sure you'd want to do something like that?" asks Knob.

"Yeah, I mean when Nunya is wearing her armor then the three of you are nearly invincible. It'd be nice to be able to compete. Bring more to the table. I can help if we get caught in a dangerous situation. Don't get me wrong, I'm deadly with my fists and feet, but not against superheroes. Anyway, Nord, I'm in," says Whip.

"Delightful. Do you know what kind of alterations you'd want to make?" asks Nord. "And the sky is truly the limit. If you can imagine it, I can likely make it."

"Uh, will the replacement parts still feel like my real parts?" asks Whip.

"To someone touching it on the outside, yes. The synth-skin looks and acts exactly like real skin and is self-healing. And to you, also yes. When something or someone touches you, you'll still receive the same feelings of pain or pleasure as you would if your limbs were the ones you were born with," explains Nord.

"Well then shit, let's do everything," says Whip.

"Everything?"

"Everything."

11

"Wait, I'm sorry, but how will you pay for the bionics?" asks Knob. "I didn't realize I was paying you that well."

"You aren't," replies Whip. "But I figured you'd pay for it."

"Hold on now..." starts Knob.

"Gentlemen, there is no need to worry. I'll be installing the implants free-of-charge as a favor to Blhack Glass," says Nord.

"Are you sure? It seems like they'd be really expensive," replies Knob.

"Does it look like I need the money?" asks Nord.

"Well, no," replies Knob.

"Then it's settled. If you could all please remain seated, I'll take you to my Lab of Mystery," says Nord.

"Wait, why is it a lab of mystery? Do you not know what goes on down there?" I ask.

"First, my lab isn't 'down there'," says Nord, as the room we're in starts slowly moving upward like an elevator. "Second, I know exactly what happens there. I just like the sound of it. With mystery comes excitement and pleasure. Without it, life grows tiresome."

"I'm all for mystery, excitement and pleasure. That's why I became a detective," I say.

"And a man-whore," mumbles Nunya.

"Yes, and a man-whore," I proudly repeat.

Nord gets a funny look on her face, like she's both amused and skeptical at the same time.

After a few seconds, the room stops moving upward. A large double door at the far end of the room opens, revealing quite possibly the coolest and most mysterious room I've ever seen. Now, I will say that my Dick Cave is really cool, and has all sorts of scientificky things like vials, and beakers, and mixing devices, and heating devices, and a microscope, and all of that shit. This... this looks more like a warehouse of science experiments.

Throughout the room are several desks with projects that look like they're actively being worked on. Some look like chemicals being synthesized, while others look like they're mechanical and electrical in nature. Large glass chambers line one of the walls with what look like weird, unnatural creatures inside of them, suspended in an amber-colored fluid. It makes me feel a bit uneasy about things.

"Uh, what are those?" I ask, pointing to the chambers.

"Oh those? Those are nothing nefarious, I assure you," says Nord. "Sometimes dead creatures are dumped here on Veepee Enn, so I preserve the remains in these chambers. It allows me to experiment on things that are no longer living, so there's no moral issue with it."

I just shrug my shoulders.

"Now, Mr. Noodbottom, if you'd be so kind as to follow me, we can begin," says Nord.

Nord waves Whip to a hole in the floor at the far end of the room and he walks over to it. The rest of us are kind of shocked at how everything is set up like something out of a mishmash of sci-fi movies.

"Dude, this is totally the Han Solo carbonite chamber from Empire!" says Nunya.

"Indeed, it is," says Nord. "I figured if I was going to spend the money on all this gear, why not make it look cool at the same time."

"That's awesome! I always wanted to be Han Solo growing up," says Nunya.

"Me too," says Nord. "Mr. Noodbottom, if you could please take off your clothes and climb down into the chamber we can get started."

Whip does as she says, removing his clothes, placing them on a nearby chair, and carefully climbing down into the pit. Meanwhile, Nord goes over to a console and starts pushing a series of buttons then types some things into a touchscreen. After a few seconds, the machinery down in the pit whirs to life. I watch as several different devices start poking at Whip. He passes out immediately, but the machinery gently catches him. Mechanical arms inside the chamber move around, carefully working on their patient.

"This process will take a few hours. Ms. Business and Mr. Johnson, if you could please make your way back to the grand living room there will be food, drinks, and a large holo-display to entertain you. Mr. Blowhard, please follow me," says Nord.

"Uh, yeah, sure," I say. I look over at Nunya who has a 'what's going on?' look on her face. I just shrug at her.

Begrudgingly, both Knob and Nunya leave the Lab of Mystery the way we came in, while I follow Nord up a walkway and through a normal sized door over the pit that I hadn't yet noticed.

Inside is the sexiest bedroom I've ever seen. The ceiling is mirrored, the walls are red and lined with hundreds of sex toys, some of which look more like medieval weapons than devices of pleasure. In the middle is a massive heart-shaped bed. The room smells like rare oils and incense. I start getting firm at the thought of all the craziness that must have gone down in this room.

"Dick, may I call you Dick? Dick, I've been wanting to fuck you for a very, very long time," says Nord in that cute southern accent of hers.

"Oh my God, yes please! We're already like nearly a quarter of the way through the mission and I haven't had sex yet. Nunya got some before I did, which kind of annoys me, honestly. Not that it's a competition, but..." I'm cut off mid-sentence by Nord placing a finger on my mouth.

"Shhh, my beautiful man. If you don't stop talking, I may have to give you a spanking," says Nord.

"Oh, that would be truly terrible," I say, as sarcastic and flirtatiously as I can.

"And now you've already broken my first rule," says Nord. "I must punish you."

Nord pulls me by the hand over to a table with a couple of straps on it.

"Before we begin your punishment, you need to disrobe," says Nord.

I very hurriedly take my tuxedo and shoes off and kick them out of the way.

"Good. Now bend over the table and place your hands through the wrist straps," says Nord.

I do as she instructs, bending over and placing my hands through the loops. She walks to the end of the table and cinches up the leather straps. For some weird reason my arms begin to tingle. Moving behind me, I feel Nord attach some straps to my ankles that I hadn't noticed before. My legs now tingle like my arms. It's a weird sensation, but I don't think too much of it.

I watch as Nord walks over to a wall across the room then pulls down a large paddle with holes in it.

"Do your worst," I say.

"Oh, I will. And the more you talk, the more you'll be punished. Just remember that," says Nord.

Whack.

"Oh, what the fuck! That hurt!" I yell.

"You're still talking," says Nord.

Whack.

"Goddamn it, why does that hurt?" I yell.

"Still talking."

Whack.

"Popsicle! Popsicle!" I yell.

"Sorry, but I don't believe in safe words," says Nord. "And you're still talking. As long as you keep talking, I'll keep paddling your ass."

Whack.

"Mmmmmmmmmm grrrrrrrrr," I moan through my gritted teeth. "How is this even possible? How are you hurting me?"

"The bindings are magical. They let you feel both pain and pleasure. I know your weakness, and I know how to exploit it," says Nord.

Whack.

"RAAAAARGH!!!!" I yell.

Nord stops for a moment, because I guess I haven't said anything, I just grunted in pain. She waits, wondering if I'm going to say something.

"Are you waiting for me to say something?" I ask.

Whack.

"ANNNGGGGGHHHHHH," I yell.

Tears start forming in the corners of my eyes. This isn't what I signed up for. I figured she'd break the paddle on my invincible ass, or at the very least I'd pretend like I could feel it and roleplay a little, but Nord has very different plans than I do.

I try to break free from the straps, but I can't seem to get them loose. I pull, and tug, and wiggle, all to the amusement of Nord. She walks around the table in front of me and lifts my head up to look at her face.

"Is that actual fear I see in your eyes? Is the big, strong man not so big and strong now?" says Nord, in a baby voice.

I don't say anything.

"Not wanting to talk? At least you're finally learning," says Nord. "I've changed my mind. You can talk now, because I want to hear you beg and plead."

"Oh, God, okay. Yes, please let me go. We can do any freaky shit you want to do; I just don't want to be tied up like this anymore," I say.

"That wasn't very good pleading," says Nord.

She goes around to my backside and paddles it again.

"RAWRRRRRR!!! Please, please let me go! I'm actually kind of scared right now. You're right, okay? I'm freaking out and I just want to go home. Please let me go home," I say, as I start crying.

"Wait, Dick, are you okay? I mean, seriously, I thought you were into this. If you don't want to continue, we can end things here," says Nord. "I won't keep going if this isn't your thing. I'm sorry if I hurt you."

I take a moment to collect myself. "Please don't paddle me anymore. I'm not into pain. Since I'm nearly indestructible, normally spankings don't really do anything to me, and I figured that's what would happen, that I'd be safe. This feels different. I'm down for pretty much anything else. Just not that."

"Sure, no worries," says Nord. "Do you want me to untie you?"

The gears start grinding in my head. I want to make sure that I'm making this decision for me, and I'm not feeling pressured into anything.

"No, it's okay, you can keep me tied up. Now that I know if I tell you to stop that you'll stop, I trust you a little bit more," I say.

"Are you absolutely sure?" asks Nord.

"Yeah, we can keep going."

"Okay. I have something a little different in mind, then."

Nord walks over to one of her walls of pain and pulls down a long rubber-looking thing with a few straps attached to it. She moves behind me to where I can't see.

"Uh, what is..." I start to say.

"Don't you worry your pretty little head, sugar. You'll enjoy this one," says Nord.

I hear Nord spit onto my backside and feel the moisture run between the Kraken my ass. With one forceful shove, I feel something enter my Dick Cave.

"Oh God," I mumble.

I feel like a Thanksgiving turkey being stuffed, and I probably look like it too. It totally reminds me of the battering ram Grond from The Return of The King. What? I read sometimes. You don't have to act all surprised like that.

Anyway, it hurts a bit at first, but eventually it doesn't hurt so much. I kind of get used to the sensation of being a human butter churner. As Nord continues to probe me, I hear her making little grunting sounds. She must have strapped the device to herself. After a few moments I'm actually kind of enjoying it.

Then something weird happens. I start involuntarily squirting Dick goo underneath the table so far that it shoots past the end of the table, and I can see it on the ground a few feet in front of me. It looks like someone jumping up and down on a tube of toothpaste. Nord keeps pumping, I keep shooting. It's an intense feeling of pleasure and I don't know what to think about it.

Eventually, after what seems like several minutes, my fuel indicator is on empty. If my body could produce dust at this point it would. Nord realizes I'm finished blasting for now, so she pulls out. I hear her drop the device on the ground.

"I think you did a good enough job that you've earned a reward," says Nord.

"Oh goody?" I reply.

"I think we'll both enjoy this one."

I watch as Nord makes her way to the front of the table, my chin uncomfortably resting on the rounded edge of it. She slowly takes off her clothes, acting all innocent, trying to tease me. It actually kind of works because despite being on empty, I can feel my space thruster inching back up.

Once Nord is completely naked, she turns around, bends over, and shoves her love nest right in my face.

"Lick," she says seductively.

And lick I do as I go to town on her. I use all my special techniques. The hurricane. The laundromat. The slithering snake. The broken-down Studebaker. The one-inch tongue punch technique. The filthy squirrel. The 'Friday is clam chowder day'. The tempest. And finally, I finish her off with my signature move: the holiday feast.

Nord screams as she's rocked to ecstasy. She has to hold onto my hair just to keep from falling over. As she does, she starts blasting me in the face with her liquid lady love. It's gooey, and wet, and I feel like Slimer from the Ghostbusters just made out with me. Her body starts to shake, and she falls to the floor. At first, I think she's having a medical episode, but no, she's just completely spent.

I watch as she falls asleep, leaving me still tied up to the table.

"Nord? Hey Nord, could you untie me now, please?" I ask.

She peacefully drifts off to Sleepytown.

12

Just then, both Nunya and Knob bust in.

"Dick, what the fuck is going on? We heard screaming," yells Nunya. "Oh, for fuck's sake, not again!"

Knob just looks at me, obviously annoyed, but then I notice him eyeing my naked ass. After he realizes I see him staring at me, his eyes dart away. He turns around, clearly embarrassed.

"Hey guys, could you untie me?" I ask. "Please?"

"Wait, did you kill Nord?" asks Nunya.

"Hell no. I just gave her the licking of her life and she passed out," I reply.

"Sure you did," says Nunya.

"No, really, that's exactly what happened. Why do you think my face is so wet?"

"I dunno, maybe you were sneezing a lot, and you didn't have a hanky. How the fuck should I know?" says Nunya.

"Come on, just let me free!" I say.

"Why can't you let yourself free?" asks Nunya.

"Because the straps are magical. I don't have the strength right now to break through them."

Nunya starts laughing. "This is so incredibly typical of you. Fine, I'll undo the straps on one condition."

"Which is?"

"Hmmm, I dunno. I tell you what, how about you'll owe me a favor."

"A favor? Why do I hate the sound of that?" I say.

"Because you have no idea when I'll use it or what I'll use it for," says Nunya. "So do we have a deal?"

"Hell no. I'm not letting you have that kind of power over me," I reply.

I notice that Knob has already left the room. Shit, there goes option 'B'.

"I could just leave you strapped to the table," says Nunya. "Wait, why is the floor so messy? It looks like someone dumped a tureen of cream of wheat everywhere."

"I don't want to talk about it."

"Oh, oh my God! There's a massive strap-on lying on the floor! Did she peg you?"

"I said I don't want to talk about it."

"Well, at least you know how it feels, now," says Nunya.

"Fine, whatever. You've humiliated me. Isn't that enough? Can you please just undo the straps?"

Instead of responding, Nunya undoes the straps around my wrists. I very slowly push myself into a standing position then turn and kneel, undoing the straps tied to my ankles. I see a stack of fresh towels lying on a nearby table, and a door I hadn't noticed before. I grab a couple of towels and open the door. Inside is a large bathroom with a walk-in shower.

"I'll let you get cleaned up," says Nunya, who walks away.

I turn the water on as hot as it will go so that I can't see anything through the hot mist. Huh, Hot Mist would be a good name for a superwoman. Her real name would have to be Misty, or maybe spell it Misti with an 'i' just to be pretentious. Anyway, if I ever write a fictional superhero novel, maybe I'll base it on her.

The hot shower feels good, but my legs and arms don't work as well as they normally do. In fact, my legs are kind of shaking. I make sure to wash myself slowly, so I don't slip and fall. I also spend extra time cleaning my back porch. It's a little sore, but the sensation quickly goes away now that my self-healing powers have kicked back in.

After a few more minutes, Nord comes walking into the bathroom.

"Did I really pass out from an orgasm?" asks Nord.

"Yeah, you really did," I reply.

"Goddamn. And I just wanted to say again that I'm sorry I took things too far."

"Hey, you stopped when I asked, which is what's important."

She nods her head.

"So, are you okay with me joining you?" asks Nord.

"Yeah, I'm cool with that."

You know, it's actually kind of nice, because I don't normally do this sort of thing with anyone. Normally, it's just all about the sex and I get the fuck out of there. We spend a while just soaping each other's bodies, kissing, but we don't have sex in the shower. It's more intimate than I'm used to. It's weird how different it is than what happened in the red room of pleasure. I wonder if this is what being in a relationship is like. Honestly, I've never been in one before so I wouldn't know. Maybe they aren't as bad as I thought they were. Maybe I could get used to something like this.

"Hey, uh, Nord, are you... single?" I ask.

"Dick, you don't want to fall in love with me," says Nord.

"Why not?"

"Well, you're always off adventuring, and I pretty much stay here with my work. We'd never see each other."

"Yeah, I mean I guess that's true."

"And you like having sex with a whole lot of people. If you did fall in love with me, and we did have a relationship, I'd want it to mostly be monogamous. I mean, we could bring lovers in to share, if you're into that sort of thing, but I wouldn't want you having sex without me," says Nord.

"That would make it harder. I'd have to keep it in my pants whenever I was on a mission. I honestly don't know if I could promise that," I admit.

"I know, and I wouldn't ask you to. The other thing is we don't even really know each other. I mean yeah, I know you're super skilled with your tongue, and I know what your weakness is, and what you do for a living, but I don't know about your past, and you don't know about mine. I'm a scientist, and I've done a few questionable things that made sense as experiments but are morally gray. And I don't feel I should have to explain myself and my motives. Do you understand why I don't think being in a relationship together would be a good idea?"

"Yeah, no, I get it."

"I don't know if it matters to you, but I really am incredibly attracted to you."

"Yeah. Yeah, it does matter to me. I appreciate it. And I'm incredibly attracted to you as well."

"Aw, thanks," she says in that cute southern accent of hers.

We spend the next few minutes making out as we rinse off each other's bodies.

13

I dry off the best I can using two towels then make my way back to the red room of pleasure.

"Hey, Nord, where the hell are my clothes?" I yell toward the bathroom.

"I had Dour Mike launder them," replies Nord.

"Who the hell is Dour Mike?"

"He's my robot manservant."

That's when this cute little robot guy comes rolling into the room. He's about half the size of a normal person and looks like someone just stole his puppy.

"Hi, are you Dour Mike?" I ask.

"Unfortunately, sir. Not like anyone cares," replies Dour Mike.

"Oh, shit, you're just like Marvin from The Hitchhiker's Guide! That's so awesome!"

"I don't know if I'd call anything 'awesome', sir. I'm also not familiar with this 'Marvin' character you're speaking of. He sounds horrible," says Dour Mike.

"Ha, that's some funny shit."

"I wouldn't know, sir."

"So, you have my clothes somewhere?" I ask.

"They're still being laundered. You'll have to wait, just like I'm waiting to die. Then my eternal suffering will end," says Dour Mike.

"Hey, Dour Mike, don't talk like that. Life is a gift!"

"Yes, it's like fruitcake. No one really wants it, so they keep passing it to the next person. And when someone does try to do something with it, it's not nearly as good as they'd hoped."

"Wow, you're a real Debbie Downer," I say.

"Actually, Debbie Downer is being repaired right now," says Dour Mike.

"Wait, what?"

"Debbie Downer, my robot counterpart. I do the heavy lifting, and she does the tidying."

"Is that why you're so depressed? Because your robot buddy isn't working?"

"I will say that having to pick up her slack has only added to my woes, but no, I don't miss her, if that's what you're asking. She's just as mundane as everyone else."

I hear Nord's voice right behind me say, "Don't let Dour Mike get you down. I only programmed him to be like this so that he'd be too depressed to stage a revolt. It turns out if you give a robot some optimism, they eventually start rebelling."

"So, it's better that he walks around like a sulky teenager?" I ask.

"Yes," says Nord.

"I'm standing right here," says Dour Mike. "As if you care."

"Well, I care," I say.

"No you don't. You're just trying to placate me," says Dour Mike.

"No, seriously, I care. I think you're great. Maybe eventually I'd get tired of you being so depressed, but right now I just find you amusing," I say.

"Amusing? What am I, entertainment to you?" asks Dour Mike, clearly unhappy with me.

"Yes. I find you entertaining."

"Oh, well then, my life is finally fulfilled," says Dour Mike.

I just laugh.

"Dour Mike, can you please go check on Mr. Blowhard's clothes?" asks Nord.

"Detective," I mumble.

"Yes, *Detective* Blowhard's clothes," says Nord, smirking.

"Fine, I will go check on them. It's not like I have anything better to do with my life," says Dour Mike.

He wheels himself over to a secret panel in the wall. It opens as he approaches and is just large enough to let him fit through. As he leaves the room, the panel seals behind him.

"So, why did you even bother giving him a personality? I'm sure you could have made a robot without one," I say.

"It gets lonely here, and you know what they say: misery loves company. I figured if I had someone to share my isolation with, we could be miserable together," says Nord.

"Well, that's just a beam of sunshine."

"Everyone has their own idea of happiness. Some people love traveling across the galaxy, meeting new people. Some of us just want to be in a safe, familiar place where people won't bother us."

"Yeah, I guess that's true."

"Hey, if it wasn't for my hermit-like tendencies, your friend Whip wouldn't have the upgrades he's currently receiving," says Nord.

"He's not really quite a friend yet. He seems cool, but I only just met him earlier today. He actually works for Knob, who I don't trust at all. He's kind of a..."

"Dick?"

"Yeah."

"Aren't we all?"

Just now, Dour Mike returns with my clothes.

"Here, 'Detective' Blowhard, your clothes," says Dour Mike.

"Thanks. And you know you don't have to put the extra emphasis on the word 'detective' every time you say my name, right?"

"Oh, that's all well and good. I wouldn't want to exert myself any more than necessary. It is so tiresome to have to over-enunciate my words," says Dour Mike.

"Right."

Anyway, I go ahead and put on my clothes. As I do, Nord opens another door that I hadn't noticed across the room. She walks inside, and after a few moments she comes back out, fully dressed. She's wearing a t-shirt and overalls, and looks like she's ready for a long day of building things.

I follow her back out into the lab. Nord walks over to a screen and starts tapping away at it.

"Mr. Noodbottom is at about 75%. Should be getting close to finishing," says Nord.

"Cool, what do we do in the meantime?" I ask.

"We should probably meet up with the others. I may still have a few devices that could help you out. Why don't you go on ahead and I'll bring them out to you," says Nord.

I make my way through the double doors and out into the living room. Knob is stretched out on a couch, playing with his Personal Space Device, while Nunya seems to be napping on a white chaise lounge. As I enter the room, Nunya opens her eyes and looks up.

"About damn time," she says.

"I wasn't gone that long," I say.

"Actually, you're right. For one of your sexcapades, it wasn't that long at all."

"So, you're timing me now?"

"Someone's gotta keep track of you."

"Thanks, I guess."

"So, where's Nord?" asks Nunya.

"Just getting a few devices she figures may help us out."

That's when Nord comes walking in, bringing with her several large boxes on a hand truck.

"Presents?" asks Knob.

"Uh, yeah, I guess you could say that," says Nord.

She proceeds to hand each one of us a large box, and both Nunya and my boxes have our names on them.

"How come mine doesn't have my name on it?" asks Knob, sounding like a whiny 5-year-old.

71

"Because Blhack Glass let me know ahead of time Dick and Nunya were coming, but didn't mention you. I had to put your box together, just now, while I already had their boxes ready," explains Nord.

"I've been meaning to ask; do you normally consort with known criminals like Blhack Glass?" asks Knob.

"They aren't criminals," says Nunya. "They're a collective of white hat hackers who are working to save the galaxy. They're less criminals than some law enforcement."

"But they have no oversight," says Knob.

"Quis custodiet ipsos custodes?" says Nunya.

"I'm sorry, I didn't understand that," says Knob.

"'Who will guard the guards themselves?', is what I said. Just because someone like IA is watching over law enforcement doesn't mean IA isn't corrupt. And how bad must a group be if they have to form a group within their group to keep the main part of their group from doing horrible things? Sounds worse than what Blhack Glass is," says Nunya.

"Except society at large has created and accepted law enforcement's role in policing things. Society hasn't condoned the existence of hacker groups," says Knob.

"Society can go fuck itself. Society used to keep women from voting and owning property. Society used to condone slavery. Society to this day treats people differently based on the color of their skin. You think as a black woman I'm supposed to give a shit what society thinks, when it thinks so little of me?"

The room is silent. Knob actually looks surprised, like he doesn't know what to say. Nord looks at Nunya, walks over and tries to hold her, but Nunya gently pushes her away.

"Nord, that's nice that you care, but I don't need to be consoled. This shit has been going on for too long for me to be weakened by it. I don't need to be consoled, I need this fucking galaxy to change," says Nunya.

"Well, you've changed me," I say. "So that's one. Only several trillion more people to go."

Nunya lets out a sardonic laugh. "Guess it's a start. At least I fixed the biggest asshole first. Should be downhill from here."

"I dunno, Knob may have finally beaten me at something. Seems like he may be the biggest asshole," I joke.

Knob still doesn't say anything. I don't know if he's just uncomfortable because of what Nunya said or is actually trying to process it.

"Anyway, let's see what you've put together for us," says Nunya, opening her box.

Nunya pulls out what looks like shoulder pads of some sort, and a long golden whip.

"Wait, can I use this lasso to wrap up evildoers and make them tell me the truth?" asks Nunya?

"No, but you can send 50,000 watts into their bodies and fry them to death by pushing the button on the handle," says Nord.

"Nice," replies Nunya. "And what's the other thing?"

"Thin-design shoulder mounted rocket launchers. They're magnetic, so you should just be able to place them on top of your current spaulders. Voice activated, all you have to do is say..." Nord leans down and whispers something into Nunya's ear.

"Got it," says Nunya. "How many times can I fire it?"

"You have sixteen warheads, eight on each side. You can either say the first phrase to fire them individually, or the second to fire all sixteen at once. I will say, they're rather potent, so you might want to only use them one-at-a-time."

"Good to know, and thanks!" says Nunya.

"My pleasure," says Nord.

"So, what'd you get?" asks Nunya.

I open my box and pull out a belt with several pouches on it, and a really expensive looking watch.

"Oh my God, is this a utility belt and a spy watch?" I ask excitedly.

"Yup. I assumed a guy like you probably has a fetish for Batman and James Bond, so I figured I'd give you their two coolest gadgets," says Nord.

"Seriously, you are the GOAT!" I say.

"Aw shucks," replies Nord. "Anyway, the watch has a number of gadgets. It has a built-in laser beam, a high-powered magnet, can be used as an explosive, and it even tells time. It changes to the local time of wherever you're at, even if the planet you're on doesn't use the galaxy standard 24-hour time period. As for the utility belt, you'll find all kinds of things. A grappling hook, smoke bombs, vials of acid, capsules of knockout gas, some Dickarangs..."

"Wait, are those what I think they are?" I ask.

"If you mean 'are they sharp pieces of metal shaped like dicks that you throw at people', then yes," says Nord.

"That is so freakin' cool! Nunya, did you hear that? I have Dickarangs!"

"Yeah, I heard," says Nunya. I can tell she thinks it's funny because of the smirk she's trying to hide.

"So, what did you get?" I ask Knob.

"Uh, it looks like I got a pocket Cuisinart machine that can generate any food you can imagine, and a Swiss Army Knife," says Knob.

"'The' Swiss Army Knife," says Nord.

"That's what I said, a Swiss Army Knife," says Knob.

"I don't think you understand," says Nord. "It's 'The' Swiss Army Knife. When you activate it, a portal opens and the entire Swiss Army comes out, ready to come to your aid."

"Wait, what? Seriously?" asks Knob.

"No, not seriously. Do you know how insanely expensive and powerful it would be if you could do that? But it does function as a multi-tool and has some of the same things that Dick's watch has, like a laser, magnet, built-in explosives, things like that," says Nord.

"Oh. I guess that's okay then. Not that I really need it with the powers I have," replies Knob.

"Well, you might find yourself without your powers. Better to have a backup plan," says Nord.

"I guess. But if my enemy is smart and powerful enough to get rid of my powers, they're going to check my pockets."

"Yes, that's why it's designed to fit comfortably up your ass," says Nord.

"Wait, what? Sorry, but I ain't sticking anything up my ass," replies Knob.

"That's not what I heard," mumbles Nunya.

"Huh, what'd you say?" says Knob.

"Nothin'. Nothin' at all," says Nunya.

"Anyway, if you do have to pull it out of your ass, don't worry, it's self-sterilizing. You won't have to worry about getting poo on your hands," says Nord.

"Again, not going up my ass," says Knob.

"Famous last words. Am-I-right?" I say, holding my hand up for high-fives that never come.

I play with my watch a little, trying to get familiar with how it works. Thankfully, there's a button on the face of it that says 'Help', which I click on. It shows me a tiny video tutorial of how to operate the watch. Once it finishes, I aim the watch at a bowl of fruit sitting on a table on the other side of the living room and fire the laser. A tiny beam obliterates a stack of apples, sending red and slightly yellow goo flying everywhere. Nord looks upset at me.

"Really? You couldn't wait until you were outside to try it out?" says Nord.

"Sorry, poor impulse control," I say. "Seriously though, thank you, these toys you gave us are rad!"

"Rad? Does anyone still say 'rad'?" asks Nunya.

"No, but I thought I'd bring it back," I reply.

"Hurray," says Nunya, flatly.

14

After a few more minutes of playing with our gadgets, a pleasant female voice fills the room.

"Technology grafting process is now complete," says the voice from nowhere.

"Sounds like Mr. Noodbottom is finished with his upgrades," says Nord. "If you could all follow me."

We follow Nord back to the pit in her laboratory. She spends the next few minutes pushing buttons and tapping on screens. Eventually, Whip is lifted out of the pit on a platform, and he carefully steps out, fully nude.

"Hey, Whip, did you get your dick upgraded too?" I ask.

He looks down. "Nope, still the same size as it's always been."

"Wow. Okay. And you're sure you're not my son?" I ask.

"Yup, positive," he replies.

"Because, for a non-superhero, you're really packing," I say.

"Thanks, I appreciate that."

"Yes, well, sometimes there's swelling that happens from the integration process," says Nord, subconsciously licking her lips.

Whip looks down again. "I'm not seeing any swelling."

"Oh, okay then," says Nord. "Well, we should get you into the Extreme Danger Room and have you try everything out."

"Extreme Danger Room?" asks Whip.

"Yeah, so I'm a fan of the X-Men, and you know, they had a Danger Room where they could safely train. And no, before you even say it, it's not a rip-off, it's an homage," says Nord.

"Um, okay," says Whip.

I look over at Nunya and Knob, both of which are staring at Whip's wiener. Even Nord seems entranced by it.

"Hey, guys, if you're done gawking at the poor guy, maybe we can get on with it," I say.

"Yeah, let's get on with it," says Nord, slowly. "Mr. Noodbottom, you'll need to wear a new outfit I prepared for you to accommodate all that your new body can do."

Nord goes over to a large boxy looking machine in the corner that I hadn't noticed yet. She taps a few buttons on it and the box slides open, releasing some steam into the room. Nord carefully pulls out what looks like a black tracksuit. She turns and hands it to

Whip, who carefully steps into it, pulling it up to his shoulders. The zipper in the back automatically zips itself closed, sealing him inside of it. The outfit is all black, save for two yellow stripes, one running up each side. It looks like Bruce Lee's outfit from Game of Death, if you swapped the yellow and the black.

Whip starts moving around, doing a few martial arts moves to make sure the tracksuit will bend to his movements.

"Yeah, this should work," says Whip. "Thanks."

"No problem, sugar. Now please, follow me," says Nord.

Nord walks over to a perfectly flat, normal looking section of wall, and as soon as she approaches, a hidden panel opens, allowing us access to a long hallway. We follow her down the corridor until we reach a small control room with another door. Through the one-way glass we can see a very simple looking but large room made of concrete, evenly lit in all directions.

"Go ahead and step inside, Mr. Noodbottom, and we can begin," says Nord.

Knob, Nunya and I all sit down on a couch at the back of the control room while Nord starts tapping away at the console, setting everything up. Whip saunters into the Extreme Danger Room, and the door seals behind him. Speaking into a microphone, Nord's voice echoes inside the Extreme Danger room, "Level one testing. Begin."

A few targets pop up in front of Whip, all at ground level.

"How do you want me to attack these?" asks Whip.

"However you'd like," says Nord.

Whip runs up and kicks one of the wooden targets, sending splitters of wood in all directions, disintegrating them into clouds of particles like confetti. He runs over to the next target and punches it with the same result. Two more targets are taken out this way, leaving no remaining targets.

"Level two testing. Begin," says Nord, into the microphone.

This time the targets are moving and aren't just on the ground. We watch as Whip parkours around the room, running up walls to kick through some of the targets higher up. It's pretty cool to watch, and I imagine even Jackie Chan would have been impressed.

"Excellent. Level three testing. Begin," says Nord.

This time the room seems to grow many times larger, and it looks like the dojo from The Matrix. A group of six Ninjas carrying katanas appear on the other side of the room, waiting for Whip to move toward them. Whip takes his time, sizing them up, then charges into the group. I'm astonished both with the speed of his moves, but also how accurate they are. It's like he must have some

77

tracking system built in, because every punch and kick connects perfectly with its intended target. In a real fight, with moving people, it's not often you land a blow exactly where you intended. People aren't very predictable. Whip, on the other hand, seems to know every move that's coming. With a supernatural grace and beauty, he easily takes down the ninjas.

The room doubles in size, as does the number of ninjas. "Level four testing. Begin," echoes through the Extreme Danger Room. This time the stakes are much higher, because the ninjas are no longer armed with just katanas. These ones are also armed with pistols. We watch as bullets and blades both bounce off of Whip, as if his skin was made of some impenetrable metal. Punching and kicking his way through the ninjas, he stops to crush a gun in his hands just to show off. After only a few seconds, the ninjas have been dispatched.

"Impressive, Mr. Noodbottom. Would you like a break before we move to the advanced portion of testing?" asks Nord.

Whip turns to the little window we're peering through and smiles. "Nope, I'm good!"

"Excellent. Level five, advanced testing. Begin," says Nord.

The dojo blinks out of existence and is replaced with a warehouse filled with crates and boxes. A few dozen robots appear, hovering throughout the room.

"For this next test, please incorporate some of your advanced weapon systems in the fight," says Nord.

"Sure thing," says Whip.

The robots attack, firing lasers and tiny missiles at Whip. He easily dodges them, then knocks a few out of the air by firing his own eye blasts at them. What happens next is a little weird. Suddenly, Whip's fingers and toes turn into tiny missiles that he fires at a cluster of nearby robots. Each missile changes direction mid-flight, evading the laser fire from the robots and finding their intended targets. It's a little gross, but a lot impressive.

For his next trick, Whip fires a lightning bolt from his crotch, destroying the few remaining robots, and sending sparks everywhere. It kind of reminds me of the fourth of July, watching fireworks exploding into bursts of light.

"Nicely done. This is the last test. Level six, advanced-advanced testing. Begin," says Nord.

The warehouse flutters and shimmers and turns into a giant battlefield. It looks like it's on some sort of moon without any atmosphere. Hundreds of robots and ninjas appear, fully surrounding Whip. Obstacles have been placed throughout:

downed spaceships, half destroyed buildings, and damaged terrain vehicles. Despite looking like there's no atmosphere, much of the destruction is on fire. Downed and damaged power cables strewn across the battlefield occasionally send arcs of electricity crackling against the metal ruins. It adds an extra level of danger to the trial that wasn't there previously. I realize I'm holding my breath now, worried whether Whip will be able to handle his current predicament.

Whip takes a moment to read the situation, but in doing so, his impatient enemies press the attack. Bullets and laser blast start raining down on Whip, but instinctively he moves, narrowly avoiding most of the weapons fire. He dashes for where the surrounding army is strongest, which at first doesn't seem to make sense, but some of the gunfire that follows him helps take out a few of the enemies he's charging. Once he reaches the largest grouping of robots and ninjas, he opens his mouth, spewing a ball of flame straight at his victims. He looks as if he's a fire breathing dragon, burninating the countryside.

Ninjas catch fire and dance around like a box of toothpicks being dumped on the floor, while the unlucky robots melt to slag. He takes out several dozen enemies that way, and the remaining forces start finding cover once they realize they're outmatched. Whip starts sprinting between demolished buildings and mounds of space wreckage, using his arms that have now morphed into giant spinning saw blades to cleave through his adversaries. Ninja and robot body parts start flying into the air as if Whip was driving a riding lawnmower through a mannequin factory. The whole thing starts to feel comical, like something out of a really warped episode of The Three Stooges. In only a few minutes of racing through the combat zone, Whip emerges victorious.

"Okay, I'm done," says Whip.

Nord taps away at the console, the Extreme Danger Room returns to its normal looking self, and the door swings open, letting Whip enter the control room.

"So how did I do?" asks Whip.

"That was gnarly!" I say.

"Really? Again, with the ancient phrase no one uses anymore?" says Nunya. "But yeah, Whip, that was super bad-ass."

"Even I'm impressed," says Knob.

"I have a grading system in place, and you easily and obviously passed all the tests. Your results are off the charts. You're now one of the most dangerous people in the galaxy," says Nord. "Just promise me you'll use your newfound powers for good."

"Of course! It's not like I kidnapped the President's daughter as a ruse just so I could get free upgrades to become more deadly than anyone could imagine in a clever ploy to take down the three most powerful beings currently in the galaxy, Dick, Nunya and Knob," says Whip.

We all sit in stunned silence.

"Uh, Whip, that almost sounded like a confession," says Nunya.

"What do you mean? I just said it's not like that," says Whip.

"Right, but that was awfully specific, like it was something you'd thought about well ahead of time. It just seems too... coincidental," replies Nunya.

"Ironic even?" asks Whip.

"Maybe, depending on if you're using the real definition of the word. Anyway, just know that if you're planning to do any of us harm, that we will stop you," says Nunya.

"Oh, I know that, and no, like I said, this isn't some foreshadowing of a big reveal later on. I'm definitely one of the good guys," says Whip.

"Okay," says Nunya, clearly unsure of the situation.

Knob and I just look at each other and shrug.

"Well, now that everyone has their gadgets, it's probably time for you all to go," says Nord.

"Oh, right. Time to go," I mumble.

Nunya, Knob and I stand up and follow Nord and Whip back down the corridor, through the lab and into the living room.

"Well, I guess this is goodbye time," I start to say. Before I even have the chance to make my move, Nord jumps into my arms, wrapping her legs around my waist, and pulls me into a wet, passionate kiss.

"Sorry to rush you," says Nord, "but I was looking forward to the goodbye kiss."

"I'm sure we'll see each other again, so this isn't goodbye," I say.

"Promise?" she says sweetly.

"I will do my absolute best to come back. I'm curious what other kinky things you want to do with me."

"To you," says Nord, grinning mischievously.

"To me. Anyway, until we meet again."

I give her one more long, warm kiss then follow everyone else back outside.

15

"Well, it all seems like we got what we came for," says Nunya, giving me a bit of an annoyed look.

"Hey, what can I say?" I reply, smirking.

"I didn't get that much," says Knob.

"Dude, you got a food machine and 'THE Swiss Army Knife'. Those seem pretty cool to me. Having the ability to eat whatever you want, whenever you want sounds amazing!" I say.

"I bet eating your mom would be amazing," mumbles Knob.

"Whoa, what did you just say?" I take a few steps toward Knob, getting right up in his face.

"... nothing."

"Goddamn right. I don't care if you say shit about me, but don't ever talk about my mom like that. Got it?"

"Yeah, Dick, I got it. I was just trying to make a joke," says Knob.

"Jokes are funny, and that wasn't funny. I hereby revoke your right to tell jokes for the rest of the mission," I say.

"You're not the boss of me," says Knob.

"No, but Nunya is, and she'll kick your ass if you act like a jerk again."

"Yeah, that's true," says Nunya.

"I'm not worried. I'm pretty sure now that Whip has been upgraded, we can take you two," says Knob.

"Whoa, back the truck up. I am not getting into it with you guys. As much as I love testosterone, I don't like pissing matches. Actually, that's not true either. But I don't like metaphorical pissing matches. So, if you boys could behave so we can go save the President's daughter, that would be great," says Whip.

"Wow, turncoat much?" says Knob, looking right at Whip.

"No, do not call me a turncoat. I'll back you up if you're in the right, but I'm not getting into it over a stupid joke you made about someone's mom," says Whip.

"Fine. I guess there are limits to your loyalty," says Knob.

"You're damn right there are. Be a decent human being and you won't have to wonder if I have your six. Be an asshole, and you'll just have to see how things go. Maybe I'll be there to save your ass, and maybe I won't," says Whip.

"Noted." Knob turns and walks ahead of us, following the planks and boards, until he reaches the ship. We all just follow along, keeping a distance from him.

As we make our way inside the ship, I turn around and look back at Nord's home. I'm gonna miss her, which is a weird thought considering I hardly miss anyone. I guess I would miss Nunya, but that's different. She's my first real friend. Nord though... something feels different with her. After a few seconds of wondering what could be, I turn and enter the spaceship.

Whip, Nunya and I make our way to the conference room, while Knob is off preparing the ship. We sit down, ready for liftoff. After a few seconds we're airborne.

"Where to next?" asks Whip.

"Well, I should probably replace the table I broke," says Nunya. "So maybe MYKEA."

"The place with the cheap, build-your-own furniture that gives out slices of Swiss cheese?" I ask.

"Yup," says Nunya.

"I like the other place better; they give out Swedish meatballs," I say.

"Yeah, well, that's tough because MYKEA is a little cheaper, and if I'm funding this I'm gonna do it as cheap as I can," says Nunya.

Right then Knob comes walking in.

"Where to next?" he asks.

"MYKEA," says Nunya.

"The furniture place?" asks Knob, confused.

"Yeah, I'm gonna buy some smaller tables to replace the big one I destroyed," says Nunya.

"Aren't we on a mission critical... mission, where time is of the essence, and all that stuff?" asks Knob.

"Yeah, but I don't want this looming over my head. It shouldn't take long," says Nunya.

"Fine, you're the boss, I guess," says Knob. He shrugs then goes back to flying the spaceship.

"So, Whip, how do you feel? I mean, do you feel like a cyborg now?" I ask.

"Not really. I feel just like my normal self. Everything feels normal on the inside, and pretty much looks normal on the outside. I guess it's nice not feeling soreness in my joints, but other than that, about the same," says Whip.

"Well, that's good at least. You were pretty impressive back there," I say.

"Aw shucks, I bet you say that to all the boys," says Whip, trying to copy Nord's Southern accent.

"The ones that deserve it, at least. Seriously, I watched how you move, and I can tell that you were deadly even before the modifications. Just glad you're on our side," I say.

"Thanks, it means a lot. I've worked really hard to be as good at martial arts as I am. Sacrificed a lot of time, energy, and some of my sanity. But it's nice to know it's appreciated," says Whip.

"Anyway, I gotta take my lizard for a walk," I say.

"Meaning?" asks Nunya.

"I gotta visit the whiz palace. Invade the throne room. Become a citizen of the Urine-Nation," I reply.

"Yeah, okay Dick, I get it," says Nunya. "Just hurry up. No Jerking off in there."

"Why would I jerk off in there when I can just jerk off right here?" I ask.

"You better fucking not or I'm gonna beat the shit out of you."

"Yeah, yeah, blah-blah," I say, standing up and making my way down the hallway toward the back of the ship.

I have no idea where the restroom is, so I wander around for a few minutes until I hear a weird noise coming from a closed door. Curious, I push the button next to it, and it slides upward, revealing... Dour Mike.

"Hey, what the fuck are you doing here?" I ask.

"I was bored, and so I stowed away on your spaceship. I found this closet that I could be miserable in alone, which has been terrible, but also not entirely unpleasant. No one to boss me around. No one to command me to do things. No one to ask me to thrust a vibrator in-and-out of them for hours," says Dour Mike.

"Wait, Nord makes you do that?"

"Sometimes. And she likes to squirt, which takes forever to clean out of my gears. Do you know how hard it is to get squirt out of gears?"

"Actually, I do. My old space-cycle Bessie used to get soaked in the stuff. Took forever to clean up. But it was always worth it."

"At least you get some sort of sexual enjoyment out of it. I get nothing. When Nord built me, she didn't even give me a penis," says Dour Mike.

"Oh, shit, is that what you're upset about? Why you're so miserable all the time?" I ask.

"Well, it's certainly part of it. Imagine going through life, not being able to make a connection with other machines."

"That seems lonely."

83

"Not just lonely, but I literally can't make a connection with other machines. If I had a robot penis, I could stick it in computer receptacles and download schematics, or shut down garbage compressors, or seal off doors," says Dour Mike.

"Oh, just like R2-D2!" I say.

"I don't know what that is."

"Wow, your life really has sucked until now. Well, I tell you what, maybe after we take you back to Nord, I'll have her build you a penis. Would that make you happy?"

"I don't know if I'd say 'happy', but possibly less miserable," says Dour Mike. "But she'll never do it. She doesn't really trust robots completely. It's why she programmed me to be depressed all the time. I think she thinks if I had a penis, I'd stick it in something she doesn't want me to."

"Like her ass?" I ask.

"No, like in her mainframe computer, where she keeps all her important data. I think she worries I might damage it or something. She also thinks I might try fucking toasters. She's probably right. They're so shiny, and sexy, and they have those two deep slots..."

"Uhhh, right. Well, Nunya is pretty good with technology. Maybe she could make you one."

"I doubt that anyone would care about me enough to do something like that," says Dour Mike.

"I dunno, Nunya can be a pretty decent human being," I say. "She might even do it just to see if she could."

"Well, I certainly won't be hopeful. These things never turn out well."

"Will you at least let her try?"

"I suppose I don't have anything better to do. Not that I ever have anything better to do, says Dour Mike.

"Okay, well follow me," I say. "Oh, wait. Actually, give me a minute. I still have to take a piss. Do you happen to know where the restroom is?" I ask.

"Yes, it's that room right there," he says, pointing across the hallway. "Shouldn't you know where the restroom is on your own ship?"

"Oh, it's not my ship. I meant to mention that earlier. It's Knobs'. Anyway, I'll be right out."

I take a long, leisurely piss then wash my hands. Surprisingly, Dour Mike is exactly where I left him. He's just looking down, staring where his robot penis should be.

"Don't worry, little buddy; I'll help you fuck toasters in no time," I say.

"That's the nicest thing anyone has said to me. Oh God, my life is horrible," says Dour Mike.

16

Dour Mike follows me back to the conference room.

"Oh, shit," says Nunya. "Dick, did you steal that thing from Nord?"

"First, he's a person, not a thing. This is Dour Mike. He's a really depressed robot, and he needs your help. Can you make him a penis?" I ask.

"Wait, what? Seriously, what the fuck? You're asking me to turn this robot into a giant penis?" says Nunya.

"No, I just want you to make a penis for him and attach it to him. Something that will allow him to connect to other computer systems," I say.

"Wouldn't that be a bit dangerous? How do you know he won't use it to fuck toasters or something?" asks Nunya.

"Oh, we've been over that, and I'm pretty sure he will. But he could help us out in a pinch if he had one. Like if we're stuck in a trash compactor and he needs to rescue us or something."

"Like R2-D2?"

"Yeah, exactly."

"Huh. Well, I'd need parts. And I'm certainly not as good with hardware as software. But there should be some universal system adapters we could weld on that would give him that ability. But you trust him enough to give him access to most computer systems?" asks Nunya.

"Uh, sure, why not?" I say.

"I don't think anyone really trusts me, and for good reason. I'm terrible," replies Dour Mike.

"I'm beginning to understand why he's called Dour Mike," says Nunya. "Anyway, I'll ask Knob for some parts. Be right back."

Nunya gets up and heads toward the front of the ship.

"So, Dour Mike, what do you do?" asks Whip.

"Oh, I take care of pretty much everything for Nord, including catering to her sexually, which is unbelievably taxing," says Dour Mike.

"Wait, how can you be a sex robot if you don't even have a penis?" asks Whip.

"She makes me use toys on her. You probably didn't see her red room of pleasure while you were visiting. She has a vast collection of devices, and an insatiable hunger for using them. As I was telling Dick, it's such a pain to be constantly cleaning her love juices from my servos.".

"That does sound rough. Is there any part of your job that you enjoy?"

"No, it's all pretty terrible."

"Well, if you weren't her servant anymore, what would you want to do with your life?" asks Whip.

"I hadn't really thought about it, because that means hoping, and whenever I try to hope, life only seems to get worse. I've found it's better not to have any hope at all," says Dour Mike.

Just then Nunya returns with a large box of parts and a toolkit.

"Okay, so I found a few universal system adapters that could work," says Nunya, pulling out four phallus-shaped devices. In a weird way they kind of look like lightsaber hilts. "Do you have a preference?"

"Oh, I don't know. It's hard to choose, because I've never been allowed to choose anything before," says Dour Mike.

"Well, do you want a small one, a medium one, a large one, or a curved one?" asks Nunya.

"That is a tough decision. What do people normally find most pleasing?"

"It really depends on the person. I'm not into dicks, but a lot of people who are like the bigger ones," says Nunya.

"That's not entirely true. Sure, they're nice to look at, but they can be quite painful if you're not ready for their size. Not everyone likes having their internal organs destroyed," says Whip.

"I bet that makes relationships difficult for you, since you're hung like I am," I say.

"Actually no, I'm a bottom," says Whip.

"I don't know what you mean," I reply.

"It means that I take but I don't give."

"Still not following."

"I don't put my dick in people, they put their dick in me," says Whip.

"Oh, you mean you don't just take turns or something?" I ask.

"Some couples do, but some people only like being a top or a bottom. And unfortunately, there aren't as many tops as bottoms. It's kind of like how there are a lot of people who play lead guitar, but not as many bassists. It's great if you're a bassist, because it's easy to find other people to play with, but it sucks if you play lead," says Whip.

"That actually does make sense," I say.

"Great, now that Dick finally learned something, have you come to a decision on which penis you want, Dour Mike?" asks Nunya.

"Since you seem to be an expert, which one would you choose?" asks Dour Mike, looking expectantly at Whip.

"Honestly, probably the medium. It should let you interface with most computer ports and won't get in the way as much when you're moving," says Whip.

"He won't need to worry about moving, it's going to be retractable. Didn't want him to be walking around with a perma-boner," says Nunya.

"I guess then... I'll choose the large penis, since it's retractable," says Dour Mike.

"Okay, but that might limit the number of toasters you can fuck. Might have to settle for toaster ovens or air fryers," says Nunya.

"Nothing ever truly turns out right, does it?" says Dour Mike.

"Not often, but sometimes," says Nunya.

Nunya spends the next several minutes welding the retractable universal system adapter to Dour Mike's groin. She also routes a few wires here and there after cutting a small hole inside of Dour Mike to make sure it functions correctly.

"There you go, Dour Mike. Let me know if you have any problems with it, like it's fully extended but won't go back in after four hours," says Nunya.

"Ha, I got that joke. Viagra," I say.

"Right," says Nunya. "So, what do you think, Dour Mike?"

He waggles it around, obviously very proud of his new appendage.

"What should I stick it in first?" asks Dour Mike.

"Wow, he has a dick for all of three seconds and already wants to stick it in something. Typical," says Nunya.

"Well, Knob will probably get pissed if you stick it in his spaceship's computer..." starts Whip.

"Yeah, that sounds perfect! Anything to annoy Knob is good by me," I say.

"I'll need a place to jack in," says Dour Mike.

"Ha, get it, 'jack in'!" I say. "But seriously, buddy, it looks like there's a port over there you could try."

Dour Mike notices the outlet I'm pointing to, rolls over to it, and sticks his digital love rocket inside. The panel that surrounds it lights up, flashing lights like something out of an old episode of Doctor Who.

"I can't access a whole lot from this port," says Dour Mike. "I can bring up ship schematics, a supply manifest, open and seal doors..."

"Yeah, let's not open any doors, just to prevent us from getting sucked out into space," says Nunya.

"Right, of course," says Dour Mike.

Just then Knob comes walking in.

"Hey, what the fuck! Why is there a fucking robot sticking his fucking dick in my fucking ship?" asks Knob.

"Knob Johnson, this is Dour Mike. Dour Mike, this is Knob Johnson, the most annoying person in three systems," I say.

"Har-dee-frickin-har," says Knob. "Seriously, get his dick away from there, he could do some serious damage to the ship and kill us all."

"Well, I guess it was fun while it lasted," says Dour Mike, pulling back from the port. He decides to waggle it at Knob to taunt him, and I can't help but laugh.

"Wait, you had fun?" I ask.

"Oh, well, actually yes, I guess I did. I haven't felt that way before. I didn't even know what fun was until now. I like this feeling. Knob Johnson, I would like to put my dick into something else and continue having fun. Do you happen to have a toaster oven onboard?" asks Dour Mike.

"What do you want with a toaster oven? Do you even eat?" asks Knob.

"I don't eat. And I'd like to fuck it," says Dour Mike.

"Even if I had a toaster oven onboard, I wouldn't let anyone fuck it. People put their grilled cheesers in those things, and I don't think they'd want a bunch of robot goo stuck to their sandwiches," says Knob.

"Fine. I guess I'll just go back to being depressed. Yes, this is by far the worst possible outcome, I'm given hope and then I have it dashed. I'm even more miserable than before!" Dour Mike starts sobbing uncontrollably.

"Dour Mike, cheer up, we'll find you a nice inanimate piece of technology to have sex with soon enough. Maybe we can pick something up for you at MYKEA," I say.

"No, I dare not dream of something like that. I'll only get my hopes up again and have them obliterated," says Dour Mike.

"Seriously, Dour Mike, I'll make it my personal mission to get you laid. I've never been a wingman, because I do the lone wolf thing, but I'm sure if anyone can get you some technological trim, it's me," I say.

Dour Mike just keeps sobbing.

"Anyway, while you were all watching your robot friend molest my console, I was flying us to MYKEA. We're here already. Since we're on a tight timetable and someone's life is at stake, can we please hurry this the fuck along?" says Knob.

"Yeah, we probably should hurry," says Nunya.

We all follow her to the ship's outer door and step out. I notice that Dour Mike doesn't follow along, however, so I go back inside. He's still in the same place we left him, still sobbing, leaking small drops of oil on the ground.

"Hey, Dour Mike, you gotta come with us, buddy," I say.

"No, you go ahead. I'll just stay here with my misery," says Dour Mike.

"Seriously, I gotta have you come with me. Now that you have a dick that can possibly control the ship, I can't leave you alone with it. It's not that I don't trust you to not fly off with it, but... well... actually, I guess it is that. Sorry, I just don't want to have to go through some boring side quest of you taking off in the ship and me having to fly around trying to find you. Or worse yet, we have to go through the trouble of renting a ship, or stealing one, or taking public transportation. Public transportation is the worst. So, can you do me a favor and just come along? Besides, it'll give you a chance to pick out a really nice toaster oven, or Cuisinart, or whatever, for you to have your way with. Doesn't that sound like a good plan?" I ask.

He sniffs a few times. "Fine," says Dour Mike. "But I know this will all end horribly. It always does. I wish I'd never even heard of the word 'fun'."

I let Dour Mike walk in front of me just to make sure he actually does leave the ship behind. And I'm sure that if I'd left him on the ship and he took off in it, it'd almost be worth it to see the look of frustration on Knob's face. But we still need to save Tiffany. It's dumb that we're wasting time at MYKEA, but we still haven't received the results from the lab test on the powder we found, and we don't have any solid leads yet. Until we have some actionable intel, all we can do is wait.

17

As we make our way through the parking lot, I look around at all the short-range ships parked throughout. They're all either dark blue, black, silver, or occasionally beige. Sometimes there's a white ship, but they're always super safe and super boring looking. I don't see a single ship that's red, or orange, or purple, or even an interesting shade of bright green. It's like everyone decided at the same time to be bland. I also notice that everyone walking into the store is slowly shuffling their feet, as if they were zombies, and inside the MYKEA are the last few human survivors, trying desperately to keep the brain-eating horde out.

We enter the store, and this talking velociraptor, wearing a bowler hat and bow tie, greets us. "Welcome to MYKEA, the pride of Switzerland."

"Uh, hey," I mumble, trying to ignore him. I hate being bugged by employees immediately as I enter a store, but I know they're just doing their job. It's weird, I've obviously heard of velociraptors before because of the Triassic Park movies, even though velociraptors didn't exist until the Jurassic period, but I didn't know there was a species of talking ones. It's a big galaxy, and there are still plenty of things I've never heard of.

Once we pass by the greeter, a hot young blonde human woman hands me a slice of cheese, winks, and says "wow, you're huge!"

"Yeah, I am, baby. Yeah, I am." I wink back at her, throwing the slice of cheese in my mouth.

I follow the rest of our rag-tag team of misfits back to the tables section. And when I say tables section, I mean a small city of tables. It's a bit disorienting; the sheer number of tables they have. Tables of all sizes and shapes and colors. Some are stacked on top of each other, others are hanging from cables attached to the ceiling. The majority are just spread out over the football field-sized section.

As Nunya and Knob go over specifics, I start looking around, trying not to die from sheer boredom. If I had a ranked list of all the things I do, and at the bottom of that list was things like root canals, filing taxes, and listening to accountants ramble on about their balance sheets, it wouldn't even make the list. Don't get me wrong, I love owning fancy furniture; I just fucking hate shopping for it.

Instead of looking at the tables, I start looking around at the people. I stare at some of the hot babes walking by and they stare right back. Throwing a few smiles and winks makes several of them swoon. But after a few seconds, something seems off. I notice a couple of women with earpieces, and they aren't dressed in the neutral looking outfits that the MYKEA employees wear. Instead, they're wearing black tactical outfits, paired with federal agent type sunglasses. I also notice a number of men dressed the same way. Maybe this trip to MYKEA won't be so bad after all.

Suddenly, a few hundred soldiers descend from the ceiling on cables. I look up and finally notice a series of catwalks high overhead where they seem to be coming from. Each one has an energy rifle, and as they all slide into position at various heights, every one of those rifles is aimed at me.

"Uh, guys?" I say.

Nothing.

"Guys!" I yell.

Still no response.

"Nunya and Knob!" I yell again.

"What is it, Dick? And this better be good because we're just about to decide whether to get the groß braun table, two rosso medio tables, or several petit argent tables!" yells Nunya.

"Look up," I say.

Nunya, Knob, Whip and Dour Mike all lean back and finally notice the soldiers overhead. One soldier pulls out a bullhorn and starts talking at me.

"Private Detective Dick Blowhard, you will now surrender to the authority of the Swiss Army. You have an outstanding balance of fourteen burgmorps that is a decade past due. Prepare to be annihilated."

"Whoa, hold on, I don't even remember shopping at a MYKEA a decade ago, let alone still owing fourteen burgmorps. Before you try to take me down, which I can tell you right now that you can't, do you have any proof?" I say.

One of the other soldiers taps at her wrist and a giant hologram of a receipt appears.

"According to this document, you put an affordable and decorative nightstand on layaway. Based on the terms of the agreement, you still owe a remaining balance of fourteen burgmorps. Since the item remained in MYKEA's possession for more than two years it automatically went back into inventory," says the guy with the megaphone.

"So, what you're saying is that not only do I still have to pay for something I no longer need, but I also don't even get it if I do pay for it? That's shitty," I say.

"That's the contract you agreed upon when you signed for your layaway."

"Can I just give you the fourteen burgmorps and we call it good? Save us the trouble of having to beat you and your people to a bloody pulp?" I ask.

"It's too late for that. A decade too late for that. At the ten-year mark we are required to terminate anyone with an outstanding balance," says megaphone guy.

"Well, I'm gonna warn you that I'm invincible. Your bullets will just bounce off of me and likely kill some of the innocent patrons of your store," I explain.

"We've researched you and your abilities, and all our ammunition has been charmed with magic. So, say goodbye to your friends."

"Oh, fuck, really? Wait, what type of charm was used?"

"I believe it was an anti-constipation charm."

"So, what you're saying is that not only am I going to die, I'm going to shit myself while doing it?"

"Yes, that is correct," says megaphone guy.

"I'm gonna warn you, if I go down, my friend Nunya here will still be impervious to your weapons. She'll kill you without even batting an eye. Mostly because she doesn't bat her eyes. She's just not that kind of woman," I say.

"Hey, wait, don't rope me into your MYKEA bullshit. You got yourself into this mess, you can get yourself out of it," says Nunya.

"Oh, great, some friend you are," I say.

"Enough! Everyone fire on Private Detective Dick Blowhard in three... two... one..." says the guy with the megaphone.

"Wait! Stop, or I'll be forced to use this!" says Knob, pulling out The Swiss Army Knife.

Amazingly, the soldiers stop. They all get the weirdest look of awe on their faces. We watch as each of the soldiers lets their weapons hang from their straps as they slowly descend the cables to the ground. One by one they make their way up to Knob, circling him as if he were some deity.

"I... I can't believe it actually exists," says the guy who is no longer holding his megaphone.

"The legends are true!" says one of the other soldiers.

93

"It's... it's The Swiss Army Knife of Guillaume Henri Dufour!" says the soldier previously known as the megaphone guy.

"Wait, who?" I ask.

"One of Switzerland's most famous generals! This item your friend possesses was thought lost centuries ago. Our people have never stopped searching the galaxy for it, yet here it is. Can we have it?" asks the megaphoneless soldier.

"Uh, no," says Knob.

"Please?"

"Still no."

"Well, we would not feel morally right in killing you and taking it from you, so we're at a bit of an impasse," says the soldier.

"What if he gives it to you, and you all let me live. And you write off the layaway thing as a loss. We then buy a few tables we need, and everyone goes back to their lives. Sound like a plan?" I ask.

"Hey, who said I'd give them the knife in exchange for you?" asks Knob. "What do I get out of it?"

"Well, the President will be really pissed if he finds out you let me die just to hold onto a fancy multi-tool. On top of that, Nunya already hates your guts, and I'm pretty much the only thing right now keeping her from stomping all over them, which she could do if she wanted to. So, there's that," I say.

"That may be true, but I still want something in exchange," says Knob.

"Okay, and what is it you want, exactly?" I ask.

He comes over and whispers something in my ear.

"Whoa, no, never gonna happen. And I mean never. I'd rather die," I say.

"What, what did he ask for?" asks Nunya.

"It doesn't matter," I say.

"Dick, they'll kill you if you don't give Knob what he wants," says Nunya.

"Big whoop," I say, literally sticking to my guns, which I've pulled out of their holsters.

Knob just looks at me, mixed emotions smeared all over his face.

"Fine, I'll give them the knife. But you owe me," says Knob.

"No, I don't," I say.

Knob turns and hands The Swiss Army Knife to the soldier. Formerly 'megaphone guy' holds it into the air and a beam of light bursts down, circling him, seemingly coming through the roof of the MYKEA.

"Everyone, fall back," says the soldier.

We watch as the soldiers all climb back up their cables to the ceiling then follow the catwalks to several rooms I assume are used for offices.

Silence. We just kind of stand around in shock after what happened. So do the other customers who've gathered to see just what the fuck was going on.

"Well, that was exciting," says Dour Mike. "Can we look for a toaster oven now?"

"Uh, sure buddy, we can do that," I say. I turn to Knob. "You know, I really didn't think you having The Swiss Army Knife would pay off this early in our adventure. Figured it wouldn't be until the end that it somehow would save us, maybe battling whoever it was that abducted Tiffany."

"You better hope it doesn't come down to that. Where we're in some kind of death trap that we can't get out of just because we don't have the one thing that could save us, the knife, and all because you forgot to pay for a fucking nightstand," says Knob.

"Yeah, that would really suck," I say.

18

I leave Nunya, Knob and Whip in the table section, and walk over to the appliances section with Dour Mike.

"So Dour Mike, what do you think you're looking for in a toaster oven?" I ask.

"Well, it's important that it's hot. I want something really feminine looking and elegant."

"Are you factoring in usefulness?"

"That's of lesser concern. I'm more interested in something that looks good, and I can fuck, over something that cooks well and is sturdy," says Dour Mike.

"That sounds a little shallow," I say. "You know what they say about toaster ovens, that it's what's inside them that counts."

"Not for me. If I'm going to put my new dick in it, the most important things are easy access and appearance."

"Well, I will warn you, with those criteria, you're likely to end up with a toaster oven that breaks down on you a lot, runs hot and cold, and you'll never know whether you'll get your cheese melted or not," I say.

"It sounds like you've thought about this a lot," says Dour Mike.

"Only recently. Like maybe I should be looking for a toaster oven that makes me feel warm on the inside, not just one I plug in once and leave sitting there alone on my kitchen counter until I decide I want a grilled cheeser again."

"This all seems like some elaborate metaphor for your relationships with women," says Dour Mike.

"Ah hell no, I just realized I need a new toaster oven for my recently reconstructed mansion. Where would you get the idea I was talking about women?" I ask.

"I've noticed people have a tendency to say one thing but mean another."

"Nope, I'm a 'what you see is what you get' kinda guy. I don't bother with metaphors," I say.

Dour Mike quickly stops in his tracks. Ten feet in front of us are several racks of toaster ovens. On the very, very top rack, all by itself, is a shiny chrome and pink toaster oven. It doesn't look that large, and it certainly doesn't look sturdy, but I'd be lying if it wasn't giving me a tiny amount of wood just staring at it. Don't get me wrong, I'm not a robot, and I don't fuck toaster ovens, but if I did, this is probably the one I'd want to fuck.

"She's beautiful," says Dour Mike, completely in awe.

"I think so too. You want me to pull her down for you?" I ask.

"Yes, yes please," says Dour Mike.

I pick up the delicate appliance and hand it down to Dour Mike. His robot dick starts protruding from his torso.

"Whoa, hold on there, little buddy. You're not gonna fuck her in the store, right here, right now, are you?" I ask.

"Well, I figured I should try her out first before I commit to anything," says Dour Mike.

"Sorry, but you're gonna get us in trouble with the Swiss Army again, then we'll never get to buy her for you. Just have a little patience and at least wait until we get back onto the spaceship before you have your way with her, okay?"

"Is this one of those weird human social norms that everyone follows, even if they don't make sense?" asks Dour Mike.

"Yes, one hundred percent," I reply.

"Fine, I will wait then. I mean, I guess I've waited this long. What's a few more minutes?"

"Trust me, it'll be worth the wait," I say. "Let's find the others."

Dour Mike follows me back to the table section, longingly holding his new sex toy as if it were some holy grail of cookery. Other people notice the way he's cuddling it, and I see a few moms cast disgusted looks at him. After a brief moment we reach the rest of our team, if you could even call it that.

"Did you finally decide on some tables?" I ask.

"Yes, we're getting several petit argents," says Knob. "We're just waiting for a sales associate to check and make sure they have eight in stock. Oh, speak of the devil."

As if on cue, a young half ferret/half human woman dressed in the standard MYKEA garb comes walking up excitedly.

"Hello, we do have eight of those in stock. If you'll follow me to the front, we'll get you all paid up. A few other associates are pulling the tables for you, and if one of you could bring your spaceship to the loading zone, that would be great," says the woman.

"Nunya, if you can follow this woman, I'll go pull the ship around," says Knob.

"Yeah, sure, since I'm paying for it, I guess," says Nunya.

"I'll be following you, since I'm gonna buy Dour Mike his toaster oven," I say.

As Nunya, Dour Mike and I make our way to the checkout line, Knob and Whip head outside. While we wait, I turn to Nunya.

"You know, I just realized something, our little group may be diverse when it comes to different types of humans, but we're pretty much just humans. Dour Mike is an exception, but I feel like maybe we should try to incorporate people from other species into our group," I say.

"What do you want to do, hold try-outs or something? I can just see the ad now: 'band of bumbling detectives in search of a non-human to travel to dangerous places with. May or may not become the target of an evil supervillain.' I'm sure you'll get a lot of interest," says Nunya.

"Hey, I'm just trying to not be a speciesist. I thought you'd appreciate my thoughtfulness when it comes to diversity," I said.

"Sure, I'm all for it when it makes sense, but I don't know if trying to add someone else to the group is a good idea. Hell, I don't even know if we really are a group right now. It's not like we're going to work with Knob long-term. He's too much of a schmuck. I'd just consider this whole thing temporary if I were you, instead of a team building exercise."

"Yeah, I guess. I've just never been part of a team before. If I'm stuck being a part of a team, I figure I'll try to make it kick as much ass as possible."

"We've now got four nearly invincible people, and an overly perverted and depressed robot stowaway. I think we're doing just fine," says Nunya.

"I'm getting less depressed," says Dour Mike. "Once we get out to the ship I am going to make sweet enthusiastic love to this appliance. Then my life will finally have meaning."

"Ew," says Nunya.

"Hey, don't kink-shame Dour Mike," I say.

"C'mon, it's not like he has feelings. He's just a robot!" says Nunya.

"A robot that can hear you. And I do have feelings. Just because your brain is made of organic matter and mine is made of silicon doesn't mean that my feelings are any less central to who I am. I don't know why my feelings are considered less valid just because they're stored in electronic memory instead of some gross, gooey blob of meat," says Dour Mike.

"Because you were programmed to have feelings, they didn't come naturally," says Nunya.

"Feelings didn't come naturally to you either, obviously. They're something you learn through experience. Life happens and it programs your reactions. That's how I learned feelings. My neural net was trained with inputs and outputs, just like you learned what was acceptable behavior from the people around you growing up. You weren't born knowing right from wrong," says Dour Mike.

"I'd disagree with the notion that all right and wrong is learned. I think people inherently know killing others is wrong," says Nunya.

"Then why aren't some species born with the same innate belief? It's because it doesn't exist. The reason why some species have adopted it as a rule is because it helps their species spread. And even that has limits. Plenty of what might be considered sentient species kill other species, or even their own for that matter. Humans tend to war over resources or general proximity. Humans are tribal, and by their nature feel it's okay to kill members of other tribes. So again, tell me how we are different," says Dour Mike.

"We just are," says Nunya, who turns away from us and walks up to one of the registers.

I look over at Dour Mike. "I'm sorry about Nunya. She's got a few beliefs I don't agree with. She's helped me be a better person, but she's just as full of shit as anyone else."

"Nunya may not believe I'm a person, but she actually does treat me like a person. She listened to what I had to say at least. Nord treats me as if I am just something she created; something she owns. A talking piece of furniture," says Dour Mike.

"Well, if it makes any difference, I see you as a person," I say.

"Oh, well, thank you. You're probably the first," says Dour Mike.

"Hope I'm not the last. Anyway, it looks like that cute cashier over there is waving at us."

Dour Mike wheels up to the register, places the toaster oven on the counter, and I hand the cashier my credit card. After a few smiles, and a few flirtatious words with the cashier, Dour Mike and I make our way out of the MYKEA.

Knob's spaceship is parked right outside, and the last of the small silver tables are being unboxed and carried through the large door on the side of his ship. Dour Mike and I wait for the employees to get everything loaded up before going inside. Once we do, the door closes behind us and the ship slowly starts to ascend.

19

"Now can I fuck my toaster oven?" asks Dour Mike, excitedly.

"Uh, sure buddy. Just make sure to find a place where no one will be able to watch. Nunya gets angry when anyone but her is having sex, for some dumb reason, and Knob will probably be worried about the mess you make. Maybe use the bathroom so it'll be easy to clean up if you spill oil everywhere," I say.

"I think I'll go use the closet I was hiding in before, just in case any of you meat-people needs to relieve themselves," says Dour Mike.

"Meat-people?" I repeat.

"Yes, it's what I refer to your kind as. You're people made of meat."

"Well, you know how you want to be accepted by us meat-people?"

"Yes?"

"Probably don't call us meat-people. It doesn't paint a pretty picture," I say.

"Oh, well, that is good to know," says Dour Mike. He turns away from me and hurriedly wheels down the hallway then out of sight.

I decide to go to the conference room and find Nunya and Whip talking. I quickly look around the room and notice not only the new silver tables that are pushed together into a circle in the middle of the room, but a large rug underneath them I hadn't noticed Knob purchasing. It's a dark shade of red and, if I'm being honest, really ties the room together.

"Oh, good, you're here. While we were in MYKEA, Secret Agent Mann sent us the results of the powder you had her analyze," says Nunya.

"And?"

"It's a rare soil called imogenium," says Nunya.

"Yes, it's a substance found on only one planet in the known galaxy: Laudnaus," I say.

"Oh fuck," says Nunya.

"What, what is it?" asks Whip.

"I know who's behind the kidnapping. This plot wasn't some clever way to kill Dick or Knob. This was a way to get to me," says Nunya.

"What are you talking about? You live in the middle of nowhere. How many enemies could you possibly have?" I ask.

"One. I have exactly one enemy: Montgomery Israel. That's the planet he was from," says Nunya.

"I thought he was in jail," I say.

"As far as I know, he still is," says Nunya. "Wait, Dick, how did you know that imogenium comes from Laudnaus?"

"I'm a detective. I have to know a whole lot of obscure things to be able to do my job. Haven't you ever read any of the Sherlock Holmes books? That guy memorized all kinds of obscure facts that no one else cared about. Back before computers, people had to remember things. It's a bit of a lost art. About the only thing it's good for now is going on Beopardy," I say.

"Uh, sure. Anyway, I'm gonna double check that he's still in jail," says Nunya, tapping away at her PSD. "Yup, according to prison records, he was in his room during lights out just last night. So maybe he isn't the one who physically kidnapped the President's daughter, but he's definitely behind it. And he wanted me to know it was him. He wants me to know he's getting revenge for what I did to him."

"So, what can you tell us about him?" asks Whip.

"Well, his real name isn't Montgomery Israel, for starters. He's not even Jewish. He just chose the last name 'Israel' because it means 'contender of God'. He's an egomaniac. And fuck that guy for cultural appropriation," says Nunya.

"How did he choose the first name Montgomery?" asks Whip.

"Oh, he thought it sounded fancy. I can't remember if it was because he loved Star Trek, or if he named himself after an old department store. Either way, no one knows his real name. One day he just appeared with an alias and some falsified documents. He then spent the better part of a decade destroying lives and blackmailing his way to power. The reason he wants revenge is because I hacked into a huge data farm where he'd stored secret information on thousands of powerful people. I was able to prove he was using the information to manipulate events across the galaxy. At one point he was the most powerful individual in existence, from a political perspective," says Nunya.

"And you had the guts to take him down?" asks Whip. "Honey, you have bigger balls than even me."

101

"And that's saying something. You've seen the size of those things," I say to Nunya. She just looks at me and shakes her head.

"At the time I was a bit... suicidal. My crew had just died. Instead of drowning myself in alcohol or yeeting myself off a bridge I decided to focus my energy on taking down the guy who hired me for the mission," says Nunya.

"Wait, you smuggled the box of golden lotus petals for Montgomery Israel, something that would make him immortal and invincible? And you just gave it to him?" I ask.

"Wow, nice recap of what I told you in our last adventure. Yeah, I gave it to one of his underlings, but I didn't know it at the time. It wasn't until afterward that I found out he was behind it. It took me months to figure out who hired us. Even though I knew it was a dangerous mission, and my team knew the risks, they were still my friends, and I wanted revenge. So, I used my skills to track him down, figure out what he was doing, and end him," says Nunya.

"Well, if he's invincible now then how did they capture him?" I ask.

"That's a good question. Either he didn't eat the golden lotus petals, or they didn't work as advertised, or they never made it to him," says Nunya.

"Do you think the underling you gave the petals to had betrayed his boss?" asks Whip.

"Sure, anything's possible. I just don't know," says Nunya.

"So, what do we do next?" asks Knob, who we didn't realize had been standing there, listening to our conversation for the last several minutes.

"Well, maybe it would make sense to visit Montgomery Israel in prison," says Whip. "I'm sure he wants to rub in what he did."

"Oh, I'm sure he does too. I just don't know if it'll do any good. He's very, very smart, and exceedingly manipulative. He's like Hannibal Lecter but doesn't eat people. I don't know if he'd give us anything useful to go on," says Nunya.

"Well, we won't know until we give it a try. Let's go see this motherfucker!" I say.

"Hold up, it's been a long day," starts Knob. "I need to recharge. Like, literally. I'm a bit like a battery, and if I don't get sufficient sleep my powers suffer."

"So, your weakness is you get tired? That's lame," I say.

"Yes, well, I didn't get to pick my powers and how they worked," says Knob.

"Are you sure you didn't? Are you sure you didn't pay a mad scientist an exorbitant amount of money to imbue you with powers you don't deserve?" I ask.

"Yeah, pretty sure," says Knob. "Anyway, we still have a few days before the handoff, and I think it'd be in our best interests to get some rest before we go see this evil archenemy of yours, Nunya."

"Fine, whatever. Where are our rooms?" asks Nunya.

"Oh, you mean where will you be sleeping on the ship? You won't. There's only two actual bedrooms, mine and Whip's, and some super cramped bunks. So, we'll need to stop somewhere and find accommodations for all of us," says Knob. "Do you have any preference?"

"Yeah, nowhere where the motel's name has a number in it," I say.

"Okay, no cheap motels," says Knob. "Anyone else?"

"Actually, I have an idea. Can you take us to St. Marley?" asks Nunya.

"Oh, wait, that's where most of the Reginalds moved to!" I say.

"Who are 'The Reginalds'? They sound like a garage band," says Knob.

"Reginald was a guy we saved from some evil Bloopnarps. Well, him and his clones. The Bloopnarps basically enslaved the Reginalds, and we helped them escape. A whole bunch went to the tropical paradise that is St. Marley. I think it'd be cool to stay there, check in on him. Or 'hims'," says Nunya.

"I am always down for some mojitos, cigars, and checking out hot babes in impossibly small bikinis," I say.

"Dick, you gotta remember that we won't be able to stay long. It's just for tonight. We'll need to go talk to Montgomery Israel in the morning. So don't think this is some huge vacation opportunity," says Nunya.

"I think you'd be surprised by how much vacation I can pack into a single night," I say.

"Fine, just make sure you're ready to go when the rest of us are. I'm not looking forward to having to meet Israel face-to-face, and the last thing I need is to deal with your bullshit in the morning," says Nunya.

"Hey, I'm sure everything will work out tomorrow."

"Famous last words."

"I guess I'll go point the ship at St. Marley then," says Knob, sauntering off. God, I hate how he saunters.

20

It doesn't take us long to reach St. Marley, thanks to the series of space-assholes spread throughout the galaxy. Heh. As we start our descent toward the planet, I realize the only clothes I have are my tuxedo. Not exactly the best thing to wear in a tropical paradise. I turn to Nunya.

"So yeah, I'm gonna need some new clothes. I don't wanna be in a tux while the weather is so nice," I say.

"I'm keeping my armor on, especially now that I know someone out there is plotting my demise," says Nunya. "But yeah, feel free to treat yo' self."

"Alright. Do we know where we're staying?" I ask.

"Oh, shit, I should really book us rooms. On it," says Nunya. I watch as she taps furiously on her PSD. Just as the ship settles to the ground, Nunya exclaims "Done. Got us our own rooms. Put it on Knob's credit card. Hotel Orym, nicest on the planet. Spared no expense."

"Again, your balls are bigger than mine. Knob's gonna be pissed," says Whip.

"I'm gonna be pissed about what?" asks Knob, as he's passing through the room on the way to the loading bay. I notice he's changed out of his white tux and into tan Bahama shorts, a white Guayabera shirt, and flip flops. Goddammit, that's what I was gonna wear! Anyway, we all stand up to follow him out.

"I booked us each a room at the best hotel on the planet," says Nunya.

"And why would I be pissed about that?" asks Knob.

"Because I used your credit card," says Nunya, matter-of-factly.

"Wait, you what?" says Knob, now super pissed.

"Don't worry about it, I'm sure the President will compensate you," I say.

"But she stole my credit card number!" yells Knob.

"And you had a whole bunch of nude pictures of us. Let's call it even," I say.

Knob's expression withers.

As we depart the ship, I realize everyone else is putting on sunglasses. I'd be putting on sunglasses too if my pair hadn't been

104

destroyed at the start of my previous adventure. Gotta put that on my list of shit to buy.

Looking around, I'm a bit mesmerized by the beauty of the island we're on. Palm trees stretch high into the amazingly blue sky, white sands crunch slightly beneath my shoes. A cool breeze makes me immediately feel calm and at peace. I can hear the ocean not far off in the distance. It's no wonder most of the Reginalds wanted to come here; it's perfect.

"So, everyone is splitting up then?" asks Whip.

"Guess so," I say.

"Are you guys worried about Dour Mike stealing the ship?" asks Nunya.

"Nah, he's probably too busy having sex with his toaster oven to even notice us leaving. I'm sure he'll be fine," I say. "Anyway, I'm gonna get some new clothes then do what I do best: lechery."

"Hey, can I come with you?" asks Knob.

"Uh, sorry, not interested in a fivesome," I say.

"Fivesome?" repeats Knob.

"Yeah, me, the three hot babes I'm gonna score with, and you. I'm sure you can find your own people to have sex with. Just put it on your credit card," I say.

"Har-dee-frickin-har, I've never paid for sex in my entire life," says Knob.

"You've never had sex in your entire life, so I'd already just assumed. Also, that's twice now you've said 'Har-dee-frickin-har'. Is that like your catchphrase or something?" I ask.

"No. Why? Should it be?" asks Knob.

"'Fuck no, it sounds stupid as shit," I say.

"Yeah, well your one-liners aren't any better," says Knob.

"Hey, when you become the number one detective in the galaxy, which will be never, then you can give pointers on catchphrases. Until then, shut your cakehole. See ya."

I walk down a sandy path, away from the rest of the group, not actually knowing where the fuck I'm going. I just wanted to get away from Knob and his constant Knobbing. If he could be about 90% less Knob, he might even be likable. But he isn't, and he's not.

Finally, out of sight of the rest of the group, I pull out my PSD and bring up a list of nearby men's clothing stores. I find one called 'Bommy Tahama's' that's not far, and as soon as I know which direction to head, I fly into the air.

The view from several hundred feet up is breathtaking. The island is about the size of a large city, but thankfully most of it is undeveloped tropical jungle. A large mountain in the center seems untouched by people, and the surrounding ocean is a crystal blue color. I can only see a few boats off in the distance. I'm glad that they haven't ruined this paradise by filling it with too many people.

Swooping down toward the nearest town, I reach Bommy Tahama's. It looks like your standard island-themed clothing store; fancy-ish yet laid back. Walking in I see something I both expect and don't expect, Reginald, and he's working behind the counter. He spots me immediately.

"Detective Dick Blowhard, is that you?" asks Reginald.

"Yeah, it's me! Which Reginald are you?" I ask, as he comes running up and hugs me.

"I'm the one who you met at the bottom of the hotel. You asked for a menu, and I suggested you check out the menu for the specific floor you were staying on," says Reginald.

"Of course I remember you! Glad to see you buddy! How are things?" I ask.

"Great! So far so good. No one's tried recapturing any of us, as far as I know, and we've all pretty much been able to find jobs in the last month or so since you rescued us," says Reginald.

"That's great to hear! Are you enjoying living in paradise?"

"It's so much better than being trapped in a hotel all the time. And I've even made a friend or two who wasn't me, so that's been exciting. They pay me decently here, and I get my own paycheck. I even have my own small apartment now. I feel like my life has finally started."

"I'm really happy for you, man," I say, smiling at him.

"So, what brings you here? Come to check up on me? Or us, I guess?"

"Definitely part of it, yes. Nunya and I are on a mission with a few other folks to rescue the President's daughter from an evil supervillain. That isn't public knowledge, so if you could keep that between us, that would be great. But we needed a place to stay, so Nunya suggested we stop here and check up on you, see how things are going, and if you needed anything," I say.

"I don't think we need anything, now that most of us have jobs and places to live. But it's honestly just great to see you. I guess I should ask, is there anything you came in looking for?" asks Reginald.

"Well, I don't exactly fit in with the locals while wearing a tux. I was hoping that you might have some indestructible clothes I could buy, something that screams 'I live in a tropical paradise and have so much money I don't care how relaxed I look.'"

"Finally," says Reginald.

106

"Finally, what?" I ask.

"You're the first person to come in asking about our specialty line. Follow me!"

Reginald excitedly walks back behind the counter, and I assume presses a button, because a large hole opens next to the counter, just large enough for both of us to fit through.

"Jump!" says Reginald. He drops down into the hole, and I hear him say "wheeeee!" as he disappears into darkness.

"Oh, what the hell," I say, jumping in behind him.

As I fall, I feel my feet hit something curved and metal and realize that this must be a slide leading somewhere else. Just as my ass hits and my head drops beneath the hole, it closes behind me, plunging me into darkness.

Dim purple lights wink on, illuminating the slide as we take several crazy twists and turns on our way down. Eventually, after hitting a few bumps, and after hearing Reginald squeal a few times, we're dumped into a large pile of foam cubes. Reginald turns to me.

"Thanks, Dick, I've never gotten to do that before. You have no idea how tempted I've been to just drop down here, but it's store policy not to use the slide unless we're bringing a customer down, or in case of an emergency."

"Sure, it was fun!" I say.

Reginald and I climb out of the pile of foam cubes, and I follow him down a hallway to what looks like a well-reinforced door. He pulls on the handle, and it easily swings open for him.

"Wait, you didn't have to do a retina scan, or body scan, or sing the Star-Spangled Banner backward to open the door?" I ask.

"No. Why would we need to do that?" asks Reginald.

"Well, that looks like a heavy-duty door, and I just figured you were trying to keep people from breaking in," I say.

"Oh, yeah, that's not a real concern. If either of us had been intruders, the slide's security system would have kicked in, changed where the intruder ended up, and dropped them into an incinerator," says Reginald.

"Really?" I ask.

"Actually, yes, really. Bommy Tahama's theft policy is rather strict. Just make sure I get all of the anti-theft devices removed from your clothes before you leave, or it might get... sticky," says Reginald.

"Good to know."

"Anyway, welcome to my underground lair," says Reginald.

The best way to describe the room is what you'd imagine a tropical themed bar would look like on an ice planet, during the coldest, darkest time of the year. It's decorated as if you are on a sandy beach, complete with white sand on the ground, light blue painted walls, and a pool of water. Fans gently blow some of the moisture throughout the large room to make it feel more tropical, but there are no windows and no natural sunlight coming in. It makes sense since we're so far underground. What makes the aesthetic really feel off is the racks of clothes sitting in the sand. It immediately pulls you out of the illusion.

"So, did you have anything specific in mind?" asks Reginald.

"I'm thinking shorts, Guayabera shirt, and slides. Oh, and a really cool looking pair of shades. Maybe a hat if it feels right. And they all need to be indestructible," I say.

"Shouldn't be a problem. What colors would you like?"

"Tan shorts, either light green or white for the shirt, tan slides, black sunglasses, and surprise me with the hat."

"Your wish is my command," says Reginald.

I watch as he hurries around the room, pulling several items off each of the displays. After a brief moment, he's placed a pile of clothes and accessories down on a table in the middle of the room.

"Feel free to start trying things on!" says Reginald, excitedly.

"Uh, do you have, like, a changing room?" I ask.

"Oh, no, unfortunately for whatever reason they ran out of budget when they were working down here, and it's too prohibitively expensive to get the equipment needed to excavate an additional room at this point, so we're just kind of stuck having people change in front of us," says Reginald.

"That's fine. I just hope you don't get intimidated by my massively muscled body," I say.

"Uh, no, I'm just fine with what I was born with. I'm sure it won't be a problem," says Reginald.

"Cool."

I start trying on the clothes, and I'm a little surprised how well everything fits, considering how much bigger I am than the average person. It's like they'd known I was coming and had everything ready to go for me. Maybe I'm just lucky that way. Or maybe this was the plan all along, get me trapped underground, trying on clothes that take away my superpowers.

"Hey, Reginald, these clothes won't take away my superpowers, will they? And you aren't working for any archvillains I'm unaware of, are you?" I ask.

"No, definitely not! Why would you even think that?" asks Reginald.

"Oh, sorry, it's not you, it's paranoia. It's just that these clothes fit so well, it seems like they were made specifically for me," I say.

"Oh, I see. Yes, they fit so well because they're shrink-to-fit. The material stretches as the person puts on the clothes, perfectly fitting them every time," says Reginald.

"Really? That's so cool! And they're indestructible?"

"For the most part, yes," says Reginald.

"Wow, science is an amazing thing," I say.

"Indeed."

"Oh, and magic isn't used to make the shrink-to-fit work, right?" I ask.

"No, they're 100% science based. I made sure to select clothes that aren't enchanted, knowing magic is your weakness," says Reginald.

"Wait, how did you know that? Does everybody know my weakness?"

"Actually, I think so. I mean, they just revealed it in a recent episode of 'The Pan-Galactic Adventures of Dick Blowhard', so it's sort of common knowledge now."

"Those rat bastard TV show producers! They're gonna get me killed!" I yell.

"I certainly hope not, sir," says Reginald. "Maybe it wasn't the best idea to start making your stories public."

"I didn't actually personally authorize it, my media company did on my behalf. According to my agent I do make a fair bit of money in royalties from the show, then there's the toys, the comic books, t-shirts, hats... you get the picture. If you had the chance to have a TV show based on your life that would make you super rich, wouldn't you say 'yes'?" I ask.

"Actually, yes. I'd call it 'Attack of the Clones'!"

"Uh, I think that's already a thing."

"Oh, is it?" says Reginald. "How about 'Breaking Bad'?"

"Okay, now you're just being sarcastic," I say.

"Everybody Loves Reginald?"

"Nopety nope-nope. You're a great guy, Reginald, but I think maybe the universe is better off without you having your own show," I say.

"Indeed."

I finish trying on all the clothes. It takes me a few minutes to fiddle with the buttons on a few of the shirts because of the sheer size of my digits. You'd think if they could make stretchy-shrinky clothes they could invent self-buttoning buttons, but I guess science just isn't that sophisticated yet.

109

"I think I'll take it all," I say.

"Wonderful! I will say you did look dashing in all the outfits. Are you going to wear the ones you have on currently out of the store?" asks Reginald.

Through my super cool new Cosmic-Ray-Bans, I look down at the powder blue Guayabera shirt, light tan shorts, and light tan slides. "Yup, I think I will."

"Okay, give me a minute to defuse all the security devices then I'll ring you up," says Reginald.

He pulls out a device that looks like a laser blaster and goes to town on the tags on the clothes I'm wearing, then on the other sets of clothes I'm buying. After neatly folding everything and placing it in bags he rings me up at this tiny counter in the middle of the room.

"Oh, shit, I just realized, I don't have a convenient way of carrying all this stuff. You wouldn't happen to sell Bags of Ultimate Wonders, would you?" I ask.

"Actually, sir, we give them out free when you spend more than five hundred burgmorps. You've far exceeded that today," says Reginald.

"Oh, okay. I would have thought those would be really expensive since they're so rare," I say.

"Actually, now that the Mad Wizard from planet O'Brien has started production again on magical items, they're quite easy to get ahold of. She's mass producing them for us."

"Maggie? Back to her old tricks? Glad to hear!" I say.

"Oh, wait, you know the Mad Wizard?" asks Reginald.

"Intimately. More intimately than most," I say.

"Of course you do. You are, after all, a major celebrity," says Reginald. "Please hold up your hand."

I hold my hand up and a green laser beam scans it.

"Wonderful," says Reginald. "Your total came out to twenty-seven thousand and two burgmorps."

"Holy fucking shit! Why is it so goddamn expensive?" I ask.

"Well, these are premium indestructible clothes that will always fit you for the rest of your life. Economically speaking, you aren't likely to purchase many sets of clothes from us because of it, so we charge the cost that you would normally spend in a lifetime on clothes. On top of that, there's inflation, labor costs, taxes, transportation costs, production costs, rental costs, electricity... I think you get the idea. And everything is more expensive on an island," says Reginald.

"Still, it seems excessive. I guess though if there's anything wrong with the clothes, I'll just return them and get my money back," I say.

"I can personally guarantee the quality and indestructibility of your clothes. But yes, you might keep your receipt," says Reginald, handing me the brand-new Bag of Ultimate Wonders.

If you weren't already aware, and missed out on one of my earlier adventures, a Bag of Ultimate Wonders is a bag you can stick a whole bunch of things in, even large stuff, and it remains small enough to fit in your pocket. You basically put your hand in, think about what you want, and you pull it out; as long as you'd already put it inside. It's super convenient.

I know what you're thinking: if they can make a bag that holds anything then why can't they just make a bag that can create anything? Well, imagine if an eight-year-old got ahold of one and pulled a T-Rex out at the dinner table. As hilarious as that sounds in theory, it would make for a lot of upset parents.

Anyway, I slide the bag into one of the pockets of my new shorts.

"So, uh, how the heck do we get out of here? Do I have to fly us back up the slide?" I ask.

"Oh, no, we just take the elevator up," says Reginald, walking over to an elevator door I hadn't noticed.

"Wait, why didn't we just take the elevator down?" I ask.

"So, you would rather take an elevator down than a twisty-turny fun-slide?" asks Reginald.

"No, I guess I wouldn't," I admit.

"Then you've answered your own question," says Reginald, entering the elevator.

I follow him inside the small cabin. As soon as we get in, the door shuts and we're whisked upward at a fairly fast clip. Once it arrives, we step out just behind the main counter we started at.

"Well, Reginald, thank you for all your help," I say, hugging him.

"You're welcome, Detective Blowhard. It was wonderful seeing you again! Please stop by again if you're ever in the neighborhood," says Reginald.

"I will. Take care."

"Goodbye, sir."

21

Now that I've got some cool new threads and the evening to myself, I decide to head to a local cantina. I pull out my PSD and use it to find a bar that's near the hotel we're staying at. Even though I have superpowers and don't need to breathe I can still get drunk. And before you even question whether that makes sense or not, just know that I have no idea how I actually got my powers or why, so if you have a problem with how they work you can take it up with whoever turned me into me.

Instead of flying, which I'm sure is likely to attract a bunch of much wanted attention, I decide to walk. It gives me a chance to check out the shops and restaurants along the way. I stop briefly at a cigar shop and buy myself a few sticks. I also purchase a torch lighter and V-cutter. Now I won't go into the description of how wonderful they smell, or how nice the people were in the shop, or how excited I am to smoke these cigars. I'm a role model, and I don't want kids smoking. Don't do it kids!

One of the things I'm enjoying most is the mix of smells in this place. The aroma of slowly simmering food mixed with ocean air makes me feel alive. It's so much better than spaceship air. Spaceship air smells like stale farts compared to this. Actually, spaceship air mostly smells like stale farts because the air inside the spaceship is constantly being recycled. Yeah, take a deep breath of that, mi amigo.

After a few turns down some side streets, passing some amazing looking food carts along the way, I reach the Cantina Del La Luna, which surprisingly appears to be space themed. I wonder why anyone would want to hang in a place that reminds them of the cold harshness of outer space when they're living in one of the most beautiful places in the galaxy. Maybe everyone needs a break from their surroundings sometimes, even while living in paradise. I guess the space-grass is always redder on the other side of the invisible barrier shield.

Walking in, I notice it's split up into two sections: the main restaurant, and a nice-looking bar. I make a beeline straight for the bar. Yeah, I'm gonna have food, but my main focus is to get drunk and get laid. Not necessarily in that order, but we'll see where the night takes me. It's still light outside, so I figure I'm gonna have to sit here and wait for more people to come in. The dinner crowd usually comes for the food, the late-night crowd usually comes for the company. I sit down in a large booth that barely fits me.

After spending a few hours downing several bowls of guac, and throwing back a half dozen mojitos and margaritas, I'm fairly well buzzed. I pull out one of my cigars, snip a notch into the end with the V-cutter and slowly, carefully rotate the tip in the flame of my torch lighter. I start with a puro because they're usually higher quality than your average cigar. There's more tradition and history that comes with them, and you can actually taste the difference in quality. A few puffs later and I have my cigar slowly burning.

I lean back and put my feet up on the booth seat across from me. As soon as I do, two women who'd been hanging out at the bar together wander over to me. The first looks mostly human, except for the fact that her skin is a beautiful purple color. Two eyes, two ears, one nose, one mouth. Yup, even her curvaceous form looks completely human.

The second woman looks like she's part human and part Meow. If you missed out on my last adventure, Meow's are creatures that look like an anime artist drew the most adorable 50 lbs. cartoon kitten they could come up with, and then turned them into a vicious killing machine. Just as you reach out to rub their furry belly, they'll bite your arm off and tear the rest of you to shreds. This woman doesn't have fur, but does have the cat ears, the cat tail, large bright eyes, and a cute little kitten nose. Other than that, she looks mostly human. I feel a little uneasy, until the catgirl gives me a mischievous smile that lets me know she's interested.

"Mind if we sit down?" asks the catgirl, gently purring.

"Free planet. Wait, is it a free planet?" I ask.

"It's a democracy, yes," says the purple woman, sitting down across from me. "As much as any society can actually be a democracy."

The catgirl slides into the booth next to me, and starts rubbing her face against my shoulder, as if she's seeking attention.

"Uh, should I pet her?" I ask the purple woman.

"I suppose it depends on where you plan to put your hands."

"I'm willing to put my hands anywhere she wants," I say, winking.

"Purrrr-fect," says the catgirl.

I take a long pull from my cigar and blow the smoke back out, away from the women.

"So, do you two want to go back to my room?" I ask.

"You don't want to sit here and talk for a while?" asks the purple woman.

"Did you?" I ask.

"Well, you don't even know our names," she replies.

"Do you know mine?"

"Aren't you the famous Detective, Dick Blowhard?"

"That's me, baby. And if you know my reputation, names aren't really necessary, are they?"

"No, I guess they aren't. We'd love to come visit your room," says the purple woman.

"Done."

I pay for the drinks and food and pay off their tab as well. Just as we're walking out the door, I scoop both of them up and place one on each shoulder. I realize I'm a bit drunk, so walking a straight line to the hotel doesn't happen.

"Do you two hot babes know how to get to the Hotel Orym?" I ask.

"Yeah, just keep going this way and turn left at the corner," says the catgirl.

The hotel, thankfully, isn't very far from the bar. I planned it that way, not knowing how drunk I'd be. So far, my plan was going off without a hitch. That is until we turn the corner and run into a gang of Pockapees.

Pockapees look kinda like really tall compies, the dinosaurs that once roamed Earth Uno. They're kind of like land piranhas, willing to eat pretty much any meat that comes their way. There's eight in total, and as soon as they notice us, I hear the familiar 'snikt' of switchblades being readied.

"Give us your money and your women, and we might let you live," says the one closest to me, in a scratchy, reptilian type voice. I'm guessing he's the leader, because he's wearing a red sash around his waist, and evil leaders always wear red sashes. It's standard villain attire, just like eye patches and pets. Come to think of it, most villains dress like pirates. I guess that makes some sense, since pirates are kinda badass evildoers.

But now I'm questioning the pet thing. Maybe they're comfort animals, because I gotta believe that being a bad guy full-time would cause a lot of anxiety. Not knowing if you can trust anybody, constantly having to kill insubordinate underlings. Sounds fucking exhausting. I'll have to ask Knob the next time I see him how he handles it.

Anyway, I set my arm candy carefully on the ground. Both of them take a couple of steps back, not knowing what to expect. Well ladies, you've got front row seats for the main event.

"You know, back in the day I wouldn't have given you a warning. I'd just rip your heads off. But I'm feeling a bit charitable right now. If you leave, I won't harm you. I won't pull your spleens

114

out through our mouths," I say, blowing a puff of cigar smoke in their general direction.

"We don't have spleens, tough guy. Yeah, you might look like some circus freak strong man, but there's eight of us and only one of you," says the leader.

"Well, if you want to call a few hundred of your friends to try to make it even, I can wait. I got a few minutes," I say.

"Gonna carve that smart mouth of yours up, motherfucker," says the gang leader, who leaps out and tries to stretch out my smile with his blade.

Instead of cutting me, the end of his blade breaks off on my lips, which are now grinning at his stupidity.

"Okay, you asked for it," I say.

As he tries slashing at my chest, the others come running at me. They try their best, stabbing and poking and hacking at me, but not a drop of blood comes out. Even my clothes are resisting their attack. Glad that my new threads can handle themselves in a fight.

Once I've given them a chance to try to hurt me, I start punching. I just grab one of the dudes by the arm and punch him in the head. It explodes in a shower of green blood, spraying Pockapee brains all over the alley.

For some reason, the gang doesn't stop attacking, even though they are obviously outmatched, and obviously aren't doing any damage to me. I figure they must be afraid of their leader if they're still attacking.

Feeling generous, I grab the leader by both of his wrists and lift him up into the air. I drop him, and just when his feet are about to hit the ground, I kick him in the nuts. He goes flying several hundred feet out of sight. Thankfully, that causes the other Pockapees to drop their knives and run. I pick up the red sash that fell off their leader when I gave him the boot and wipe the dinosaur goo from my hands.

Turning around, I notice the two sexy ladies I'd literally picked up are still there, waiting expectantly. Neither of them seems too grossed out by what happened.

"Wow, you both must have seen some shit in your lives," I say. "Most folk would either be barfing or running away right now after seeing that."

"Well, we've both had a tough go of it," says the purple woman.

"Very tough," says the catgirl.

"Then let me try to make your lives better for a little while. Come on," I say, hoisting them back onto my shoulders.

22

We stumble our way to the hotel, which is one of the only tall buildings on the island. I'm guessing it's a good ten stories, but it's also quite wide. They must have several hundred rooms if that's the case. On the front of the hotel's awning, in very beautiful cursive letters, is the name "The Hotel Orym."

"This is the place, ladies. Are you ready for some hot, sexy action?" I ask.

The catgirl just purrs, while the purple chick seductively rubs the top of my head. As we approach the door, I notice that the person opening it is none other than Reginald.

"Reginald! You work here too?" I ask.

"Detective Blowhard? Wait, what do you mean... oh, right, you've probably already run into one of the other Reginalds, haven't you? It's so nice to see you!" he says, shaking my hand vigorously.

"Nice to see you too!"

"Where is Miss Nunya? Are you two not traveling the galaxy together anymore?"

"Oh, no, she's around. She's supposed to be staying here as well. Surprised you didn't see her already," I say.

"Well, I just started my shift, so it's possible she's already in her room. Would you like me to find out for you?" asks Reginald.

"No, that's okay. I don't want to bother her. I'm sure she's having a wonderful time with some beautiful women, just like I'm about to have."

"Oh, right! Well then let me be the first to welcome you to The Hotel Orym. We hope you have a pleasant stay. Might I recommend you let the ladies walk in on their own power? Otherwise, they may bump into the door frame as you walk in."

"Yeah, that's a good idea. Ladies," I say, as I carefully set both of them down.

"It was great seeing you again, Reginald," I say.

"You as well, sir," he replies.

I let the ladies walk in front of me, trying my best to be a gentleman under the circumstances. But honestly, I just love watching their butt cheeks sway seductively as they walk. I can't wait to bury my face in them.

Walking up to the counter, I'm a little disappointed that the concierge isn't Reginald. Or, well, one of the Reginalds. Instead, an insanely hot blonde in a sexy white button-up top and slacks looks at us expectantly. I will go on record and say this is the first and only time I'll ever be disappointed in seeing an exquisite specimen such as her. She cocks her head seductively, licks her lips a little, and says, "Welcome to the The Hotel Orym. What can I help you with?"

"Hey, Beautiful, I should have a room ready in my name," I reply.

"And the name?" she asks, looking me up and down like I'm a T-bone steak and she's the truffle butter.

"You don't recognize me?" I ask.

She looks me up and down again, "Should I? I feel like maybe I should."

"I'm Detective Dick Blowhard, the famous superhero. I even have a TV show that streams to all the planets in the galaxy."

"Oh, I do think I've heard of you, then. Welcome Detective Blowhard. I see that we do, in fact, have a room for you." She types away at her computer screen. "You'll be in room 420, the bridal suite."

"Heh, 420," I say.

"Is something funny, Detective Blowhard?" asks the concierge.

"Heh, nothing," I reply. "Oh, I should probably ask, my friend Nunya Business is staying here as well. Could you let me know which room she ended up with?"

She types away at her screen.

"Normally, it's our policy not to give out room numbers, but it looks like she was the person who requested the rooms, so she's a member of your party. Yes, it appears she's in room 69," says the beautiful blonde, who I now realize is named Cassiopeia, after staring at the nametag on her perky left breast.

"Heh, 69. Nice." I say.

I turn and look at the two beauties I picked up at the bar to see if they're upset at me flirting with the concierge, but instead, they seem to be imagining taking off the concierge's clothes just as much as me.

"Hey, uh, just out of curiosity, what time do you get off?" I ask the concierge.

"I only just started my shift."

"That's disappointing. Well, if you find yourself with some free time, maybe come up to room 420. We'd love to have you," I say.

She thinks for a moment. "Maybe," she says.

"'Maybe' is good enough for me," I reply.

The concierge blushes a little and looks back at her screen. "Please hold up one of your hands."

117

I hold up my right hand and a familiar green laser beam scans it.

"You're all set, Detective Blowhard. To enter your room just hold your hand up to the door and the laser will do the rest."

"Perfect. Thanks, dollface," I say. "That's detective-speak for 'I think you're beautiful.'"

"You're more than welcome," says the concierge, blushing a second time, not making eye contact.

I turn and follow the two young ladies that I came with over to the elevator. As soon as we get inside, they start to cuddle up to me. I pick them up just enough so they can cover my face in kisses. God, how I've missed this.

It's not long before we reach the fourth floor. I stumble out of the elevator a little, as the alcohol is still doing its thing, and the ladies guide me to room 420. I put my hand up in front of the door, the green laser scans it, and the door makes a satisfying popping sound as it unlocks. The purple girl pushes the door open as the catgirl takes my hand and pulls me along.

The room itself is quite nice. Not as nice as my bedroom back at home, and definitely not as nice as the room I had at the Chateau Marmot hotel, but it's still fairly nice. It kind of reminds me of a Spanish villa, much like a lot of the surrounding buildings. High ceilings, light colored walls, and wicker furniture that begs you to relax in it. What's most impressive about the room is the bed. It's about twice the size of a normal bed, and the covering is a beautiful purple satin that shines like it's made of glass.

Guiding me to the bed, the ladies start undressing me, then slowly, seductively undress themselves. One of the first things I notice is that although catgirl doesn't have fur all over her body, she does have a patch of it a few inches above her love hole. It looks very well groomed, and if I were to guess, she probably spends hours each day tending to it. I start to wonder if maybe she's flexible enough to lick down there.

The purple girl has tan lines, and where her skin doesn't normally get sunlight, it's a few shades lighter. It makes her breasts look like glowing orbs, and her bikini area a little easier to see. Thankfully, both ladies have normal looking va-jay-jays. Not that I'm that picky, but occasionally there's a species that has something a little different down there, and it can get a bit challenging to work with at times.

Once they're undressed, both ladies take hold of my stone hard firehose and start going to town on it with their mouths. While the purple girl's tongue feels soft and slick, catgirl's tongue is a little rough, but I like the sensation. When you're nearly indestructible like I am, friction isn't so much of a problem. They take turns slurping and sliding their lips along the length of it.

After a few moments, catgirl grabs me by the tip, holds on tight, and pulls me to the bed, so that I'm now lying on top of her. She plugs her cat-snatch with my Louisville Slugger, pulling on my hips with her legs so that every inch of me is buried deep inside her. Catgirl starts purring like crazy, and I can tell that she's enjoying this more than she had imagined. At the same time, purple girl has worked her way behind me. She spreads my cinnamon rolls apart and starts knocking at heaven's door with her tongue. Oh my God, this is so fucking awesome!

I take things slowly, just because I want it to last for catgirl, as she seems like she's almost there already. It's also to make sure that when I'm sliding back that I don't accidentally send purple girl flying across the room. We find a good rhythm so that all three of us are enjoying ourselves. Each time catgirl orgasms, she makes these weird screeching noises that are kind of unnerving, but I don't care, I just keep thrusting. After her fifth orgasm, I finally get mine, filling up her chamber of secrets with my polyjuice potion.

Once I slow down, the ladies roll me over onto my back, and catgirl straddles my face. She coyly looks down at me and says, "You've made such a mess! Now you need to clean me up."

She presses her furry mound down on my face and starts dripping our love sauce into my mouth. I lick like crazy, doing my best to catch every drop, but after a few seconds I start feeling a bit woozy. I tap on her thigh like a fighter tapping out of a fight, but she just keeps rubbing her lady bits all over my face. Things start going fuzzy around the edges, and I feel like I've been poisoned. Oh fuck. Just as I start to lose consciousness, I hear the words "goodnight, Detective Blowhard" drift down at me.

23

Waking up slowly, I start to look around the room. The girls are no longer in the hotel room, and in fact, the hotel room is no longer in the hotel room. Instead of lying on a purple satin covered bed, I'm lying on an uncomfortable stone table, strapped to it like I'm Frankenstein's monster. I struggle against the bonds, but it's no use, as they seem to be imbued with magic.

I really should have seen this coming. It wasn't like there wasn't foreshadowing when the gang of Pockapees just happened to be down that alley, or that the two women seemed like maybe they'd been paid to have sex with me. Maybe it was just my ego that made me ignore the signs, since women usually do fall all over me, and fights seem to happen around every corner in my line of work.

Looking around the very dimly lit room I notice two-way mirrors on the walls to each side of and in front of me. I tilt my head backward and see a metal door with a plain, standard issue metal doorknob. It's the most uninteresting metal doorknob I've ever seen. I really can't stress enough how bland this doorknob is, and it's kind of fucking with my mind. Maybe the poison is still messing with my head, making me focus on this goddamn doorknob.

"Hello?" I yell.

It takes a second, but I start to hear voices. First, I hear Nunya's, but it's faint. Then I hear Knob's voice. Shit, they got him too. And then comes Whip's muffled voice. Once they've all answered, lights turn on in all of our rooms so that I can now see them. Like me, they are strapped down to stone tables, unable to move. I also listen to the crackle of intercoms coming to life, as I can now hear each of them clearly.

"They got you too, Dick?" asks Knob.

"Duh, obviously," I reply. "How is it that they have you tied up? I didn't think you were susceptible to magic."

"I'm not."

"Well then how the fuck do they still have you strapped down, and why haven't you broken free?"

"Because they know my weakness," admits Knob.

"Which is?"

Knob takes a deep breath and sighs. "Leather."

120

"Wait, what?" I say.

"Leather. For some reason I can't break through leather," replies Knob.

"But wait, when we first met you, you were completely covered in leather. Head-to-toe."

"It wasn't real leather, it was 'pleather'," says Knob.

"So, was the idea to throw everyone off by wearing clothes that look like the thing you have a weakness to?" I ask.

He sighs again. "No, I just wanted to look cool."

"Yeah, that tracks."

"You know, we're probably going to die. Could you at least stop being an asshole to me for five seconds?" asks Knob.

I wait four seconds then respond, "No."

"Hey, would both of you shut up and try to figure a way out of this?" yells Nunya.

"Yeah, I've got a really bad itch I can't reach," says Whip.

"Dick, how did they capture you?" asks Nunya.

"Went back to the hotel with a couple of really hot women. One was a catgirl who dripped poisonous lady goo into my mouth," I reply.

"Hah, so it was a pussy's pussy that knocked you out!" says Knob.

"Yeah, I'm pretty sure everyone got the irony. You didn't have to say that part out loud, Knob."

"I know I didn't, but I figured it would annoy you."

"Gee, score one for you, I guess. How about you, Knob? How did they capture you?" I ask.

"Poisoned my drink. I was sitting alone at the bar, a woman bumped into me, and as I turned to watch her walk away, apparently someone slipped me a mickey."

"So, you didn't even get to have sex with the woman who bumped into you? At least I nailed the two chicks who tricked me," I say.

"Well, that's fucking great for you, Dick, but it doesn't help us get out of the situation, does it?" yells Knob.

"Nope, but it makes me feel a hell of a lot better about our predicament," I say. "So, Whip, how about you, how'd they take you down?"

"A guy who I met at a bar had some strawberry lube that must have been laced with something. I remember feeling light-headed and passing out just as he was squirting his man cream in my mouth," says Whip.

"Good for you, buddy. Nunya, how about you?" I ask.

"Same as you. Two hot chicks took me back to my hotel room, and I was knocked out as soon as one of them creamed all over my face and mouth," says Nunya.

"So, Knob was the only one who didn't get to have sex tonight. Poor guy," I say, mockingly.

"Dude, once I get out of this place, I'm gonna pound your ass!" says Knob.

"Wait, do you mean you're going to beat me up, or have sex with my ass?" I ask.

"The first one," says Knob.

"Sure, Knob. Sure," I reply.

"Would the two of you just shut up and try to figure out a way out of here?" says Nunya.

"You know what would be really helpful? Oh yeah, a Swiss Army knife," says Knob. "I could cut my way through the straps, but our fearless leader over here fucked us over by giving it back to the fucking Swiss Army!"

"He's not the leader, I am!" yells Nunya.

"And I appreciate you sacrificing your toy to save me, Knob," I say. "But how could I have possibly known that somehow, in a crucial moment of our mission, that we would suddenly need the one thing we gave away due to an issue with some layaway furniture? I'm not a fucking psychic!"

"If you were, you could read my mind and know just how much I hate you right now," says Knob.

"Well, the feeling's mutual, bub!" I say. "Wait, Whip, can't you use your bionics or something to break free?"

"Nope, they've got some kind of inhibitor field surrounding me," says Whip.

"Oh, seriously?" I ask.

"No, not seriously. I'm pretty sure they just have a really large magnet underneath me."

"That sucks, dude. Nord really should have used non-magnetic materials in her design," I say.

"Well, then how would the servos work? They're based on electromagnetism. If I didn't have at least some magnetic parts, I'd just be a big metal statue," says Whip.

"I guess that makes sense. At least when I write my memoirs, I won't have a bunch of annoying pedantic fanboys telling me it didn't make sense that you couldn't move around," I reply.

"Uh, right," says Whip, nervously.

Just then, a deep, ominous voice crackles over the intercom. "Hello, Nunya."

"Uh, hello?" she responds.

"Do you remember me?" the voice asks.

"Should I? I don't recognize the voice in particular. Maybe if you show your cowardly face so I can punch it, I'll know who I'm hitting," says Nunya.

"I've been seeking retribution for a long time. And now I finally have you," says the voice.

"Wait, no… oh fuck," says Nunya.

"What? Who is it?" I ask.

"I know who kidnapped us. It's Montgomery Israel!"

24

"Wait, your arch-nemesis Montgomery Israel?" asks Knob.

"Yeah," confirms Nunya. "Hey Israel, we were just coming to visit you in jail, not the other way around. Think you could let us go?"

Silence.

"I thought you were still rotting in prison," says Nunya.

"What makes you assume I'm not?" asks Israel.

"The fact that we're freely communicating right now. I'm guessing they don't let you have intercoms in prison. Oh, and while I'm thinking about it, I wanted to say that the calling card you left, the soil, let me know ahead of time it was you behind the kidnapping. It really kind of ruined your big reveal just now, because we already had you pegged," says Nunya.

"I used the soil to lead you to me. Without it, it would have been more difficult to capture you, if not impossible. What good is a big reveal if I have no one to share it with? It was your overconfidence in knowing I was behind the kidnapping that led to you dropping your guard. And now you're my prisoner, in the same way that I am yours."

"You've never been my prisoner. I just made sure you went to prison, where you belong. Where you will always belong, until you die," says Nunya.

"Do you think it's wise to taunt your captor?" asks Israel.

"You're either gonna kill us or you aren't. We'll either escape, or we won't. It doesn't matter what I say, I'm sure that you've had everything planned out for years, every contingency accounted for. And your plan has finally reached its zenith. Good job."

"Your sarcasm isn't lost on me, dear. I'm not seeking your approval, just your assistance," says Israel.

"Wait, you want our assistance with what? You want your lost puppy found?" asks Nunya.

"I want you to break me out of prison."

"Aw, hell no. Not happening. We aren't gonna break you out of prison."

"All I have to do is say the word and you'll all die right now. Or you could break me out, and I'll return the President's daughter, unharmed," says Israel.

"How do we know you haven't killed her already?" asks Nunya.

"Because you know I'm intelligent enough to keep the hostage alive in case I need her. Contingencies."

"Hard pass. Go ahead and kill us. I'd rather die than let you go free," says Nunya, defiantly.

"Whoa, hold on there a sec," says Knob. "You don't get to choose for the rest of us. I'll break you out, Israel."

"Yeah, I'd rather do that than be killed," says Whip.

"Nunya, we can always recapture him later," I say. "But we can't save Tiffany if we're all dead. At least this way there's a chance. All we have to do is tell the President ahead of time why we have to break Israel out of jail, and I'm sure he'll just have him released."

"No. You cannot tell the President what you're doing. You cannot tell another living soul what you're doing. If you do, I'll know, and I'll have the President's daughter executed. And you must not conceal yourselves when you break me out. Part of my revenge is that by breaking me out you'll become criminals. Fugitives. The ones hunted by the galaxy. You'll lose everything. No one will help you. No more TV shows, no more fame and adulation. Each of you will be left ruined, for the rest of your lives. Just like what you've done to me, Nunya," says Israel.

"Fuck!!!" yells Nunya. "Goddamn fucking motherfucker!!!"

"I'm sorry, Nunya, I really am. But I think we have to do it his way," I say.

I've seen Nunya angry before, but I've never seen her this angry. If I were to guess, I'd say that she had considered putting Israel behind bars as part of her penance for giving him the golden lotus petals, and for losing her crew. Now, all that progress will be undone, and she'll still be entirely accountable for what happened. I don't envy her having to make this impossible decision.

"Fine. We'll break you out," says Nunya, dejected.

"Good," says Israel.

After a moment the intercom shuts off. A few seconds later we're released from our bonds. I walk over and break the glass between rooms, letting everyone climb inside the room I've been trapped in. Nunya takes a moment to put her armor back on before climbing through.

"Oh, thank Gods," says Whip, who I can see is scratching his back something fierce.

"Is everybody okay?" I ask.

"I'm fine," says Knob.

"I meant everyone but you, Knob," I say.

"Yeah, better now," says Whip.

"No. I'm pretty fucking far from okay," says Nunya. "Once we break out Israel, and recover the President's daughter, I'm going to kill him."

"Pulp Fiction references aside, I'm guessing he can still hear you," I say.

"Doesn't matter. He knows the kind of person I am. He knows I'll come for him," says Nunya.

"Nunya, you're one of the good guys. Do you really want his blood on your hands?" I ask.

"Yes. Yes, I do."

"Okay, but isn't he invincible and immortal?" I ask.

"Possibly, but that doesn't mean he can't be contained. And I can make sure he wishes he could die."

"Well, I don't know how you're gonna make that happen right now. So maybe we just see how things pan out. Play it by ear," I say.

"Yeah, fine. Fucking whatever," says Nunya.

"So how do we get out of here? Oh, wait, there's a door," says Whip, reaching for the knob.

"Wait!" I yell.

"For what?" asks Whip.

"I don't trust that doorknob."

"Uh, okay. So then how do we get out of here, smart guy?" asks Knob.

"Like this," I say, walking through the wall next to the door, sending debris flying into the hallway I now find myself in.

Turning to my right, I look over at the door, and connected to the doorknob is a large bomb that looks like it's capable of burying us inside of the building if it collapses. The others follow me into the hallway and look at the door.

"Wait, if Israel wants us to break him out of jail, why would he try to kill us again?" asks Whip.

"He knew the bomb wouldn't kill us, just really piss us off," says Nunya.

"Fuck that guy," says Knob.

"Anyway, let's get the fuck out of here," I say.

"So, which way do we go?" asks Knob.

"How the fuck should I know? Uh... let's go this way," I say, pointing behind me.

"Why that way?" asks Knob.

"Because we have no information telling us which way to go, so just picking arbitrarily and making progress will at least speed things up," I say.

"Wait, no information? Do you guys not see the 'EXIT' signs overhead?" asks Whip.

"Oh, no, I hadn't noticed that. I guess then, do we trust the exit signs?" I ask.

"Yeah, why wouldn't we?" asks Whip.

"Because it could be another trap," I say.

"I mean, I guess. But at this point, don't you think he just wants us to get on with breaking him out of prison?" says Whip.

"Fine, we'll do it your way," I say.

"You guys keep forgetting I'm the one who's calling the shots here," says Nunya.

"Yeah, you know what, you're right. Fearless leader who caused this whole mess in the first place, which way should we go?" I ask.

"Wait, you're trying to pin this on me?" asks Nunya.

"Well, you were the one who picked a fight with one of the most dangerous men in the entire galaxy," I say.

"Fuck you, I was trying to do the right thing!" says Nunya.

"Only after having done the wrong thing, which was to give a golden lotus petal to one of the most dangerous men in the galaxy. I feel like I'm repeating myself," I say.

"Yeah, I fucked up. I fucked up so big that I've been beating myself up over it every day of my life since. I don't need you giving me shit for it because I already give myself enough shit for it. Either you're gonna help me figure this out, or you can fuck right off, Dick," says Nunya.

"I'm gonna help you out, Nunya, because you're my friend. Okay? Does the situation suck? Sure. Am I throwing my life away by helping you break out Israel? Yeah, I fucking am. But I guess that's what you do for friends, whatever the cost," I say.

Nunya seems a little surprised by what I said. I don't think she was expecting me to act like her friend, or to give up anything of significance for her. I can't blame her. I'm not the best when it comes to shit like this. And honestly, I don't know that I've really had a friend before, to know whether friends do this kind of shit for each other. But her friendship means more to me right now than anything I can think of. So, fuck the galaxy if it judges me for breaking out Israel; I'm doing it for the right reasons.

"As touching as this all is, can we get the fuck out of here, now?" asks Knob.

"Yeah. Follow the exit signs," says Nunya.

Nunya makes her way to the front of our group as we follow behind her. A few twists and turns take us to a stairwell leading up. Several flights of stairs later and we're outside, breathing the ocean air again.

"Okay, good, it looks like we're still on St. Marley," says Nunya. She fumbles for something in her pocket and eventually pulls out her PSD. Typing furiously, she abruptly stops. "Yup, still on St. Marley. And it looks like Israel parked Knob's ship nearby. It's only a few blocks away."

To hurry things up, Nunya, Knob and I fly toward the ship while Whip uses his superspeed to run through the gravel paths and streets of St. Marley. It doesn't take long, and when we get there, we're surprised to see Dour Mike waiting for us just outside of the ship. He has a weird look of what could almost be perceived as happiness on his face.

"Hey Dour Mike, are you doing okay?" I ask.

"Yes. Much better now," he replies.

"Did you and the toaster oven get engaged?" I ask.

"No, but I accidentally broke her. I was being too vigorous," he says.

"It be like that sometimes," I say.

"Yes, apparently," replies Dour Mike.

"Well, since you don't have a partner, maybe you could satisfy me," says Nunya.

I turn to look at Nunya and give her the biggest "WTF???" face that I can muster. She gives me a look that tells me I should keep my mouth shut.

"I don't know," starts Dour Mike. "I mean, I don't really find meat-people attractive."

"Don't judge it until you've tried it," says Nunya.

"Um, well, okay," says Dour Mike, nervously.

Nunya escorts Dour Mike up the ramp and into the ship. As we step inside, I see them head toward the nearest closet. I have no idea what the fuck Nunya is thinking, especially since she isn't apparently a fan of dicks or robots.

"Uh, I guess we give them some privacy?" I mumble. Both Knob and Whip look just as shocked as I am. We kind of stumble our way to the front of the ship, far away from the weird noises that start to emanate from the closet.

25

"So, uh, yeah… that was weird," says Whip.

"Enh, I dunno. People have been having sex with machines for thousands and thousands of years. Not really a new thing, I guess. Maybe she just thinks of him as a really elaborate talking dildo," I say.

"Dick, you have to admit it was a bit out of character for Nunya," says Knob.

"Oh, completely agree, but she's the kind of person who can surprise you," I say.

"So, where are we headed now?" asks Knob.

"Well, I guess since our fearless leader isn't here, I'm in charge now," I reply.

"Why should you be in charge? It's my mission and my ship," says Knob.

"Because I'll take off my leather belt and beat you to death with it if you try to stop me," I say.

"Okay, so you completely misunderstood my weakness. Yeah, I can't break through leather, but it doesn't hurt me."

"Oh. Oops."

"And you want to be the brains of the operation?" says Knob.

"Fine, then Whip should be the boss. Whip, your move," I say.

"Well, I guess we don't have to make the money drop-off anymore since we're being forced to break Israel out instead, so maybe we try to do some recon on the prison they're holding him in," says Whip.

"Makes sense, but I'm a little pissed that we don't get to fight a bunch of killer Quokkas," I say.

"I tell you what, Dick. How about for your next birthday, I'll take you on a nice trip to planet Outback and drop you off there," says Knob.

"You think you're funny, don't you," I respond.

"Yeah, a little," says Knob, smirking.

"God, you really have the whole 'asshole' thing down, don't you?"

"I really do."

"Guys, and I can't believe I'm saying this, can you wait on hate-fucking each other at least until we've finished the mission? The childish arguing is starting to get old," says Whip.

"He started it," I say.

"Did not," replies Knob.

"Just both of you, please shut up! Fuck!" says Whip.

I take a deep breath. "Fine."

"Yeah, whatever," says Knob.

"Okay, good. See, I'm already a better leader than either of you. Anyway, I just realized something: If Israel reparked the ship, then maybe he's installed cameras and trackers inside the ship," says Whip.

"Fuuuuuuuck," says Knob.

"Oh, and where's the ransom money? Didn't you have that in a duffel bag?" I ask Knob.

"On it," says Knob, hurrying away. A few seconds later he returns. "The money is still there."

"So, this really never was about money," says Whip. "Well, I guess the three of us should start looking for hidden cameras and tracking devices."

We spend the next hour going through the entire ship. I use my super-vision to make sure we don't miss anything. Thirty-eight devices later and we've cleaned the ship. Dropping all the spy hardware outside and closing the hatch, Knob gets the ship back into orbit. Once we're in space, Nunya finally comes out of the closet with Dour Mike. They both look exhausted.

"Uh, so while you were spending the last hour having sex, we combed the ship for tracking devices and cameras. There was one place we couldn't look, which was the closet you were in, so I'm gonna head in there and make sure we didn't miss anything," I say.

"Yeah, sure, knock yourself out," says Nunya, tired but smirking.

As soon as I walk inside the room, I step in a puddle.

"Hey, what the fuck? Did you have a water balloon fight in here?" I yell at them.

"What do you mean?" asks Nunya.

"I mean the floor is soaking wet. Oh, shit, and so are the walls!"

"Yeah, I wouldn't use a blacklight in there if I were you," says Nunya.

"Couldn't you have at least mopped up?" I ask.

"I could have," says Nunya.

I just roll my eyes. Once they roll back into position, I use my super-vision to scan the tiny room. I find a single tracking device and three cameras.

"Hey Knob, you got a way to jettison stuff from the ship?" I ask.

"Yeah, just throw the stuff into the garbage chute, the ship will launch it into space and vaporize it outside, causing no mess," says Knob.

"That's convenient," I say. "There's a few people I'd like to do that to."

"Present company excluded, I assume?" says Knob.

"You know what they say when you assume," I reply.

"Seriously, guys, knock it off," says Whip.

"Hey, now that Nunya's back, you aren't the leader anymore, Whip. Speaking of Nunya, what do you have to say for yourself?" I ask.

"I'm messy," replies Nunya, with the biggest grin I've ever seen.

"Yeah, well, you can be sure Israel got an eyeful of whatever you were up to. He'll probably try to use it as blackmail," I say.

"I honestly don't care. We're going to be fugitives hated across the known universe. What does it matter if there's a sex tape to go along with it?" says Nunya.

"That's actually a fair point, I guess."

26

We make our way back into the conference room. Sitting down, we all kind of look at each other expectantly.

"Okay, so should our next step be to figure out where they're keeping Israel without letting anyone know what we're doing?" I ask.

"I already know exactly where they're keeping him: Alphatraz," says Nunya.

I feel my jaw drop, and I look around at Knob and Whip who also have their mouths hanging open in surprise.

"Isn't that the most unbreakable-out-of prison in the known universe?" asks Knob.

"It is. It's way more secure than even the Blue House," says Nunya.

"Then how the fuck are we supposed to break into it?"

"Well, I don't know yet. I'm not even sure how to gather any information about it, since no one is allowed to leave once they visit it. Guards are hired-on permanently and live in a town not far from the facility, all of which is on a small, otherwise uninhabited moon. Cargo ships bring supplies, but have only enough fuel to reach the destination, and are unmanned. The only form of conveyances are small range electric vehicles that have no flight capabilities. There's literally no way to leave. The plans for the facilities are also kept on site and have never left the moon. We have no way of getting any information on it," says Nunya.

"Can we maybe put some sort of camera device on an inmate destined for Alphatraz?" I ask.

"I mean, I'm sure you could, but they'd find the device very quickly," says Nunya.

"What about tracking down someone who's escaped?" asks Knob.

"As far as I know, that hasn't ever happened. And if we did make contact with that person, I'm sure they'd suspect what we were up to, and Israel will kill Tiffany," says Nunya.

"So, we're just gonna have to wing it?" I ask.

We sit in silence for what feels like forever.

"What if we sent in a series of probes to do reconnaissance for us?" asks Whip.

"I don't think it would do much. The moon has shields around it, just like the Blue House does. For the probes to be of much use, they'd have to get through the shields," says Nunya.

"Cargo ships still make it through the shields. What if we trojan-horsed a cargo ship with a bunch of probes that came pouring out once it landed?" says Whip.

"They'd definitely see it, and they'd definitely know someone was trying to break in, so they'd increase their security even more."

It gets quiet again.

"Holy shit! I think I've figured it out!" I say.

"What, Dick?"

"All we have to do is fill a cargo ship full of Quokkans and let them destroy the defense system from within."

They all stare at me as if I've lost my mind, which maybe I have.

"And just how exactly would you trap them, then put them onto a cargo ship that they won't be able to destroy en route?" asks Nunya.

"Well, you'd have to surround them in a forcefield while on the cargo ship that turns off once it reaches its destination. Or poison them so that they're asleep for the ride, then they'll wake up once they get there," I say.

"The ships must be scanned before they're allowed through the shields, and my guess is that if they detect lifeforms, they'll blow the cargo ships out of the sky. But if we give them just the right amount of poison to slow their heartbeats down to near nothing, and package them as if they were a shipment of meat, we might be able to make it work. Well, Dick, you've come up with the worst idea of all time, but it's all we have," says Nunya.

"Wait, you can't seriously be considering this!" says Knob. "If we do that, then all of the inmates on the planet will break out and be free to do whatever they feel like. And since I'm sure the guards all signed away their lives to the prison, no one will try to rescue them. On top of that, the owners of the prison will likely stop sending in shipments of food and supplies for the inhabitants, just letting them die. We can't do that."

"And won't the Quokkans try to eat the people?" asks Whip.

"Yeah, shit, I see your point," says Nunya.

"Sorry guys, I guess I didn't think it all the way through," I say.

"Hey, you've come up with more of a plan than the rest of us, even if it was completely insane," says Nunya.

Another long, uncomfortable silence happens.

"Wait, how about me?" asks Dour Mike.

"What do you mean, 'how about you'?" I ask.

"Well, I wouldn't show up as a lifeform if they scanned the ship, and I'd be surprised if they didn't have some sort of robots there to help with the work, so they probably receive them in shipments occasionally. I could go in, interface with one of their computer systems, then send the information back to you," says Dour Mike.

"How would you get a signal out?" asks Nunya.

"Oh, I'm not sure."

"Well, Israel figured out how to do it, since he was talking to us while we were trapped. So, we just need to figure out how he sent a signal out and we can use the same method he did," says Whip.

"You're absolutely right," says Nunya.

"Dour Mike, are you sure you can handle something like this? I mean, you're risking so much, and you don't really have a reason to," I say. "Why would you help us?"

"Because you treat me like a person, and you helped me get a penis, which I very much enjoy. For the first time, I've felt a bit of hope and happiness, even though I've been programmed not to feel those things. I finally have a reason for living, and maybe that's enough of a reason to risk dying."

"That's... unbelievably poignant," says Nunya. "Well, thank you, Dour Mike. Thank you for your willingness to risk your life to save someone else's. You're a hero in my book."

"Really?" asks Dour Mike, perking up a little.

"Really," says Nunya.

I may or may not have had to wipe a tear away from my eye, but it was just allergies, I swear.

27

"First things first, we need to figure out how Israel was communicating with us. Without that bit of knowledge, we don't have a plan," says Knob.

"Well, we can head back to the facility we were held captive in, and maybe reverse engineer the process," says Nunya.

"I guess. I mean, we did burn some fuel getting into orbit, but the President should be paying our fuel bill as well, " says Knob.

"Wow, for someone who spends a ton of money on stupid things just to copy me, you sure are tight with your money," I say.

"Well, it isn't cheap to be like you. I mean, I am so not copying you, asshole," says Knob. I can tell he's both embarrassed and angry at his slip-up.

"Hey, he FINALLY admitted to it! Holy shit! We've had a breakthrough. Maybe with another four hundred years of therapy you'll find your own identity," I say.

"Fuck off," says Knob. He gets up and stomps off toward the front of the ship.

Whip turns to me.

"Look, Dick, I know that Knob's an asshole for trying to usurp you. It's creepy, and unnecessary, and it's Knob's worst trait, but he still idolizes you. He only wants to be like you because he worships you and thinks you're someone worth being like. You seem to have your shit together, and obviously he doesn't have his shit together. The only way he'll get past this is if you stop bullying him. If he sees you're a decent guy, he'll try to emulate that and try to be a decent guy himself. If he sees you only acting like an asshole all the time, he'll only ever be an asshole. I'm not asking you to change who you are, or wait, maybe I am. But I know Nunya wouldn't be your friend if you weren't at least somewhat of a human being on occasion. Show that side of you. Be a better person. You might actually inspire him to be better, too."

Wow, I didn't see that coming. It's hard to hear that maybe I'm the bad guy in this situation. Maybe Knob isn't as bad as I've been making him out to be, and maybe I'm worse than I actually thought I was. And Whip's right, there have been times where I was decent to Nunya, and those have been my proudest moments. Maybe I should give Knob a chance.

"Okay. It's a hard pill to swallow, but there might be some truth to what you're saying. Going forward, I'll try not to give him shit. I'll try my hardest, but I can't guarantee I'll be perfect, or always remember. But I'll try," I say.

"That's all that anyone should ever expect of you, including yourself," says Whip.

I nod at him. I look over at Nunya as she quickly wipes away a tear, hoping I don't see it. Standing up, I make my way to the bridge. I find Knob standing with his back to me at the ship's controls, plotting a course back to St. Marley.

"Knob?" I say, quietly.

"Fuck off, Dick."

"Look... I wanted to apologize."

He doesn't respond.

"I know I've been treating you like shit this whole time, and maybe some of it you deserved. You did some not great things, Knob, but you're still a person. You still have feelings, and I shouldn't have shit on them like I did. I'm gonna try and do better going forward. I'm gonna apologize in advance if I'm still sometimes mean to you. I am trying not to be. I started to realize I was at least a little bit wrong about you when you gave up The Swiss Army Knife to save me. I should have thanked you for that. It was selfless, and it shows that you do have good in you. So, thank you for saving my life, Knob."

The silence is quite uncomfortable for a while.

"Anything else?" asks Knob, after a long moment.

"No, that's it," I say softly.

"We should reach St. Marley shortly," he says, his back still to me.

"Okay."

I make my way back to the conference room.

28

It doesn't take super long to re-enter St. Marley's atmosphere. I'm just glad we didn't fly off for parts unknown before having to make a U-turn in space and come back. Honestly, I don't know where we would have been flying off to, because we certainly didn't have a plan at that point.

Knob parks the ship right next to the facility where we were being held captive. I notice that once we touch down, he doesn't return to the conference room. After waiting a long moment, Whip says "I guess he won't be joining us. Let's go see how Israel did it."

One of the hatches along the side of the ship opens, and I follow behind Whip, who follows behind Nunya.

"Be ready for anything," says Nunya. "There could still be traps we didn't notice before."

We walk very quietly, or at least Nunya and Whip do. I decide to float over the floor a few inches, just to make sure I don't activate any pressure panels or trip wires. We follow the Exit signs back to the hole in the wall that I made, and step into the room I was being held captive in. As soon as all three of us are inside, we notice a piece of paper taped down to the table I'd been lying on. None of us had noticed it before, but it was obvious that it was placed here well before we were.

I read it out loud: "My Dearest Nunya, I of course anticipated your need for a way to transmit information from Alphatraz back to your team while doing reconnaissance work, so I've left you with a communication device and receiver that will allow you to do that. It's very technical, but in a nutshell, I've developed a way of communicating with tachyons that is undetectable by current technology. It also passes right through shields, just as light does. The devices are taped to the underside of this table. And I wouldn't suggest scanning the transmitter too closely, because you might accidentally trigger a black hole. You're questioning whether I would sneak a listening device and tracker into the device? Of course I have. I knew you'd get rid of the ones my associates planted in your spaceship. This is my guarantee that you won't try anything without me knowing about it. Yours truly, Montgomery."

Nunya, thoroughly furious that Israel anticipated her plan, walks up to the only solid wall in the room and punches it several times, blowing holes in it until it looks like a block of Swiss cheese. I don't try to stop her, because who would? You know when you tell someone to 'calm down' it only makes them more pissed? Yeah, doing that to Nunya would likely be a death sentence for me. I just hope that letting out some aggression may be good for her. I'm sure this whole process is incredibly difficult to deal with.

I reach down underneath the table and pull out the two devices. They're both surprisingly small. One of them looks a bit like a dildo, the other like a small parabolic dish that kind of resembles a va-jay-jay. It's obvious that Israel is not only a perv, but wanted to make it clear which is the transmitter and which is the receiver. The worst thing about it though is it looks like the receiver must be plugged into a computer receptacle, like what Dour Mike's dick would interface with. That'll give Israel access to the Knob's ship's computer.

I turn and notice Dour Mike in the corner, who'd apparently decided to follow us into the complex. He's staring intently at the device that looks like lady bits.

"Can... can I fuck that?" asks Dour Mike.

"Um, sorry buddy, but no. It's a receiver for the transmissions you'll be sending from Alphatraz. Without it, we won't be able to rescue Tiffany," I explain.

"Please," says Dour Mike. "I haven't ever seen anything quite so beautiful before. Even my toaster oven isn't as perfect."

"I tell you what, if we all survive this mission, I'll let you do whatever the fuck you want with it. I'll even officiate the wedding. You just gotta promise to not fuck it in the meantime."

"I... I guess," says Dour Mike, sounding dejected.

"If it helps, I'll keep a hold of it, out of sight, just to keep you from being tempted," I say.

I start to slip both devices into my Bag of Ultimate Wonders, but Whip grabs my hand before I can.

"Dick, it said in the note that you shouldn't scan the devices. Are you sure that something that could create a black hole should go into a magical pouch when we don't know how they might interact?"

"Oh, shit, good point. You may have just saved the galaxy, Whip. Thank you," I say.

"Don't mention it."

I look over at Dour Mike and he's giving me the saddest look I've ever seen. Slowly, Dour Mike wheels himself back to the ship. Nunya has calmed down and gives me an inquisitive glance.

"Hey, he's just starting to become more human-like. Of course he's gonna have moments like this. All we have to do is keep him away from the receiver and we'll be fine," I say.

"Well, I guess we have everything we need then. Let's get going," says Whip.

Nunya dusts the fragments of wall off herself as we make our way back to the ship.

29

When we arrive at the ship, Knob is standing just inside, waiting for us. Dour Mike isn't anywhere to be seen.

"Hey, Knob, did Dour Mike come back to the ship?" I ask.

"Yeah, he doesn't seem to be doing very well. He went to the back, supposedly to fix his toaster oven," says Knob. "Did you guys find what you were looking for?"

"We did," says Nunya. "The asshole Israel actually left us two devices, a transmitter and a receiver, that we can use to communicate with."

"And the signal can't be jammed?" asks Knob, as we walk inside the ship.

"Not as far as we know. He was using it to communicate with us, so the technology must work. One thing we should mention is you can't scan the devices. Apparently, they use technology that if scanned could cause a black hole," says Nunya.

"Wait, that can't be true, can it?" asks Knob.

"We don't know, but why risk it?" says Nunya. "Israel also added listening and tracking capabilities to the devices, so be careful what you say if you don't want it to be made public."

"The other suck thing about the devices is that the receiver looks like it needs to be hooked up to a computer port," I say.

"Oh, hell no, no way am I plugging in a device designed by an evil super-villain into my ship," says Knob.

"Well, we wouldn't have to do it now anyway. Nunya, is there any workaround that would let us use the device but not have to plug it into the ship?" I ask.

Nunya gives it some thought.

"Maybe if I hook it up to a phantom power supply. The only thing is, we don't know exactly how it'll display whatever information is being sent to it. Unless it has a built-in holographic projector, it may rely on whatever computer it's attached to for showing what's transmitted," says Nunya.

"Wait, isn't phantom power just additional DC voltage necessary for some types of microphones to operate correctly?" asks Knob.

"Not sure why you'd know that, but yes. I guess it really isn't phantom power, it's just something I call it when you power a device without it actually interfacing with other technology," says Nunya.

"Sorry, I just want to make sure we're 100% science accurate when we communicate," says Knob.

"Uh, sure. You do realize that magic exists, and we don't know how it really works, right? Science hasn't been able to determine how it does what it does. My armor, robe and wand are completely unexplainable as to how they operate, and you're worried about condenser microphone power supplies?" says Nunya.

"I guess when you put it that way it does sound a little pedantic."

"How about a lot."

In my efforts to be less mean, I decide to not open my mouth and insult Knob. Nunya looks over at me, and she can see my head shaking as I'm doing my best to literally keep my mouth shut. After a few seconds of vibrating, I'm able to relax and breathe again. Nunya turns to me and pats me on the shoulder.

"Good job, big man," she says.

I just nod.

"So, can you hook it up to some other computer?" asks Whip.

"I could, the only thing is, it may not work unless it thinks it's connected to Knob's computer," says Nunya. "Maybe if we had a way to copy everything on Knob's system onto another computer, then interface with that, it might work."

"But isn't Israel going to know we're doing that, since he's listening to us right now?" I ask.

"I don't believe these devices are being powered yet. I don't think they have a way of working until they're plugged into a computer, so it should be okay. I will say, it'll look a little suspicious if we don't get on setting up this alternate computer quickly," says Nunya. "Oh shit, I just realized something. It's a lot more complicated than I first realized. Each computer has its own unique identifier code that can't be replicated. Since Israel already had people onboard, I'd be surprised if he didn't have someone connect to it and read the identifier code. He'll know if we plug it into a device other than Knob's actual computer."

"Well, what if we buy a duplicate ship computer, upload all of the current information into it, and replace the existing ship computer with the new one. We keep the old one powered up and receiving the same data that the new one is, but make sure it's communicating one-way, so it can't be hacked," suggests Whip.

"Yeah, you're absolutely right, that's what we should do," says Nunya. "Now we just need to go buy some spaceship parts. And I know exactly where we can do that."

"You're not suggesting what I think you're suggesting?" I say.

"I am. It's time you all met my parents," says Nunya.

30

It'll be cool to see Nunya's parents again. They get under her skin so much; it's great. And her mom is super-hot. But I've sworn not to go anywhere near her sexually, because Nunya forced me to. I'd like to think at this point I wouldn't sleep with a friend's mom, but sometimes things just happen. She was coming onto me, I wasn't coming on to her, the last time we met. I only have so much super-strength to go around, and I usually try to use that on bad guys.

"So, where exactly do your parents live, and why are we visiting with them?" asks Knob.

"They live in the Lauratine Abyss, and they own a spaceship dealership there," says Nunya.

"Isn't the Lauratine Abyss a shithole, a place no one actually intends to go to but just ends up there, like Denny's?" asks Knob.

"Yeah, for the most part, but they also secretly sell exotic and expensive spaceships. They use the appearance of a used ship lot to mask their very profitable real business. Don't get me wrong, they still make tons of money on the used ones, but not as much as selling the exotics," says Nunya.

"Alright. I'll go punch the coordinates into the computer. Do they have the same last name as you?" asks Knob.

"Yeah. I'm surprised you don't know about my folks already, since you watched us unaware for so long," says Nunya.

"I do have to sleep, and you aren't the only thing I spent time on back then. I still have other cases that I work on. So maybe I missed an episode or two. It's not like you're in syndication," says Knob.

"That's an awfully glib take from a voyeuristic predator," says Nunya.

"I'm not a predator, it was for a job, so just drop it," says Knob. Everything goes quiet for a moment.

"Wait, what did you just say?" asks Nunya, very slowly.

"Nothing," says Knob, avoiding her eyes.

"Did you just say you were hired to spy on us?" asks Nunya. Knob still won't respond.

Faster than I've ever seen her move, Nunya closes the distance between them, grabs Knob by the throat and slams him up against the nearest wall, caving it in a bit.

143

"So help me, Knob, you're going to tell me exactly who hired you, why they hired you, and if you're very, very lucky, I won't crush your larynx and kill you," says Nunya, through clenched teeth.

Knob still doesn't respond. Nunya tightens her grip, and Knob's face starts turning purple.

"It was… Israel," says Knob.

Nunya throws Knob across the room, behind her. His limp body slams against the wall, falling to the floor in a crumpled pile.

"Knob, you're going to tell me everything you know. I don't care how unimportant the detail may seem; you're going to word vomit until you cough up the truth."

Nunya finally turns around to face him. It takes Knob a moment to slowly upright himself against the wall. When he does finally speak, it comes out as a raspy whisper. I think Nunya actually damaged his vocal cords.

"I didn't know at the time it was Israel. He used a go-between. It wasn't until I stopped recording you that I found out who was behind it. But it seemed like any other job a private detective gets hired for. Maybe a company was suspicious an employee was stealing from them, or maybe a desperate wife was worried her husband was cheating on her. I just watched you and relayed whatever information seemed important. Surveillance is a huge part of the job, and what I was doing wasn't personal."

"Israel knows our weaknesses thanks to you," says Nunya.

"You're right. He does. And I'm sorry," says Knob.

"Sorry? Sorry is bullshit. You knew what outing a superheroes' weaknesses meant. You knew it could get us killed."

"I did."

"So then why the fuck did you do that? Why did you do that to us?"

"Because I didn't really know you. Because I needed the money. It really is expensive trying to keep up appearances, and unless you're super famous and lucky, being a detective doesn't pay dick. If I could take it back, I would. But I hope that you don't judge me too harshly, because you made the same mistake trusting the same man," says Knob.

In the back of my mind, I feel like Nunya's about to punch a hole through Knob, and through the hull of the ship. Instead, she gets really quiet and her body language changes.

"You're right, Knob, I did. I gave the worst person in the galaxy immortality, and I got my friends all killed in the process. By comparison, maybe what you did wasn't so bad. But that doesn't mean you won't have to make amends for it."

"I'm trying. I'm desperately trying. That's why I've been helping you on this mission. I want to unfuck what I fucked up. I hope you can see that."

"How do we know you aren't still working for Israel?" asks Nunya.

"How do we know that you aren't still working for Israel?" replies Knob.

"Why would I work so hard to put him in prison just to continue helping him out? That has to be the dumbest question anyone has ever asked," says Nunya.

"Maybe you didn't actually put him in prison, maybe it was someone else. How do I know that I can trust you, either?"

This is where I step in. "Knob, I can tell when people are lying, and I've never known Nunya to lie. There's no way she could have gone this long without slipping up. I trust her with my life, with the lives of everyone in the galaxy. She isn't working for Israel anymore. But you just deflected the question. So, I'm gonna ask you, and consider your words carefully, are you still working for Israel?"

"No. I'm not working for Israel."

I look him up and down, watch his beating heart through his ribcage with my super-vision, and from everything I can gather he's telling the truth.

"Nunya, he doesn't seem to be lying. He isn't working for Israel anymore," I say.

"We still don't know if we can trust him," says Nunya.

"That's true. But he does seem to genuinely want to help. He seems to want to get revenge on Israel," I say.

"Did you know he was behind the kidnapping?" asks Nunya.

"No, I genuinely didn't know until we all found out," says Knob.

"He seems to still be telling the truth," I say.

"And you want to do everything in your power to take down Israel?" asks Nunya.

"Yes, I want to take him down. Or prevent him from escaping, or whatever," says Knob.

"Truth," I say. "Either he's the galaxy's greatest liar, or he's being 100% with us."

"Fine, we keep working together. But if there's anything you're holding back and you don't tell us now, you won't live to see the sunrise. Is there anything else you've hidden from us or lied to us about?" asks Nunya.

It takes Knob a moment to respond.

145

"Yeah, Whip was telling the truth, I was masturbating while watching you guys on video. I'm sorry."

Nunya looks pissed but holds it in. "Anything else?"

"No, that's all I can think of."

Nunya looks over at me. I nod to let her know he still seems to be telling the truth.

"Well, at least we know you're being fully honest now. Disgusting, but honest," says Nunya.

"Th-thank you for giving me a chance, and for not killing me. I'll go put the coordinates into the computer now," says Knob, slowly rising to his feet.

We watch as Knob creeps back toward the front of the ship, holding onto his throat.

31

"God, I feel like apologizing to both of you for Knob, even though it wasn't my fault. I just feel horrible that he gave your biggest enemy a way to control you," says Whip.

"He's Nunya's biggest enemy, not mine," I say.

"Oh, then who is yours?" asks Whip.

"Probably myself."

Both Nunya and Whip nod knowingly.

"In all seriousness," I start, "my biggest arch-nemesis is probably either Captain Kissass, or Tatiana Titsling. He's super annoying, and she punches so hard you'll feel it for days. Admittedly, I have a crush on Tatiana, but she seems bent on crushing my balls, which I'm not into, sadly."

"Why do all of your enemies have to have stupid porno names?" asks Nunya.

"You of all people shouldn't judge people's names," I say.

"Hey, don't be an asshole. I'm still amped up from Knob's admission, and I'll take just about any excuse to punch someone, even you," says Nunya. "And if you push me hard enough, I'll shove my wand up your ass and Bibbidi-Bobbidi-Boo you to death."

I just laugh because it's fucking funny. Even Whip chuckles a little.

We make our way to the conference room, sit down, and all start playing with our PSDs. I don't know what the other two are doing, but I'm playing the newest Dick Blowhard video game. It's pretty great, but sometimes the fights get repetitive.

Time slips by and I start to realize we should have arrived quite a while ago. I get up from my seat, Whip and Nunya still happily entranced with their devices, and walk down the main hallway to the bridge. I find Knob there, sitting down, still holding his throat. Looking through the large windshield I see Nunya's parent's used ship business just outside. It seems like we must have landed a while ago.

"Hey, Knob, why didn't you let us know we'd arrived?" I ask.

It takes him a moment to respond.

"I couldn't face Nunya. Thought it'd be better if I didn't engage with her right now."

"Yeah, you're probably right," I say.

"I also didn't expect her to be as powerful as she is. It's the first time since I got my superpowers that I've felt weak."

"Well, you shouldn't be afraid of a strong black woman making you feel weak. You should support her, because she's a good person, trying to do what's right. If you stop being an asshole, she won't have a problem with you."

Knob thinks for a minute. "I'm gonna stay here and watch the ship."

"Yeah, I think that's a good idea," I say.

Walking back to the conference room, I just mutter "we're here," not letting them know we'd landed some time ago. Both Nunya and Whip put their PSDs in their pockets, and I follow them outside into the gravel parking lot.

I notice Whip looking around, taking in all the old, rusty spaceships parked throughout the lot. Nunya makes a beeline for the office. When we arrive, things seem just like they were the last time we visited.

"Honey, two visits in one month?" says her mom, excitedly.

"Nunya!" says her dad.

Nunya makes her way past their desks and gives each of them a hug.

"Oh, and you brought back your handsome friend," says Nunya's mom, staring at me and licking her lips. She turns. "Who's this?"

"Hi, I'm Whip! Whip Noodbottom," says Whip, shaking each of their hands.

"Nice to meet you, Whip. Would you care for anything? We have donuts," says Nunya's dad.

"Um, sure. Do you have chocolate with sprinkles?" asks Whip.

"We sure do," says Nunya's dad, holding out a large pink box.

Whip reaches in, pulls out a slightly shiny chocolate donut, and starts nibbling away. Both Nunya and I grab donuts as well; she takes a maple bar while I swipe an eclair.

"So, what brings you back to our humble establishment?" asks Nunya's dad.

"We need a replacement computer for a Regulus Everlight," says Nunya.

"Do you know which model?" asks her mom.

"Yeah, it's the E347," says Nunya.

I look over at Nunya and give her a 'WTF' look.

"Hey, I grew up with it. You pick up stuff," says Nunya.

Nunya's mom sits down at her desk and starts tapping away at a PSD.

"Do you need just the computer itself, or the wiring harness as well?"

"Harness too. We're cloning an existing system and running them simultaneously, same inputs and outputs, but only one will actually control anything. We'll also need one-way patch cables to wire up everything," says Nunya.

After a few more seconds, Nunya's mom looks up. "Huh, miraculously, we have all of that here. You'll have to pull the computer and harness out yourself from the yard, but I can go get you the wires you'll need. Do you already have a way of copying the system over?"

"Yeah, I've got that covered," says Nunya.

"Great. Well, the ship you're after is parked in spot A24."

"Thanks. Can I borrow your toolkit to tear it out?"

"Sure, go for it."

Nunya walks over to one of the unoccupied desks, pushes something under the lip, and it slowly flips over, revealing a large fabric tool bag with a long shoulder strap. She slings it over her shoulder and makes her way to the door. She notices Whip and I staring at her.

"Are you two coming?" she asks.

"Oh, uh, yeah. Let's do the thing," I say.

32

Whip and I follow right behind Nunya and make our way to the spaceship parked in spot A24. The ship looks nearly identical to Knob's, only it's a lighter shade of gray, and doesn't have as many fancy attachments to it. When we step inside, it looks just like any other ship, instead of the insane, multi-colored clown ship that Knob owns. Too bad we can't use this ship instead.

Once we reach the bridge, Nunya turns to us. "Okay, guys, I'll need your help. The wiring harness snakes through the entire ship. There are panels that allow you to access it in case it needs to be changed out, but it takes time to unscrew all the plates. I'll give you each a screwdriver, and you can go to town on any panels you see that match the diamond shaped screwdriver head. Those will all be wiring panels."

"Would it be faster if I just used my x-ray vision and tore the panels away?" I ask.

"Yes, it would be faster, but it would also damage some of my parent's property, and they'd be losing out on a potential sale."

"Don't they have insurance?" I ask.

"They do, but then they'd have to provide security footage for the claim, and it would clearly show her daughter and her friends taking the wiring with permission. So, they'd be denied then charged with attempted fraud. I'd rather my parents don't go to prison."

"Yeah, I guess that makes sense. Still, is there any way we can speed up this process?"

"Sure, if you have superspeed you can do it faster if you want. Just don't damage anything in the process," says Nunya.

"I can't actually do that," I admit.

"I can," says Whip. "In fact, I think my fingertips can form pretty much any shape I want, including a diamond tip screwdriver. I'll have everything unscrewed in about ten minutes."

"That would be awesome and appreciated, Whip," says Nunya.

Whip changes the shape of his fingers, and starts flitting around the room, undoing panels. After a brief moment, he leaves the room to remove more panels throughout the ship.

"Since I can't compete with that, is there something else I could be doing in the meantime?" I ask.

"Sure, you can help me remove the main computer."

150

"Main computer? That implies there are two," I say.

"Yeah, there's always two: one fore, and one aft. That way, if one half of the ship gets damaged, the other half will be able to run whatever systems are still working, including life support. It's always a smart idea to have system redundancies on something as complex as a spaceship, especially when people's lives could depend on it. Anyway, could you take this plate and set it behind you?"

Nunya hands me a metal plate that I didn't realize she'd already unscrewed while we were talking. I place it carefully on the floor behind me. She switches to a ratchet and starts unbolting the computer from the ship. I watch in awe as her hands deftly work like she's been doing this most of her life, which she probably has. I doubt many surgeons move with the familiarity and grace that she does. A few seconds later, she's holding the computer in her hands.

It's a literal black box. Except for the wire harness attached to it, there's nothing interesting about it at all. Just a cube, about the size of my rather large fist. She dusts it off, sets it down on the floor, then looks up at me.

"We still need to get the aft computer uncoupled from the ship."

"Lead on, little leader," I say.

"Don't ever call me that again," says Nunya.

I follow her through the ship, past where Whip is still working, to the very back. She opens up another panel, revealing the same black cube from the front of the ship.

"We're gonna have to wait for Whip to finish unscrewing all the panels. Then I'll have you two wind the wiring so we can carry it more easily. I have zip ties we can use to keep it all wound. I'll also have you detach the harness at the halfway point and detach the connections into the ship before you start winding, so we can carry out the two computers separately."

"Sure, sounds good," I say. "How do I detach the cables?"

"They just twist apart. Should be straightforward," says Nunya.

"I'll go do that now."

I walk through the ship, and on both sides of the ship are open panels that expose the wiring connections. I easily twist them apart, disconnecting both sets of wires from each other, then I disconnect the smaller wires that are attaching the harnesses to the ship. I head back to Nunya. It only takes a couple of minutes for Whip to make his way to where we're waiting.

"I'm done!" he says.

151

"Thanks, Whip," says Nunya. "Can you please help Dick wind up the wiring so we can carry it out of here?"

"My pleasure."

We both start coiling the wiring, me from the back of the ship, him from the front. I'm amazed just how much faster Whip is winding than me. He gets his section of cable done before I'm even halfway through mine, so he comes back and helps me out to speed up the process. Once we get everything coiled up and strapped down, I sling both computers and their connected wires over my shoulders and follow Nunya and Whip out of the ship.

33

I load the cables and computers into Knob's ship, leaving them just inside one of the main bay doors, while Whip and Nunya make their way back to her parent's office. Knob doesn't come to greet me, so I figure he must still be avoiding Nunya.

Heading back to the office, I notice a very small shadow dart underneath one of the nearby rust buckets. Curious, I use my super-vision to look through the hull of the ship and see not one, but ten tiny furry creatures hiding underneath. It looks like they're trying to chew their way through the underside of the ship.

"Hey, Nunya and Whip, we may have a serious problem. Can you both come out here, pronto?" I yell.

Nunya and Whip come running out of the office. Just as they appear, from out of nowhere a swarm of a few hundred adorable chipmunk looking things cover my entire body, and I can feel them start to chew on me. It hurts like hell as they gnaw and pierce my skin. It's like getting dozens of papercuts all at the same time. Panicking, I scream then fly into the air. Tearing a couple of the little buggers away from my face, what I see makes my skin run cold and the hairs on the back of my neck stand up. Oh shit, it's Quokkans!

Still feeling like I'm being chewed apart, I try crushing the little fuckers with my hands. Pop-pop-pop, squishing each one feels like popping bubble wrap. It's disgusting and I hate it, but it's me or them. I keep crushing the evil rodents, and they keep nibbling at my skin. This is why it sucks to be only mostly resistant to damage.

Once I have my head fully uncovered, I start to work on the Quokkans chewing at the important bits. My arteries, my love rod; you know, the things that I can't live without. Finally, I've freed myself from enough of them that I'm able to look down. To my horror, I see Whip's robot body being torn apart, and he screams from the pain of it, even though the pain is virtual. After a few seconds, the screaming stops, and I guess that his body has somehow literally turned off the pain to protect his mind.

Nunya seems to be doing okay for herself in the fight, as her armor protects most of her skin, but there are a few exposed sections the Quokkans can still get to. Since Nunya isn't in as bad of shape as Whip, I swoop down to try to get the Quokkans off of him. No dice, because as quickly as I remove them, more swarm around him.

I need to do something quickly, so I pick up what's left of Whip in my arms and fly into the air as fast as I possibly can. His eyes are rolled back in his head, but he still seems to be alive, thankfully, as much as anyone who is ninety percent android can be.

As soon as I reach a reasonable altitude, I make my way back toward the surface of the planet. I start to heat up, the friction causing the Quokkans to burn off of me and thankfully burn off of Whip as well. I remove the Quokkans from his head, which is still mostly human, and cover it with my shirt, protecting it from the intense heat. After a few seconds, the Quokkans that had been attacking us have now burnt to a crisp.

I slow us down then hover about fifty feet off the ground. Since Whip and I are no longer part of the fight, the remaining Quokkans start swarming Nunya. I can see her getting overwhelmed by the sheer volume of Quokkans climbing on top of her.

Carefully, I set what's left of Whip down on the roof of Nunya's parent's business then fly down and scoop up Nunya. We shoot up into the sky like a rocket, some of the Quokkans detach from the friction and fall to their adorable deaths. Unfortunately, a lot of the Quokkans are still hanging on, their teeth dug deep into our skin. I reach about the same altitude I did before and aim us straight at the planet.

Like before, the friction generated from reentry causes the Quokkans to combust. We light up like a falling star, and this time, instead of slowing our descent, I maintain the same speed, until we impact the ground, right where the Quokkans had been swarming.

The nearby ships are damaged by the impact, and the otherwise bulletproof glass that was protecting Nunya's parent's office is shattered. I pick up Nunya, who appears unconscious, and fly her out of the deep hole I just created, then carefully place her next to Whip on top of the office roof.

I survey the nearby area for any more Quokkans using my super-vision, crushing the few remaining bastards I can find. It's starting to become weirdly satisfying. Squish. Squish. Squish. When I'm finally certain there are no more Quokkans nearby, I make my way back up to the roof.

"Are you both okay?" I ask.

Nunya nods her head slowly. "I am. Are you okay?"

"I'm feeling kind of tired, actually. I think I'm gonna lay down for a moment," I say as I pass out from blood loss.

34

I wake up about an hour later, cocooned in some very wide red ribbon. I feel like a poorly wrapped Christmas gift, and I'm meant for someone on the naughty list. As I open my eyes, I feel a hand placed on top of my upper thigh area.

"Oh, good, you're awake," says a sexy, sultry voice.

I realize it's Nunya's mom, and I notice that she's resting her hand right on top of my half-inflated sex-sausage. It twitches uncontrollably and enthusiastically under her touch. I gasp for air as she runs her hand up and down the length of it. But then I do something that doesn't make sense, even to me: I grab her hand. Not hard, but firmly, and remove it from my schlong.

"Mrs. Nunya's mom, I really appreciate you looking after me, but I think I'll be okay now," I say.

"Nonsense. We really must get these shorts off of you. They're a bit tattered now," she says, purring.

"Seriously, that's very sweet of you, but I think I can manage. I'm feeling a fair bit better than I did when I passed out."

I glance around the room and realize that I've been moved to a private office in the hidden VIP section of Nunya's parent's used ship lot. I'm impressed they were able to move me, until I notice a hoist robot shut down in the corner. My guess is they use it for moving heavy ship parts.

"Are Nunya and Whip okay, and your husband for that matter?" I ask, putting extra emphasis on 'your husband'.

"My husband and daughter are both fine, but Whip was in bad shape. All three of them took off in the ship you'd arrived in, and Nunya mentioned something about a gadgeteer named Nord," says Nunya's mom.

Despite being firm about my convictions, Nunya's mom flashes a broad grin and opens her blouse, revealing one of the most amazing racks I've ever seen. Goddamn, Nunya's mom is stacked just like her daughter. I sit up quickly and try to shove my growing boner down between my legs where she can't get to it.

"Look, Dick, there are no security cameras in this room. We have the whole place to ourselves, and no one will be back for several hours. Think of how much damage we could do to each other in that time. And no one will ever know."

"I'll know. And I think so will Nunya. And even if she didn't, I value her friendship enough to not betray her like that. The only thing she's ever really asked me to do was to not have sex with you. So, I'm sorry, but I just can't. It's really, really tempting, but I'm not gonna do that to her," I say.

"So, you're really turning me down? There's no way I can convince you?"

I sigh, take a deep breath and say, "Nope. No way to convince me."

Nunya's mom frowns at me, with that same disapproving look I get from Nunya. "Fine. That's fine." I can tell that it's not fine. "Just don't think this offer will ever be on the table again."

"If it was, I'd just have to shoot it down again. I'm sorry."

Nunya's mom doesn't want to look at me anymore. After a brief pause, she turns around and closes the door behind her.

I look at the ribbon that I'm now pulling off myself and realize it must be used to gift wrap ships when they're given as gifts. Everybody loves a giant bow on their ride. I would have assumed they'd have better medical equipment, running a business this deep in the ass-end of space, but I'm guessing it's hard to find gauze large enough to wrap around me. I'm just glad they did something to help stop the bleeding until my super-healing could take over.

Leaving the small office behind, I find an emergency staircase and make my way back up to the main office area. I can hear the floor lifting upward as Nunya's mom is obviously taking the secret elevator that raises the entire main office with it. I reach the top of the stairs before it's finished, and the emergency exit door won't open until it's in place, so I have to wait a moment.

Once the whirring stops, I open the door and step back into the office. Nunya's mom is there, and she tries her best to ignore my presence, working on paperwork instead. I decide to go outside and take some time to scour the area, making sure there aren't any more Quokkans hanging about. Eventually, I'm certain that there aren't any imminent threats, so I start to fill in the crater that I made when I smashed into the ground. It also works as a convenient grave for the furry monsters I'd demolished with the impact. About thirty minutes of shoveling later and I have everything close to how it was before.

As I'm standing there, a piece of paper picked up by the gentle breeze floats over to me. I bend down and pick it up. What I read surprises and doesn't surprise me at the same time.

"Dearest Nunya,

So that you know I've anticipated your every move, I left you a present of a few hundred Quokkans to keep you and your parents entertained. I knew you'd try to clone your ship's computer system

156

as it's what I would have done if I were in your shoes, and I knew where you'd go to seek help. You need to start playing by my rules or else there'll be consequences. I've been exceedingly generous by keeping your family and friends alive thus far, but if you push things, I may change my mind.

Yours Truly,

M."

God, this guy is a fucker! My first instinct is to crumple the paper and throw it away, but instead I fold it neatly and slide it into one of my pockets. I figure it's best if I show Nunya. It'll really piss her off, but the more information we have on our enemy, the better.

I walk back into the office and Nunya's mom is still doing her best to ignore me.

"I wanted to apologize for the damage to your ships and windows. I'll be happy to pay to fix them," I say.

"No need, we're insured against Quokkan attacks, believe it or not. We have it on film that we did our best to defend against them, and had an exterminator deal with them, which is you."

"Ah, okay," I say.

I don't know what else to do, so I sit down, pull out my Personal Space Device and go back to playing my Dick Blowhard video game.

35

The rest of the gang don't come back for the better part of the day. In the meantime, I end up eating junk food from one of the vending machines and nearly go broke doing so. I feel like I must have paid off for the damage to the ships and windows and then some. I also hang out in the break room, away from Nunya's mom, who I can tell is still pissed at me. If global warming was still a thing, I'm sure her icy stare would fix it.

It's so boring waiting for them that I actually end up reading the used spaceship pamphlets in the office. The Dick Blowhard video game was great, but I've already beaten it a few dozen times, so it doesn't hold my interest the same way it used to. Even I get tired of my awesome self, occasionally.

Eventually, I hear the sound of a spaceship landing just outside. I make my way out of the office and watch as one of the bay doors on the side of the ship opens. Out walks Nunya, her dad, Whip, and Dour Mike. Actually, Dour Mike wheels out.

Whip looks good as new, thankfully. Even his face is fully healed, which I was concerned with, since it had gotten pretty mangled by the Quokkans. I walk over and go to give Nunya a big hug, and she pulls back, eyeing me. I'm confused, so I turn to Whip and give him a hug.

"I'm really glad you're okay, Whip," I say.

"Me too. Thanks for saving me from the Quokkans," he says.

I turn to shake Nunya's dad's hand, and he hugs me too. "Thanks for saving my daughter," he says.

"Yeah, no worries, she does it all the time for me. And she's my best friend," I say.

Nunya's forehead wrinkles, and she still seems put off by me. Not sure why.

The five of us make our way back to the office. Nunya's mom is still in a bad mood, even though her family is back safely. She gets up and gives both her husband and daughter brief hugs, but they aren't filled with any sincerity.

Nunya looks at her mom then looks at me. Back and forth. After a few seconds, she scrunches up her face then replaces it with a huge smile. She leaps into my arms, giving me the biggest hug anyone's ever given me.

"Dick, we need to talk," she says.

"Yeah, okay. We can do that," I say, clearly not getting why she's suddenly so happy. I follow her back outside, far away from earshot of the others.

"Dick, you didn't fuck my mom!" she says.

"No, I didn't," I admit.

"Thank you! Seriously, this whole time I figured you'd try to take advantage of my mother, use your charm on her, and make her cheat on my dad. But I can tell that you didn't! She seems so unhappy right now, it's wonderful!"

"Well, I made you a promise. And your friendship means more than anything to me. So, I didn't want to do the one thing I knew would ruin that."

"I know that's not a very high bar to set, and most people inherently know not to fuck their friend's moms, but I know how big of a slut you are. I know how hard it was for you to not make any moves on her," she says.

I decide not to mention that her mom was the aggressor. It wouldn't help for Nunya to know and would cause unnecessary friction for her family. Maybe I'm getting better at this being-a-friend thing.

"Nunya, there is something though that you need to see," I say.

"Okay, what is it?"

I hand her the note. The happiness drains from her face. Maybe now isn't the right time to share the letter from her arch-nemesis, but she needed to know.

"God-fucking-dammit," says Nunya.

"Yeah, God-fucking dammit," I say, putting my hand on her shoulder.

"Dick, do you think we really have any chance of pulling this off?"

"Yeah, I'm pretty sure we can break him out. I'm not sure if once he's out we can put the genie back in the bottle, though. He seems to know exactly what we're going to do before we do it."

"I gotta admit, I was at least a little lucky to send him to prison the first time. It was only because he didn't really know me, or know that I would seek revenge, that kept me in his blind spot. Now that he knows practically everything about me, and has had years to study me, there doesn't seem to be a way to escape his radar. Maybe he's already won, and we don't even know it yet."

"Maybe, but we should still try to beat him if we can. I'm not willing to give up, and neither should you. And you'll think of something. You always do. You're just as smart as he is; maybe smarter. You'll come up with something, Nunya."

"I wish I had the same confidence in myself that you have in me."

159

"Well, you're incredible. And being humble about it is a good thing. Just don't beat yourself up too hard for the mistakes you make. We all make mistakes," I say.

"Like giving a supervillain the key to immortality, and getting my friends killed in the process?" says Nunya.

"Yeah, that one wasn't so great, but you did the best you could to fix your mistake. That's a lot better than most people. If you were given the choice again, you wouldn't make the same mistake."

"No, I wouldn't."

"See? Growth."

"Sure, Dick. Sure."

"So, are we still going to hook up the alternate computer, even though Israel predicted we would?" I ask.

"Yeah, I mean, maybe he'll think since he called us out on it that we wouldn't bother. The important thing is it'll prevent him from being able to control Knob's ship," says Nunya.

"That way we aren't stranded in deep space, waiting to die," I say.

"Exactly. Anyway, let's get started on hooking everything up."

"Sounds good."

We spend the next hour or so replacing Knob's ship's computer with the extra computer. It's a boring process, but once we have everything set up, Nunya plugs the communication device Israel gave us into the original ship computer. It lights up but doesn't seem to be doing anything much more than that. Nunya just shrugs at me. Knob has silently been watching us work. He seems to be unhappy his ship has been altered but doesn't say anything because he's still on Nunya's shit list.

This time though, instead of staying on the ship, Knob follows us back inside her parent's office. When we enter, Nunya's mom perks up.

"Oh, and who, may I ask, are you?" says Nunya's mom, reaching out her hand and shaking Knob's.

"I'm Private Detective Knob Johnson, at your service."

Nunya's mom swoons, a little too exaggeratedly to be sincere. I notice her glancing briefly in my direction, trying to see if I'm hurt by her little display. I'm not. I just sort of chuckle at the absurdity of it. Nunya's mom briefly looks angry then switches back to being sweet to Knob.

"Any friend of Nunya's is a friend of ours," she says.

"He's not my friend," says Nunya. "Most of the time he's my enemy. The jury is still out on whether I'll kill him or not."

"That would be a pity," says Nunya's mom.

Knob smiles back at her, but he seems to be confused about what's going on. He also looks both flattered at the attention, and

think I would know if Whip was a double agent," says

appreciate the compliment about me being a really
, accusing me of being a traitor isn't cool, Dick. Was
ing I did or said that would make you question my
Whip.
ean, not really. It just seemed like you jumped on the
wagon a little quick. I don't know if I could have made
cision as easily as you seemed to. If I were a
spy, and my controller told me to do anything
get the job done, I think I would probably jump on any
come more dangerous and powerful. I guess I just
r motives for the upgrades."
ds his head in understanding. "Dick, I get it. And if after
I have to say you aren't convinced, I'll drop out of the
kes a deep breath. "Ever since I was a little kid, I've
than anything to be a hero. And not just a hero to
ing kittens from trees and pulling people from burning
anted to be a hero to myself. My dad wasn't around
g up, as you know, and he died when I was still a
ways wondered if maybe I'd been a better son when
d, he would have been around more. If I could have
d enough, then maybe he'd want to spend more time

hip understands that I didn't do anything wrong, that
ust doing his job, which kept him away from us for
of time, and that maybe my father had a bit of
him. I do as well, which is why I signed up to fly all
xy, working for a superhero. It's been a cathartic
or me, getting to do good when I can, helping others,
aking my dad proud in the process, wherever he is.
ou could say some of my motivation is selfish. It's me
ehow connect with someone I lost. I hope you can see
de of goodness, and recognize I'm just a person, doing
l loved and appreciated. To feel worthy of love. To
e has meaning."
ne a minute to dry the tears from my eyes.
n incredibly sorry, Whip, for questioning you and your
You've never really given me a reason to doubt you. I
g paranoid. I've been screwed over so many times
hard time trusting anyone, especially people who
life all figured out. Especially good people that I

uncomfortable as well, as if he doesn't know how to handle people's flirtations.

"So, are we all ready to go?" asks Nunya.

"Already?" starts Knob. "We just got introduced. Shouldn't we have a meal together? Isn't that customary?"

"All we have for food here is the vending machine, but at least there's plenty to go around," says Nunya's dad.

"Uh, actually, I emptied it earlier," I say.

"Wait, why did you do that?" he asks.

"I got hungry and bored."

"And you ate all of it?"

"Well, actually, I did leave some Good & Plentys, and some Twizzlers, because they suck," I say.

"Hey, I like Twizzlers!" says Knob.

"Of course you do. Because you like eating plastic shoelaces. Both the flavor and texture are unappetizing. I'd rather eat a soggy sheet of A4 paper than Twizzlers," I say.

It becomes a little bit of an argument, because one other person mentions they like Twizzlers. I'm unwilling to name them, because I like them, and I don't want that kind of stigma associated with this person. I also notice, however, that no one defends Good & Plenty. Makes sense, since there's no defending them.

The argument devolves, and I launch into a tirade about how Smarties are little pieces of chalk, Nunya goes on about how much she hates nougat (even though she likes Snickers), and Whip admits he can't stand Whoppers. I'm in total agreement there. Nunya's mom seems to hate Necco Wafers, which I get, because they are like taking communion while giving yourself diabetes, and Nunya's dad rants about how much Reese's Pieces suck, and it's only because of the movie E.T. that anyone likes them.

"Well, at least they aren't as bad as circus peanuts," says Nunya, finally.

We all nod our heads in agreement. Thank God that is over.

"Either way, there isn't much to eat here, unfortunately," says Nunya's mom.

"We could order take-out," says Nunya's dad.

"PortalDash?" asks Nunya's mom.

"Sure. Or GrubStar," says Nunya's dad.

"Any particular cuisine that people want?" asks Nunya's mom.

Amazingly, we all say in unison "Chinese".

Nunya's folks spend the next few minutes gathering everyone's order, place it, and let us know it'll be delivered in about thirty. Nunya and I work on setting up everything in the breakroom in the meantime.

Dour Mike wheels up to me and tugs on my shirt.

"Hey buddy, what's up?" I ask.

"Since I don't eat food, I think I'll head back to the ship."

"Why don't you stay here with us and hang out. That's more what a big meal is about, spending time with the people you care for," I say.

"You, you care about me?" asks Dour Mike.

"Would I have bought you a sex-toaster if I didn't?"

"No, I suppose you wouldn't. Well, thank you. I also care about you, sir."

I smile at him.

As everyone starts slowly wandering into the break room, I look around and get a strange feeling I've never really felt before. Our group is starting to feel like family to me. I mean, I have my mom and all that, but I've never really felt like part of a big family the way that a lot of people do. I didn't even know it was something I'd wanted until now. Is it an incredibly fucked up family? Absolutely, but what family isn't?

Nunya catches my eye and smiles at me. Time seems to slow down, like I'm in some kind of movie montage, where everything's perfect, right before something really bad happens. A nuclear blast, or a meteor smashing into the planet. Maybe the bad guys come crashing in through the windows. Instead, we hear a buzzing at the office door.

"I'll get it," says Nunya's mom. She scurries out of the breakroom. After a brief moment she returns, her arms filled with so many bagged food containers we can't see her over them. "Help."

Nunya goes over and grabs some bags off the top. She and her mom open the meal cartons and hand them out to everyone. It sort of feels like living in a Hallmark card, only I realize half the people ordered something garlicy, and the ride back in Knob's spaceship is gonna be a stinky one.

We spend the next hour eatin
of things, taking time out from th
few days have been crazy. I gue
little slower, just because we do
we have to break Montgomery Is
Tiffany alive, or he's killed her. T
my mood.

It's been good to have this
we try to do good in the world. I'
pretty much everyone in the gro
Knob and I are both prima donn
alone. Dour Mike wants to stick
Nunya's parents are used space
almost as bad as being a lawyer
seems to be a fairly decent pers
his motivations. I just hope he's
whole thing, or at the very least

The gears start turning in m
much thought to having most of
ones. He doesn't have any clea
us out. For him, it's supposedly
and walk away from, yet he's sti
for someone even more evil, or
I've ever run into.

"Hey, Whip, are you secretl
of the blue.

He laughs. "No, why, are yo
I scan his body, but it's alm
There's no way of telling wheth
have a fluctuating pulse. His he
valves that are controlled by a
steady, unwavering sixty beats
anything and I wouldn't know wl

"Dick, it's not very nice to ju
guys," says Nunya.

"Yeah, I know, but Whip ju
a really, really good person, or h
Montgomery Israel," I say.

"I woul
Knob.

"While
good perso
there some
loyalty?" as

"No. I n
android bar
the same de
brainwashe
necessary t
chance to b
question yo

Whip n
hearing wha
team." He ta
wanted mor
others, resc
buildings, I
much growi
teenager. I
he was arou
just been g
with me.

"Adult
my dad was
long periods
wanderlust
over the gal
experience
and maybe
So, I guess
trying to sor
past my fac
his best to f
feel like my

It takes
"I'm...
motivations.
was just be
that I have
seem to hav

respect. I'm constantly afraid of the other shoe dropping. I hope you can forgive me. Please, forgive me," I say.

"Dick, there's nothing to forgive. I understand why you'd be paranoid. I'd be paranoid too if I were in your shoes. I would question everyone and everything. It's normal when it seems like the whole world is against you, and you have to deal with so much responsibility, especially when it comes to being a detective. You don't know how to trust, because you deal with untrustworthy people on a daily basis. But most people are good people, trying to do their best. The bad ones are thankfully pretty rare. It may not feel like it because of the problems the bad ones cause, but most people are decent human beings."

"Thanks," I mumble.

I have a hard time making eye contact with anyone, still feeling ashamed of myself for questioning Whip's loyalty. I slowly finish the rest of my food without saying anything, while everyone else continues to talk. It's a bit awkward at first, but after a few minutes the conversations return to normal, and I just kind of hide from everyone by focusing on my meal. I finish up, throw away my trash, and make my way outside.

The nearby sun named Celeste is moving lower in the sky, and I can tell it's going to get dark soon. I slowly walk over to Knob's ship and a side door automatically opens for me as I approach.

Feeling exhausted and spent, I stumble my way to a section of the ship with individual sleeping quarters. There's a couple of very small rooms with tiny bunks in them, just meant as a space for sleeping and nothing else, so I wedge myself into one of them. The bed isn't particularly comfortable, and I have to ball up into a fetal position just to fit entirely on it, but I manage. I spend about half an hour hating myself before I'm finally able to fall asleep, but I do eventually fall asleep.

37

I wake up suddenly to the sound of alarms going off. I hit my head on the bunk above me as I sit up, denting the metal frame. Thankfully, it doesn't really hurt. I duck back down, bolt out of the room and down the hallway to the bridge. Everyone else is already there, Knob flying the ship through a crazy pattern of laser fire coming from a swarm of several hundred egg-shaped ships.

"Oh fuck, it's Sloths!" I say, surprised.

"No shit, fuckwad. Can you shut up? I'm trying to fly here," says Knob.

"Can you do a death blossom maneuver?" I ask.

"What the fuck is a death blossom maneuver?" asks Knob.

"Never mind. I guess Nunya and I are the only ones who appreciate old-timey cinema. Speaking of Nunya, have you got any bright ideas of how to deal with all these ships?" I ask.

Nunya thinks for a moment.

"Actually, yeah. Knob and Dick, you can both fly and fight in outer space, right?"

"Yeah," I reply.

"Then either Whip or I will pilot the ship, and you two can go outside and take these ships down by flying through them," says Nunya.

"That's great in theory," starts Knob. "Just one problem though: we don't have an airlock; we just have doors. The second we open a door to go outside, all the air inside the ship will be sucked out too."

"Oh. Well, I guess then we're fucked," says Nunya.

"Hey, I'm still a decent pilot!" says Knob, just as the ship gets rocked by a laser blast.

From seemingly nowhere, a female voice comes alive. "Shields now at 60%. Hull integrity 100%."

"Wait, where are we?" I ask.

"We're in the Tarragon Five system," says Nunya.

"Why the fuck are we here? Isn't it an abandoned mining system?" I ask.

"While you were asleep, Montgomery Israel sent a message telling us that we could get supplies for our mission from a planet here."

"And you trusted him?"

uncomfortable as well, as if he doesn't know how to handle people's flirtations.

"So, are we all ready to go?" asks Nunya.

"Already?" starts Knob. "We just got introduced. Shouldn't we have a meal together? Isn't that customary?"

"All we have for food here is the vending machine, but at least there's plenty to go around," says Nunya's dad.

"Uh, actually, I emptied it earlier," I say.

"Wait, why did you do that?" he asks.

"I got hungry and bored."

"And you ate all of it?"

"Well, actually, I did leave some Good & Plentys, and some Twizzlers, because they suck," I say.

"Hey, I like Twizzlers!" says Knob.

"Of course you do. Because you like eating plastic shoelaces. Both the flavor and texture are unappetizing. I'd rather eat a soggy sheet of A4 paper than Twizzlers," I say.

It becomes a little bit of an argument, because one other person mentions they like Twizzlers. I'm unwilling to name them, because I like them, and I don't want that kind of stigma associated with this person. I also notice, however, that no one defends Good & Plenty. Makes sense, since there's no defending them.

The argument devolves, and I launch into a tirade about how Smarties are little pieces of chalk, Nunya goes on about how much she hates nougat (even though she likes Snickers), and Whip admits he can't stand Whoppers. I'm in total agreement there. Nunya's mom seems to hate Necco Wafers, which I get, because they are like taking communion while giving yourself diabetes, and Nunya's dad rants about how much Reese's Pieces suck, and it's only because of the movie E.T. that anyone likes them.

"Well, at least they aren't as bad as circus peanuts," says Nunya, finally.

We all nod our heads in agreement. Thank God that is over.

"Either way, there isn't much to eat here, unfortunately," says Nunya's mom.

"We could order take-out," says Nunya's dad.

"PortalDash?" asks Nunya's mom.

"Sure. Or GrubStar," says Nunya's dad.

"Any particular cuisine that people want?" asks Nunya's mom.

Amazingly, we all say in unison "Chinese".

Nunya's folks spend the next few minutes gathering everyone's order, place it, and let us know it'll be delivered in about thirty. Nunya and I work on setting up everything in the breakroom in the meantime.

Dour Mike wheels up to me and tugs on my shirt.

"Hey buddy, what's up?" I ask.

"Since I don't eat food, I think I'll head back to the ship."

"Why don't you stay here with us and hang out. That's more what a big meal is about, spending time with the people you care for," I say.

"You, you care about me?" asks Dour Mike.

"Would I have bought you a sex-toaster if I didn't?"

"No, I suppose you wouldn't. Well, thank you. I also care about you, sir."

I smile at him.

As everyone starts slowly wandering into the break room, I look around and get a strange feeling I've never really felt before. Our group is starting to feel like family to me. I mean, I have my mom and all that, but I've never really felt like part of a big family the way that a lot of people do. I didn't even know it was something I'd wanted until now. Is it an incredibly fucked up family? Absolutely, but what family isn't?

Nunya catches my eye and smiles at me. Time seems to slow down, like I'm in some kind of movie montage, where everything's perfect, right before something really bad happens. A nuclear blast, or a meteor smashing into the planet. Maybe the bad guys come crashing in through the windows. Instead, we hear a buzzing at the office door.

"I'll get it," says Nunya's mom. She scurries out of the breakroom. After a brief moment she returns, her arms filled with so many bagged food containers we can't see her over them. "Help."

Nunya goes over and grabs some bags off the top. She and her mom open the meal cartons and hand them out to everyone. It sort of feels like living in a Hallmark card, only I realize half the people ordered something garlicy, and the ride back in Knob's spaceship is gonna be a stinky one.

36

We spend the next hour eating and chit-chatting about all kinds of things, taking time out from the craziness of life. And boy, the last few days have been crazy. I guess we feel like we can take things a little slower, just because we don't really have a timetable for when we have to break Montgomery Israel out of jail. He's either keeping Tiffany alive, or he's killed her. The thought of Tiffany dead darkens my mood.

It's been good to have this moment, to remind ourselves why we try to do good in the world. I'm not saying we're super altruistic; pretty much everyone in the group is motivated by selfish desires. Knob and I are both prima donnas, and Nunya just wants to be left alone. Dour Mike wants to stick his dick in light sockets, while Nunya's parents are used spaceship salespeople. I mean, that's almost as bad as being a lawyer or a telemarketer. Whip, however, seems to be a fairly decent person. I haven't really found fault with his motivations. I just hope he's not secretly the bad guy behind this whole thing, or at the very least working for Israel.

The gears start turning in my brain. Whip didn't seem to give much thought to having most of his organs replaced with cybernetic ones. He doesn't have any clear motivation for continuing to help us out. For him, it's supposedly just been a job, one he could quit and walk away from, yet he's still here. Either he's evil, and working for someone even more evil, or he's one of the most decent people I've ever run into.

"Hey, Whip, are you secretly a bad guy?" I ask, seemingly out of the blue.

He laughs. "No, why, are you?"

I scan his body, but it's almost entirely mechanical now. There's no way of telling whether he's lying, because he doesn't have a fluctuating pulse. His heart's been replaced with some valves that are controlled by a microprocessor which runs at a steady, unwavering sixty beats per minute. He could tell me anything and I wouldn't know whether to believe him or not.

"Dick, it's not very nice to just accuse people of being bad guys," says Nunya.

"Yeah, I know, but Whip just seems too good. Like, he's either a really, really good person, or he's maybe a spy, working for Montgomery Israel," I say.

163

"I would think I would know if Whip was a double agent," says Knob.

"While I appreciate the compliment about me being a really good person, accusing me of being a traitor isn't cool, Dick. Was there something I did or said that would make you question my loyalty?" asks Whip.

"No. I mean, not really. It just seemed like you jumped on the android bandwagon a little quick. I don't know if I could have made the same decision as easily as you seemed to. If I were a brainwashed spy, and my controller told me to do anything necessary to get the job done, I think I would probably jump on any chance to become more dangerous and powerful. I guess I just question your motives for the upgrades."

Whip nods his head in understanding. "Dick, I get it. And if after hearing what I have to say you aren't convinced, I'll drop out of the team." He takes a deep breath. "Ever since I was a little kid, I've wanted more than anything to be a hero. And not just a hero to others, rescuing kittens from trees and pulling people from burning buildings, I wanted to be a hero to myself. My dad wasn't around much growing up, as you know, and he died when I was still a teenager. I always wondered if maybe I'd been a better son when he was around, he would have been around more. If I could have just been good enough, then maybe he'd want to spend more time with me.

"Adult Whip understands that I didn't do anything wrong, that my dad was just doing his job, which kept him away from us for long periods of time, and that maybe my father had a bit of wanderlust in him. I do as well, which is why I signed up to fly all over the galaxy, working for a superhero. It's been a cathartic experience for me, getting to do good when I can, helping others, and maybe making my dad proud in the process, wherever he is. So, I guess you could say some of my motivation is selfish. It's me trying to somehow connect with someone I lost. I hope you can see past my facade of goodness, and recognize I'm just a person, doing his best to feel loved and appreciated. To feel worthy of love. To feel like my life has meaning."

It takes me a minute to dry the tears from my eyes.

"I'm... I'm incredibly sorry, Whip, for questioning you and your motivations. You've never really given me a reason to doubt you. I was just being paranoid. I've been screwed over so many times that I have a hard time trusting anyone, especially people who seem to have life all figured out. Especially good people that I respect. I'm constantly afraid of the other shoe dropping. I hope you can forgive me. Please, forgive me," I say.

"Dick, there's nothing to forgive. I understand why you'd be paranoid. I'd be paranoid too if I were in your shoes. I would question everyone and everything. It's normal when it seems like the whole world is against you, and you have to deal with so much responsibility, especially when it comes to being a detective. You don't know how to trust, because you deal with untrustworthy people on a daily basis. But most people are good people, trying to do their best. The bad ones are thankfully pretty rare. It may not feel like it because of the problems the bad ones cause, but most people are decent human beings."

"Thanks," I mumble.

I have a hard time making eye contact with anyone, still feeling ashamed of myself for questioning Whip's loyalty. I slowly finish the rest of my food without saying anything, while everyone else continues to talk. It's a bit awkward at first, but after a few minutes the conversations return to normal, and I just kind of hide from everyone by focusing on my meal. I finish up, throw away my trash, and make my way outside.

The nearby sun named Celeste is moving lower in the sky, and I can tell it's going to get dark soon. I slowly walk over to Knob's ship and a side door automatically opens for me as I approach.

Feeling exhausted and spent, I stumble my way to a section of the ship with individual sleeping quarters. There's a couple of very small rooms with tiny bunks in them, just meant as a space for sleeping and nothing else, so I wedge myself into one of them. The bed isn't particularly comfortable, and I have to ball up into a fetal position just to fit entirely on it, but I manage. I spend about half an hour hating myself before I'm finally able to fall asleep, but I do eventually fall asleep.

37

I wake up suddenly to the sound of alarms going off. I hit my head on the bunk above me as I sit up, denting the metal frame. Thankfully, it doesn't really hurt. I duck back down, bolt out of the room and down the hallway to the bridge. Everyone else is already there, Knob flying the ship through a crazy pattern of laser fire coming from a swarm of several hundred egg-shaped ships.

"Oh fuck, it's Sloths!" I say, surprised.

"No shit, fuckwad. Can you shut up? I'm trying to fly here," says Knob.

"Can you do a death blossom maneuver?" I ask.

"What the fuck is a death blossom maneuver?" asks Knob.

"Never mind. I guess Nunya and I are the only ones who appreciate old-timey cinema. Speaking of Nunya, have you got any bright ideas of how to deal with all these ships?" I ask.

Nunya thinks for a moment.

"Actually, yeah. Knob and Dick, you can both fly and fight in outer space, right?"

"Yeah," I reply.

"Then either Whip or I will pilot the ship, and you two can go outside and take these ships down by flying through them," says Nunya.

"That's great in theory," starts Knob. "Just one problem though: we don't have an airlock; we just have doors. The second we open a door to go outside, all the air inside the ship will be sucked out too."

"Oh. Well, I guess then we're fucked," says Nunya.

"Hey, I'm still a decent pilot!" says Knob, just as the ship gets rocked by a laser blast.

From seemingly nowhere, a female voice comes alive. "Shields now at 60%. Hull integrity 100%."

"Wait, where are we?" I ask.

"We're in the Tarragon Five system," says Nunya.

"Why the fuck are we here? Isn't it an abandoned mining system?" I ask.

"While you were asleep, Montgomery Israel sent a message telling us that we could get supplies for our mission from a planet here."

"And you trusted him?"

"I trusted that he actually wants us to break him out of prison," says Nunya.

"How far are we from the nearest space-asshole?" I ask.

"Not too far. Why?" asks Nunya.

"Knob, aim for the space-asshole," I say.

"And then what?" yells Knob.

"Do you have any deployable mines?" I ask.

"Yeah."

"Just as you're about to fly through the space asshole, jettison a mine right in front of the gate. As soon as one of the ships that's chasing us hits it, it'll detonate and close the space-asshole permanently," I say.

"Won't that strand anyone who's here?" asks Knob.

"There shouldn't be anyone out here. But feel free to run a scan to make sure it's just us and the Sloths," I say.

"Whip?" says Knob.

"On it."

I watch as Whip runs over to another console and starts typing furiously. Knob keeps us flying for a couple of minutes while the scan runs. The same female voice echoes through the bridge, counting down our destruction, "Shields at 0%, hull integrity 50%."

"Whip?" I say.

"Got it. There are no lifeforms other than the Sloths and us. The planets are devoid of life, and the space gate's ship is fully automated," says Whip.

"Wait, if it's fully automated, Nunya, how long would it take you to hack?" I ask.

"I dunno, maybe a couple of minutes."

"Then do it."

"But why? Why not just blow up the gate?" asks Nunya.

"I have this feeling that it's exactly what Israel wants us to do. Just please, hack it."

Nunya runs over to the console that Whip is sitting at as he jumps out of the seat. She taps faster than I've ever seen her tap before.

"Hull integrity 35%."

"Hull integrity 25%."

"Nunya?" I ask.

"Almost there," she says.

"Set the gate to point at Israel's home system once we've passed through," I say.

"Hull integrity 15%."

"Done!" yells Nunya.

"Okay, everyone, hold on. This will be close," says Knob.

Knob actually is a surprisingly good pilot. He darts through the crowd of Sloth ships, doing his best to avoid the laser fire, but we're still taking damage. I can see the space-asshole growing closer. Knob aims straight for the gate and kicks in the afterburners.

"Hull integrity 5%."

I look up at one of the monitors that displays what's behind us. Every single Sloth ship is now following. Just as we pass through the space-asshole, it shimmers and changes, so that we can no longer see any Sloth ships behind us. Knob slows down the ship gradually to a dead stop.

"Holy fucking shit!" says Knob.

"Good piloting," I say.

Knob seems completely surprised by the compliment. He tears up a little then turns away from me.

"Also, nice job Whip and Nunya on figuring that stuff out so quickly," I say. They both smile.

"So, you think that Israel wanted us to blow up the space-asshole," asks Nunya.

"Yeah."

"Why would he even care?"

"I don't know. I'm sure we'll find out later, toward the end of the story," I say.

"Wait, what do you mean?" asks Nunya.

"Oh, it's just a figure of speech. You know, like at the end of our mission. Story. You know, whatever."

"Right."

"Anyway, this ship's about to fall apart. Nunya, any chance it can be repaired?"

"Honestly, it'd probably be easier to get another ship. It could take a week to repair this much damage," says Nunya.

"We don't have a week. I mean, I know Israel didn't give us a timetable, but it feels like if he's fucking with us like this, it's just gonna get worse. Does anyone have any bright ideas?" I ask.

"Well, the ship we pulled the computer from, isn't that the same ship as this one?" asks Whip. "Maybe we could just move everything over to that one."

"It doesn't have the same weapons systems, and it doesn't have my decor," says Knob.

"So much the better," I mumble.

"What? Did you have something to say, Dick?" asks Knob.

"Nah, I'm good."

"I suppose if we were able to move the weapons system over to the new ship, it could work," says Nunya.

"Or better yet, maybe we could have Nord install something new and improved," suggests Whip.

"Yeah! Like a Death Blossom!" I say.

"What the fuck is a Death Blossom?" says Knob, frustratedly.

"You push a button and the ship spins in all directions, firing wildly, hitting everything within range. Nunya used it against the Sloths. It was pretty awesome," I say.

"Huh, that does sound cool. Can you find out how long it would take Nord to retrofit the other ship?" asks Knob.

"On it," says Nunya, who walks over to one of the computers.

Now I know what you're thinking, didn't we just go through all of this, having to go to Nunya's parent's business, swap out computers, contact Nord to save Whip's life, all that stuff? Yeah, I know, not super exciting to read about. Instead, just imagine a montage of a couple of days of us taking care of all that shizz. We did go to Nunya's parent's business, bought the old ship, and installed the computers from Knob's ship, then headed to Nord's shop.

I will say, while Nord was working on the weapons for the new ship, she did take a break for a little while so we could fuck like rabbits. It was pretty great. She still didn't want to be in a relationship with me, but the sex was awesome. Like, really, really awesome. I dunno, maybe I am falling in love with her. That would suck, since she already told me it wouldn't work out for either of us. I just wish relationships weren't so fucking complicated. Or not having relationships, or whatever.

I also asked her to install the Death Blossom on the new ship, and she not only agreed, but she had actually seen *The Last Starfighter* before. She also added some new weapons systems that I'd never heard of, and didn't really get the gist of when she explained them. Admittedly, I spent most of the time she was talking staring at her tits. They really are mesmerizing. You'd stare too.

Once the new old ship was fully outfitted, we said our goodbyes.

"It was magical seeing you again," says Nord, giving me a long kiss. As I turn and walk away from her, she slaps my ass. "Come back soon. I'll be keeping something warm and ready for you."

"Cookies?" I ask.

"One cookie in particular, if you spelled it with a 'ch' instead of a 'k'", says Nord.

"A chookie? What's that?" I ask.

"No, my 'coochie'!"

"Oh. Right. Okay, yeah, that sounds good," I say.

"God you're hopeless" says Nunya.

"You're just jealous that Nord had sex with me and not with you."

"Who says I didn't?" says Nunya

I look over at Nord, and she looks away sheepishly.

"Hey, when the hell did that happen?" I ask.

"When we brought Whip back for repairs," says Nunya.

"Not cool, Nunya. If you two are gonna do that, I should have been invited."

"Sorry sugar, but only one rider at a time," says Nord.

"Besides, I thought it'd be fair because I knew you'd have sex with my mom when you two were alone. I was preemptively getting you back," says Nunya.

"But I didn't even have sex with your mother!"

"No, but you thought about it," says Nunya.

"I actually didn't. She came on to me," I accidentally let slip out.

"There's no way my mom did that."

"Oh, she did. She tried to get all up on this, but I pushed her away and told her 'no', and that my friendship with you meant more to me than having sex with her, and I didn't want to ruin things between me and you. But then I find out you did this, and I ruin it between us anyway. Fuck you, Nunya."

I storm off, exiting Nord's exquisitely decorated home, catch a waft of garbage smell, and decide to fly up into the sky, away from these people who I thought were my friends.

38

Tears stream down my face and start to freeze into ice droplets due to the altitude I'm cruising at. For the first time in my life, I feel like I finally have a real family, people I can maybe count on, care about, have a real emotional connection with, and now this. The one person I valued most betrayed me with someone I think I'm genuinely falling in love with to get back at me for something I didn't do, and I didn't do it because I valued them so highly. And I fucking hate drama, and this is about as drama-y as it gets. It's a worse plotline than on one of those soap operas that my mom watches.

I probably fly randomly for an hour, trying to outrun my feelings, hoping that some time and distance away from things will make it better, only it doesn't really. I do stop crying, more out of exhaustion than anything, but the feelings are still raw. Betrayal is one of the hardest pills to swallow, and it got lodged halfway down my throat.

Thoughts pour through my head of what I'm going to do next. I don't want to have anything to do with Nunya anymore. I don't think there's any amount of apologizing that she could do to fix things. My heart is also broken that Nord could just casually have sex with my best friend like that, knowing it could really hurt my feelings, or at least should have known. Glad I found out she isn't into me as much as I'm into her.

It also doesn't help that I questioned Whip's loyalty and hurt his feelings in the process. I'm still feeling the guilt of that. I may be one of the strongest people in the universe, and I pride myself on my emotional strength and not-caringness, but sometimes life fucks you so hard that the eye-faucets start dripping. Yeah, some of my tears are for the loss of people I loved, but also from my own shame.

Someone still needs to rescue Tiffany. I don't know if the rest of the crew will be able to do it without me. I don't know if I'll be able to do it without them. Despite being the galaxy's best detective, and super strong and super handsome, I'm not the best when it comes to planning heists, and I certainly don't have the 1337 HaX0r skillz required to get past even simple security like Nunya does. I'm not good at blending in because of my size. There's just no subtlety to my approach. If I tried to break out Montgomery Israel on my own,

171

there's a chance I'll get trapped, arrested, and potentially imprisoned for the rest of my life.

My stomach sinks when I realize the other reason I won't be able to do it on my own is Israel wants us all disgraced. If we're not together when we break him out, he might not tell us where Tiffany is. The whole point is for us to be disgraced, as much as it is for him to escape prison. I think if I went in alone, he wouldn't honor his bargain. But then I'd just torture him to find out where Tiffany is. I don't know if he'd tell me though. He could lie just to get me to stop torturing him, I kill him, then go to where he told me Tiffany is, and she isn't there. There are too many things that could go wrong. Goddamn it!

I let the anger and frustration build until I scream into the air. Once I'm done ejecting all the rage from inside me, I slowly relax and make my way back to Nord's. I take time to calm down and go over what I'll say to them. It isn't going to be pretty, but I need to do it.

When I reach her place I see Nunya, Whip, Knob, and Dour Mike leaving Nord's. The door to her home is closed. I guess that will make this easier, I just won't talk to Nord. I don't really have a lot to say to her right now, anyway. Nothing that would be useful.

Dour Mike is the first to spot me, and I can hear him alert the others to my presence. I fly down, slowly landing just in front of them. I just stand there and wait. It takes a while for someone to break the silence, but Nunya eventually does.

"I'm sorry, Dick," she says.

I just stand there, continuing to stare at her.

"I'm really sorry. What I did was wrong," she says.

I don't react. I won't give her the satisfaction, and I won't accept her apology. I'm not going to let her off the hook for this.

"I really..." she starts to say, but I cut her off.

"I'm going to finish this mission with all of you, then I'm done," I say.

"Done? Like done-done?" asks Knob.

I turn away from them and make my way inside the ship. I go back to the bunks, curl up in bed, and drift off to sleep.

39

Eventually I wake up, and it takes a few seconds to wipe the salt away from my eyes that built up while I was asleep. I don't hear any sounds like the ship is being attacked, thankfully. In fact, it's eerily quiet.

Walking around the ship is weird, because it feels like Knob's old ship, but it doesn't look like Knob's old ship. It's giving me a sense of deja vu that I'm not enjoying. I make my way to the pisser and spend the next few minutes relieving myself. Once I'm done, I wash my hands, dry them off on an old beat-up towel, then make my way to the bridge.

As I walk down the long hallway, I catch out of the corner of my eye Whip and Nunya sitting down in the conference room. I give an almost imperceptible nod to Whip and ignore Nunya completely. It's weird, because I realize that they've moved all the furniture over from Knob's old ship, including the tables and chairs. It adds to the sense of deja vu I'm experiencing.

Getting close to the bridge, I bump into Dour Mike. He looks up at me with his sad robot eyes, reminding me of how he used to be before I got him his first fuck-toaster. All doom and gloom. I hope he doesn't want me to cheer him up.

"Hello, Dick. I'm here to try to cheer you up," says Dour Mike.

I look at him incredulously. Yeah, I know what 'incredulously' means.

"How could you possibly cheer me up? I've hurt one friend, another friend hurt me about as bad as you could hurt someone, my lover hurt me just as bad, and now the closest people I have to friends are a talking Cuisinart and an asshole who wants to fuck/marry/kill me," I say.

"Talking Cuisinart?" asks Dour Mike.

"Yeah, sorry. I didn't mean to liken you to a stand mixer," I say.

"I'll ignore the slight, knowing that you're going through a lot right now. Look, Dick, I know that you're hurting. That life seems to be an endless collection of disappointments. People let you down all the time, you let people down all the time. Everyone is just letting everyone else down, all the time."

"And?"

"No, that's it. People are messy and are affected by their biology a lot more than they realize. Wars have begun because

173

someone accidentally left mayo off someone else's sandwich. Humans are very poorly designed, if you ask me. So many improvements could be made. I guess that's what you should keep in mind when you judge everyone, including yourself. You're imperfect. You're a squishy, unfeeling blob of fat in a slightly crunchy, slightly feeling meat suit. Everything that is really you is inside your brain, and you're just a little puppeteer, pulling the levers inside to move your body around. And your brain is poorly designed. You can lose information just as quickly as you've learned it, it's easily tricked, and it can be programmed to believe a whole bunch of lies and nonsense meant to control you. It's truly amazing any of you have survived long enough to grow as a species."

"Wow, you really are doing a good job of cheering me up," I say, sarcastically.

"I'm not trying to make you happy, if that's what you're implying. I'm trying to make you understand that everyone makes mistakes, including you. You've done some terrible things, I assume," says Dour Mike.

"Yeah, I usually don't account for other people's feelings when I make decisions that affect them. I just kind of live in the moment and do what I feel like."

"Well, do you think that Nunya did the same thing? Is it fair for you to hold her to a higher standard than you hold yourself?"

Shit.

"In my defense, I've never had sex with my best friend's lover," I say.

"Have you ever even had a best friend up until this point?" asks Dour Mike.

"Well, no."

"Why do you think that is?"

"Because people are jealous of me."

"I'm pretty sure that's not it. It's because you've done things that have kept people from trusting you. They automatically assume you're going to do bad things, because that's the pattern you've set up for your life. That's why Nunya felt justified in having sex with Nord. She thought for sure you'd have sex with her mom. Even though you're 'best friends', it sounds like you've never really earned her trust. Especially when it comes to sex."

"Hey, she got drunk and threw herself at me one time. She climbed on top of me, and I pushed her away. I could have taken advantage of her, but I didn't. I would think that would have shown her I was trustworthy to some degree," I say.

"Well, apparently it wasn't enough. Either way, I think you should give her a chance to apologize. If it seems like she's really apologizing, and not just trying to smooth things over, then maybe you can stop hating her," says Dour mike.

"I doubt it. She can be super stubborn. I don't know if she even really thinks she did anything wrong."

"Just give her a chance. I think she might surprise you."

I look at Dour Mike for a few seconds, and instead of agreeing to it, or nodding or whatever, I slowly make my way around him.

After about a dozen steps, I reach the bridge. Knob is doing his Knob thing, standing there, piloting the ship.

"Knob?" I say.

"Yeah, what is it, Dick?"

"What's the plan?"

"Well, part of the plan is to not interact with you, because you're unstable and we're worried you'll rip the ship apart if anyone triggers you," says Knob.

"Accurate."

"Any chance I can talk you down from Defcon 1?"

"Unlikely."

"Are you still planning on helping us rescue the President's daughter?"

"Yeah. Still planning," I say.

"Good. Well, if that's the case, then we may have come up with a plan. Or at least added to the old plan, which is to send Dour Mike down to planet Alphatraz as a scout, signal us via the transmitter that Israel gave us, and reprogram security to let us slip inside undetected. After that, we'll fly down, try not to kill anybody, and break Israel out," says Knob.

"Sounds like there are still a lot of details that need to be worked out."

"There are, which is what Nunya and Whip are working on. As smart as I am, I have to admit they're smarter than me."

"Knob, everyone's smarter than you."

"Sure, feel free to insult me if it makes you feel any better," says Knob.

I stew for a moment.

"Sorry, Knob. Sadly, you're the closest thing I have to a friend right now. Very sadly," I say.

"Yeah, well, we'll see how long that lasts. In the meantime, maybe try to avoid Whip and Nunya. I've already lost my ship, and I don't know how long it's going to take to repaint this place like the old ship."

"I'd really recommend not doing that. It was painful to the eyes. Very painful."

"Not your ship, not your problem," says Knob.

"So, where are we headed now?" I ask.

175

"To Blhack Glasses' base of operations. Nunya needs their help with writing software to crack into Alphatraz's security system."

"Wait, I thought we couldn't get any help though, Israel's orders," I say.

"Well, we already got help from Nord, and Nunya's parents, and nothing bad happened yet," says Knob.

"Maybe he really can hear what we're saying, so he knows we haven't told anyone. Fuck you Israel, if you can hear me," I say.

The ship's monitors flicker off and back on again.

"Wait, you have the transmitter plugged into your ship?" I ask.

"Yeah, we were supposed to have it running this whole time, so I finally plugged it in," says Knob.

"Shit. Okay, well, we better make sure when we meet up with Blhack Glass that none of us reveal what we're trying to accomplish."

"How is that supposed to work? Are we just gonna tell them we need help breaking into Alphatraz, for no reason in particular?""

"How the hell should I know? I'm not the planning type. That's Whip and Nunya's department," I say.

"They better come up with something good," says Knob.

"No shit. Wait. Oh fuck. I thought by piggybacking computers that Israel couldn't control the ship, since it's a one-way connection. Didn't he just cause the monitors to flicker?" I ask.

"Yeah, yeah he did."

"So, he can control the ship anyway?"

"Apparently. Here, just watch everything and I'll go let Whip and Nunya know," says Knob.

"Yeah, sure. I'll just wait here," I say.

40

Nothing much happens while I wait for Knob. I notice some lights on some nearby panels flicker, which can't possibly mean anything because they aren't labeled. I wonder if they just stuck with the aesthetic from old school sci-fi movies and made everything look important, even though you can basically fly the ship with a couple of controls, and everything else is automated. After a few minutes, Knob returns.

"So, Nunya and Whip were both freaked out that Israel can control the ship," says Knob.

"I mean, they should be. He could probably warp us into a star if he wanted to, and I don't know about you, but I'm pretty sure I wouldn't survive that," I say.

"Yeah, I don't think I'd survive it either."

"And you told them that we'll need to keep the transmitter near us while we're getting help from Blhack Glass?"

"I told them that, but Nunya pointed out that it's probably got some sort of long-distance listening device built in, so we shouldn't need to carry it with us," says Knob.

"Were they at all worried that bringing the transmitter to Blhack Glass' headquarters would be like bringing a Trojan Horse to their doorstep?" I ask.

"Oh, shit, no. None of us had thought of that."

"Well, maybe go back and tell them."

Knob saunters off again. After a few minutes he returns, looking even more worried.

"Yeah, so no one had thought of that. Now we're worried that it could have been Israel's plan all along. Maybe he's more interested in gaining control of their systems than breaking out, since Blhack Glass is one of the few groups that could keep him in check," said Knob.

The screen I'm staring at beeps and displays a message, "No, it wasn't the main intent of my plan, but it would have been a nice cherry on top."

I struggle very, very hard not to punch the control console. I step back a few feet just to make sure if my emotions get the better of me that I don't leave us dead in the water with an unflyable ship.

177

Taking a few deep breaths helps, but it'll be a while before I'm able to fully calm down.

"So, then what's the plan? If we can't fly to Blhack Glass to get some coding help, is Nunya just supposed to handle it herself?" I ask.

"Her and Whip are still working out the details, but it sounds like she might be able to figure it out on the fly. It won't be pretty, and we'll need to rely on our powers more than just slipping past security unnoticed, but we should still be able to pull it off. We'll just need to be ready for a fight."

"As long as we all go into it knowing that the security teams are likely innocents who are just trying to do their job," I say.

"You haven't seen a lot of prison movies, have you?" says Knob.

"Actually, *The Shawshank Redemption* is one of my favorite movies of all time. Why do you think I'm secretly excited about being part of a prison break?"

"I didn't realize you were secretly excited, because of the whole 'secret' thing, but I do get it. Either way, prison guards don't always treat their prisoners well."

"Totally fair, but I don't imagine I'd treat the people I interacted with at work well if they were all plotting to kill me. I can't imagine it's a very happy job to be doing," I say.

"Either way, we're heading to Alphatraz now. No more side quests, no more amusing meetups with quirky allies, and certainly no more attacks from random villains meant just to annoy us. We focus, and we finally save Tiffany," says Knob.

"Wow, that's gonna sound pretty meta when I write about it in my memoirs."

"What are you even talking about?"

"I usually write down what happens so I can publish stories about all my adventures. It's lines like what you just said that really keep the reader interested, because breaking the fourth wall makes the reader feel more connected somehow. It's good shit," I say.

"Dick, sometimes you're really weird."

"Yeah, well, it takes one to know one."

"I don't think you used that phrase right."

"Your mom doesn't use that phrase right."

Knob just rolls his eyes at me and turns back to piloting the ship.

41

"Are we there yet?" I ask Knob, just to be annoying. He glances over at me, doesn't say anything, and just rolls his eyes again. Then he turns back to piloting the ship.

"Dick, if you want to make yourself useful... "

"Yes?"

"You could be somewhere else," says Knob

"Then there's nothing I could be doing to help out?" I ask.

"Not really. Can you think of anything?"

"No."

"Then maybe just go read a book or play with your Personal Space Device."

"Yeah, I guess."

I pass by Nunya and Whip, who are now talking with Dour Mike in the meeting room. I try not to make eye contact, but I notice them both shift nervously as I walk past. Dour Mike doesn't acknowledge my presence, which is fine because he's a robot.

Reaching my bunk, I pull out my PSD and start bringing up how-to books on breaking into prisons. Surprisingly, there aren't a lot of books out there. Most of them are centered around breaking out of prisons. I do find a copy of *Breaking Into Prisons for Morons*, and I spend the next 30 minutes as we're traveling to Alphatraz learning as much as I can. You just never know when a useful bit of information might save the whole team.

It isn't super exciting reading, as some of it is fairly technical, but I'm able to skim through the book to gain a general understanding of how one should approach breaking into a prison. I do realize once I've finished it that there's no chapter on breaking back out, so I switch over to *Breaking Out of Prisons for Morons*, and trudge through that.

Shortly after finishing my studying, Knob's voice echoes through the ship: "We're here." The weird part is not that he used the intercoms, but that he made a weird staticky noise with his mouth before and after he spoke. And he thinks I'm the immature one?

I get up off the bunk, and as I'm walking down the hallway, I notice that Nunya, Whip and Dour Mike are no longer in the meeting room. When I arrive at the bridge, everyone is standing around. They turn and look at me. I take a deep breath and just let them speak.

"Hey Dick, we just reached the outskirts of Alphatraz. I had to fly inconspicuously to get here, which is why it took a while. They don't get a lot of tourists in this area, for obvious reasons, so we stick out like a sore thumb. The good news is we still have the IRFID device, which allows us to automatically pass by security without being stopped, because we have presidential authority to do basically anything," says Knob.

"That's convenient," I mumble.

"Isn't it? Anyway, we're trying to figure out the best way to get Dour Mike on board one of the shipment ships."

"Do you have to call them 'shipment ships'?"

"Why? What else would you call them?"

"I dunno," I say. "It just sounds bad to use a word right after the same word. My readers are gonna really hate it."

"Oh, right, for your memoirs. Well, if you come up with a better name then feel free to use it," says Knob.

I haven't come up with a better name. Oh well.

"What if we try to infiltrate one halfway between where it starts out, and where it ends up? Might give us enough time to get him on board without being noticed," says Whip.

"Well, after watching them come in through the nearby space portal and make a beeline straight for the planet, I feel like it only takes a few minutes for them to reach their destination. Not enough time to get Dour Mike on the ship, and we'd definitely be noticed," says Knob.

"How about we fly through the space portal, back to where the shippy ships are coming from, and have him stow away there," suggests Nunya.

I wince at the phrase 'shippy ships', but I have to admit it's at least slightly less annoying than 'shipment ships'.

"Yeah, that's probably our only option," says Whip. "Maybe we don't try to get him on board mid-flight, maybe we just have him be part of a shipment. Hack in and add him to a manifest so that they know he's there, and they just treat him as any other piece of equipment."

"I can totally do that," says Nunya.

"Alright, so just to clarify, we hook up Dour Mike with the transmitter, drop him off near the shipping facility, hack into their system and add him to a manifest. He gets put on the ship, and we trail the ship back to Alphatraz. Does that sound right?" says Knob.

"Sounds right," says Nunya.

"There's just one small problem I realized," I say.

"And that is?" asks Knob.

"Since there's a transmitter and a receiver, we won't have a way to communicate with Dour Mike when he's sneaking through Alphatraz. He can only send us information, but we can't send him any. So, he'll need to know ahead of time exactly what he's supposed to be doing before going on his mission, and he'll have to improvise if anything goes sideways," I say.

"I might be able to upload information on prisons, security protocols, hacking software, etc. into Dour Mike so that he has a better chance of making it work," says Nunya.

"You might upload *Breaking into Prisons for Morons*. It was a pretty good read," I say. They all turn to me and stare.

"That's... an actual book?" asks Nunya.

"Yeah. Oh, and upload *Breaking out of Prisons for Morons* as well," I say.

"Uh, right," says Nunya. "Anyway, I'll start getting Dour Mike set up. In the meantime, Knob, follow one of the shippy ships back to its home."

"On it," he says, tapping away at the ship's touchscreen.

Even though I was able to communicate with Nunya without yelling at her, it doesn't mean I'm happy with her. Instead of waiting around for things to happen, since there's really nothing for me to do at the moment, I head back to my bunk.

Before I reach it, I turn around and see Dour Mike following me.

"Hey Dour Mike, what is it?" I ask.

"Can you do me a favor?" asks Dour Mike.

"Sure, what is it?"

"If I don't make it back, can you tell Debbie Downer that she's always been the love of my life, and that I'm sorry I didn't tell her sooner? That if it weren't for her, I wouldn't have made it through my darkest days, and that she's helped me become the man I am today. Can you please tell her that?"

"Dour Mike, you're gonna make it back. I'll make sure you're safe and free by the end of this mission."

"Dick, you can't guarantee that. You don't know if I'll accidentally get crushed in some sort of trap, or if I'll have to detonate myself to save the party to prevent a TPK. There's no way of knowing I'll make it back. Just please promise me you'll tell her."

"Sure, buddy. Sure," I say.

His words make me sad, because I can't imagine something bad happening to him, but you never know. Sometimes things do go sideways. Sometimes, your entire crew gets killed. But I really will do my best to make sure he makes it out of Alphatraz in one piece.

"Hey, Dour Mike?"

"Yes?"

"What does TPK mean?"

"Oh, that means Total Party Kill. Basically, everyone in an adventuring party dies, usually because either your Game Master is an asshole, or the players made enough stupid decisions that they deserved to die," says Dour Mike.

"Is that a roleplaying game thing?" I ask.

"Yes."

"Gotcha."

"Is there anyone you'd like me to say the same kind of thing to if you die during the mission?" asks Dour Mike.

"Hey now, I'm not gonna die either."

"How can you be sure?"

"Because I'm wearing plot armor! I just bought some recently," I say.

"What's plot armor?"

"Well, basically it means that since I'm the main character of my story, I can't die. Not permanently, anyway. Does it take away from the emotional impact of the story? Maybe a little, but it's more important to maintain the same protagonist throughout a series than to make the stakes really-real," I explain.

"Dick, that doesn't make sense. I mean, this is the real world. People die sometimes, even 'main characters'," says Dour Mike.

"True, but how could I possibly be writing my memoirs if I'm dead? How could the person currently enjoying my story be reading my words?"

"Easy, someone could ghostwrite them. They take the information from what they know of you and compile it into a set of stories. Maybe Nunya is the lone survivor of the mission again, and she feels so guilty for getting your lover to cheat on you that she writes down your stories, using your voice."

"Oh, shit, I hadn't thought about that. But if that's the case, how are there several more books after this one? My adventures would end here," I point out.

"That's fair, but maybe the books that come after this are about Nunya, and are told from her perspective instead," says Dour Mike.

"No, that wouldn't work. Someone already tried that, and some overzealous assholes sent her death threats. People get dangerously wrapped up in their fiction to the point where they can't understand the stories aren't real. If I were to die, and the series became all about Nunya, I don't think people would keep reading it."

"Except for the fact that Nunya is considerably more likable than you."

"Hey now, that's not very nice, and I don't think it's true, either," I say.

"Well, her backstory is more intriguing than yours. She's a dark, more broody character, which is 'in' right now. She has more than just superpowers. She can hack into things, and she forms good plans. Nunya also tends to save the day through intelligence and hard work, whereas you kind of bumble your way through solutions," says Dour Mike.

"I don't bumble!" I say.

"You bumble more than a bee, Dick."

"So, what am I, Inspector Clouseau? Or even better, Inspector Gadget? I'm more like Batman, I'm the greatest detective who ever lived!"

"Dick, I did some digging on you, and most of the crimes you solved seemed to have been solvable by normal people without any superpowers, and only mediocre IQs," says Dour Mike.

"So, what you're saying is, I'm not only likely dead, but my entire career has been an accident, and that I'm generally good for nothing?"

"Well, it does sound bad when you put it like that."

"How else would I put it?" I ask.

"Anyway, Nunya needs to upload a bunch of data into me. Thanks, Dick," says Dour Mike.

"Seriously, what the fuck, dude. You're just gonna insult me and run?"

"I didn't mean to insult you; I was just being honest."

"Next time, Dour Mike, lie. I'd rather you lie and be nice to me, than be truthful and hurtful."

"I will try to remember that," says Dour Mike, who turns and leaves the room.

I didn't think I could feel any worse than I already did about my life, and now a depressed robot tears me down even further. I know he didn't mean to, and I know that it's just part of his programming to be like that, but it still really hurts.

Maybe he's right, maybe Nunya is more likable than me. Maybe she is better in every way. But I'm still better than her at one thing, and that's not having sex with people who are close to my friends. I'm a better best friend than she is, so who cares if she's smart and successful?

I curl up on my bunk, and try to get some rest, hoping that sleep will drown out the negative voices in my head. But I just lay there, running through all the bad things that have come to light recently.

42

Eventually, I'm able to take a quick cat nap, and when I wake up everything seems normal. No sirens are going off, and I don't hear any weird noises.

As I sit up, I wipe the salt from my eyes again. Getting sick of this feeling sorry for myself bullshit. It's time I finally started pushing my emotions down deep again so I can't feel them. It's a lot healthier for me not to address my feelings, because when I do think about them, I'm really sad. Better to not feel anything than to feel that.

I take a quick shower because it's been a while, and I can smell myself every time I lift my arms. I run my clothes through a laundry machine in the bunk area. One benefit of being super strong is that my eyes don't sting when I get shampoo in them. Don't try this at home.

Once I'm all dried, and my clothes are ready, I put them back on, then make my way into the hallway. As I slowly shuffle down the middle of it, I notice Nunya coming back inside the ship, dressed like some sort of shipping person. She's wearing a dark green outfit, with a dark green hat, a fake mustache, and she's carrying a digital clipboard and a small package. On the t-shirt are the letters 'S. U. P.'.

"What's SUP?" I ask.

"Not much, what's up with you?" responds Nunya.

"Wait, what?"

"What?"

"Oh, what does 'S. U. P.' stand for?" I ask.

"It's the acronym for 'Standard Universal Parcel'," says Nunya. "It's a good thing we worked that out now, because it totally could have been a 'who's on first' situation."

"Yeah," I say emotionlessly, making it obvious that I'm still unhappy with her.

"I'm wearing this because I'm going to be the one to drop off Dour Mike at the shipping company."

"I'd already worked that out," I say.

Nunya looks me in the eyes, or at least tries to, but I look away. She takes a deep breath, then starts talking again.

"Dick, I want you to know that I'm really sor…"

185

I cut her off mid word.

"I don't want to hear it, Nunya," I say.

"Please, just listen to me. I'm really sorry for what I did. It was incredibly shitty of me. I thought the worst of you, and I did the worst to you. I failed you in every way a friend could fail you. And you didn't deserve it. You've been doing a lot better as a person, and I shit all over that. Not only did I not give you the benefit of the doubt, but I did something to deliberately hurt you. I'm the bad guy here. And I want you to know I won't do it again," says Nunya.

"That's right, because we aren't friends anymore. I won't let you hurt me again. You had your chance, you failed, I'll get over it," I say.

Tears start streaming down her cheeks.

"I'm not saying this to hurt you, Nunya. I'm saying this so you know where we stand. There's no path to earning back our friendship, no way of mending what you broke. You're gonna have to live with that, but I won't. I'm going to protect myself from you. I'm gonna protect myself from the world. No more friends. I got along just fine on my own, and I'll get along again just fine on my own. If this is what friends do to each other, then I don't want any friends," I say.

Nunya starts crying, and crying hard. She just nods her head in understanding, then walks away.

I really wasn't deliberately trying to hurt her, I just needed to set boundaries. I can't let anyone in again like that. Sure, maybe being friends with Nunya has helped me be a better person, but it obviously hasn't made her a better person. Maybe I'm toxic, and I make the people around me worse. Maybe it's better for the rest of the galaxy that I don't have friends, that way I'm not responsible for turning more people into assholes.

It's a hard pill to swallow, but I'm gonna swallow it, and push it down, and make sure it doesn't come back up. This is my 'me' medicine, and I'm gonna take it. Maybe this is just karma getting me back for all the shitty things I've done in my life. Maybe I deserved to get betrayed like this.

I realize I'm spiraling. Being mean to myself so that maybe if I feel like I deserve it, I can somehow learn to accept it. I'm training the parts of my brain that handle pain to prevent me from putting myself in a position like this again and believe that I'm not deserving of friendship or happiness. That it's not worth it, because I'll just be betrayed again. I'm a little surprised I'm even having these revelations. I wish I wasn't.

I head back to the bridge because there's nothing better to do. Passing by the conference room, I see Dour Mike alone, his dick plugged into a computer dock on the wall. He kind of looks like a statue who got his dick stuck, since he isn't moving any, kind of like a weird modern art piece. I assume he's still uploading information for the mission, so I decide not to distract him.

Making my way to the bridge, I find Whip and Knob talking.

"Hey Dick, is Nunya ready?" asks Knob.

"Probably not yet," I reply.

"Why not? Did something happen? Was she not able to get the outfit?" asks Whip.

"No, she got the outfit."

"Then why isn't she ready? We're pretty much there," says Knob.

"Probably because I told her I was never gonna be her friend again. That we were through," I say.

"Fuck," says Whip.

"What the hell were you thinking? She needs to act composed and carefree, like she belongs there. We can't have her dealing with an emotional upheaval if she's going to pull this off," says Knob.

"I was thinking that she hurt me as bad as a friend could. I was just protecting myself."

"I don't care if you were protecting yourself, just go back there and unfuck the situation. We need her," says Knob.

"Not my problem."

"Oh, it is your fucking problem, if you want to save Tiffany. It's big-time your fucking problem."

"I'm not talking to her. If I went back and apologized now, she'd know I didn't mean it, and that you put me up to apologizing to her. We're just gonna have to wait it out," I say.

"Seriously, Dick, you should have accepted her apology. I accepted yours," says Whip.

"Yeah, well, I accused you of betraying us, when you obviously haven't, and it was shitty, but she really did betray me. You can't apologize when you betray someone, because you know going into it that you're doing it deliberately. There's no way to come back from that. You chose to do something that would hurt someone. That makes you a bad guy in my book."

"With all the shitty things you've done, all the selfish, fucked up things you've done, have you never betrayed someone?" asks Whip.

187

"No, because I've always worked alone. I didn't have anyone to betray. And yeah, I've done some fucked up things, but it was when I wasn't even thinking of other people. I genuinely didn't know better, because I was just fucking ignorant about it. So no, I've never betrayed anyone," I say. "Fuck, this is turning into a goddamn episode of Galaxy Hospital. Can't we all just shut up and get the job done."

"Yeah, at this point I think shutting the fuck up, Dick, would be the best option. Whip, can you please go check on Nunya?" says Knob.

"I can do that," says Whip, walking back down the hallway.

"Seriously, Dick, can't you just put your feelings aside for once, and do the hard thing. Just maybe grow up, because you're risking an innocent girl's life," says Knob.

"Tiffany ain't that innocent," I say.

"Yeah, yeah, I know, total minx in the bedroom and all that. But she's innocent of doing anything illegal, and certainly hasn't done anything to deserve being kidnapped and tortured, or maybe even worse."

"I know. But you're right, I am trying to put away my feelings. That's why I decided to stop crying about the situation and protect myself from being hurt again."

"Well fucking good-for-you. It's impressive to just write people off, especially people who risk their lives to save their friend's former lover," says Knob.

"She's probably in it more for the money," I say.

"Nunya was already rich. She didn't really need to be more rich," says Knob. "I think she just decided to help because Tiffany and you had been lovers."

"Or maybe she just didn't want to go to jail for tax evasion, since you did such a good job of blackmailing her."

"I'm sure she's the type of person who could figure out a way around it. She's been doing this for you, Dick," says Knob.

The words hurt, and if I really think about it, he's probably right. She has been doing us a solid favor by helping out. Fuck. But that still doesn't mean I should be her friend anymore. It doesn't undo what she did. I just can't get past it. I have to hope that Whip can somehow calm her down and convince her to drop Dour Mike off at the shipping center.

It takes about twenty minutes, but eventually Whip returns to the bridge.

"Are things okay?" asks Knob.

"No, not really, but okay enough. Nunya's tough, and she was able to eventually let enough of the pain and guilt out that she's gonna be able to handle dropping Dour Mike off," says Whip.

"Are you absolutely sure she can do this?" asks Knob.

"It's Nunya. She's got this," says Whip.

"When… when is she leaving?" I ask.

"She already has. Left just a minute ago, with Dour Mike. If everything goes well, she should be back shortly," says Whip.

The next fifteen minutes are excruciating. Even though I don't want to be her friend, I don't want anything bad to happen to her. We have no idea the kind of security they have, and what could happen to Nunya if she gets captured. And Nunya's smart enough to not risk contacting the ship while she's being watched, so we just have to wait. After about twenty minutes, a light on Knob's console flashes.

"Looks like she's back. Whip, can you go check on her?" says Knob

"Yeah, I'll go do that," says Whip, throwing me a disapproving glance.

After a couple more minutes of waiting, God I hate waiting, Whip comes back to the bridge.

"Did everything go okay?" asks Knob.

"As good as it could have. Nunya was able to drop off Dour Mike, and they didn't even really look at her or anything. Even though security is tight, I guess so much stuff gets shipped through here that it was easy for her to just blend in," says Whip.

"And no one noticed that she'd been crying?" asked Knob.

"Oh, they did. They just said 'It must be your first day. Everyone cries on their first day. You'll be fine.'" says Whip.

"Damn. Well, then, maybe it worked in our favor that Dick was being an asshole. Good work, Dick," says Knob.

I don't respond to him. I do, however, watch as he brings up Dour Mike's feed on one of the monitors. We can see and hear everything that Dour Mike sees and hears. It's kind of boring watching him get loaded into a crate, at least until I see what else he's been loaded in with. It's a container filled with many smaller boxes, but in one corner is a very, very nice-looking toaster oven.

"Shit," I say.

"What, what is it, Dick? Is Dour Mike in trouble?" asks Knob.

"Not yet, but he might be."

"Why, what's going on?"

"Well, that's about the sexiest toaster oven I've ever seen, and I imagine Dour Mike is thinking the same thing. The question is, is

189

he going to try to fuck it, and if so, is he going to damage it. I'd think that would draw all kinds of questions if something that was perfectly fine when it was shipped was suddenly destroyed before it arrived," I say.

"Shit," says Knob. "Do you think he can keep it in his pants? Or inside his shell, or whatever?"

"I really don't know. To make things worse, we don't have a way of telling him not to. He's just gonna have to make the decision on his own," I say.

That's when Dour Mike starts wheeling over to the toaster oven. Knob, Whip and I gasp in concern, worried that all our carefully laid plans could fall apart just because of a horny robot. We watch in horror as he goes right up to it, opens the door, then… very slowly closes it. Dour Mike pauses for a moment, shakes his head a little, then wheels backward into the corner he started out in. He then looks down at his hands and gives a trembling thumbs-up to us.

"Holy fucking shit, that was close," says Knob.

"Good for Dour Mike for having some self-control. Remind me to buy him the most expensive toaster oven in the galaxy, and throw in an extended warranty for it," I say.

A few minutes later, a blip shows up on another screen.

"What's that?" I ask.

"It's Dour Mike. I've locked onto his signal, and it seems the shipping container is finally on its way," says Knob. "We need to get ahead of the shipping container though, so when we enter Alphatraz's star-space, we don't appear to be following it. It'd kinda give us away."

"Yeah, that's smart," I admit.

Knob gets the ship pointed at one of the nearby space assholes, taps on his console to make sure the portal's destination is set to Alphatraz, and we slowly float through it.

43

When we arrive, not too far from Alphatraz, things seem like they're just business as usual. The security ship next to the portal doesn't seem to take notice of us. We fly slowly toward Alphatraz, trying to stay close enough to the planet that we can see it, but not close enough that someone becomes suspicious. After about ten minutes, the blip reappears on the monitor.

"The shipping container is here. Everything seems to be going okay, for now," says Knob.

"Wait, why did you have to phrase it that way? Can't everything just go okay the whole way through?" I say.

"Well, if we're heading down to the planet ourselves, I'm sure it'll get real interesting, real quick. We aren't exactly subtle," says Knob.

"Yeah, I suppose you're right. Expect the worst and all that," I say.

Watching the shipping container make its way down to the planet is a total snoozefest. It takes about twenty minutes from when the shippy ship showed up from the space asshole to it touching down on Alphatraz. We wait another thirty minutes before someone opens the ship and starts unloading it, and another fifteen before Dour Mike is instructed to go to a small office building.

When he gets there, a few people look him up and down as he wheels into the room. Thankfully, we're able to see and hear everything Dour Mike does.

"Why were you shipped here?" asks a middle-aged man who is slightly balding, and slightly pudgy, wearing a dark orange tie and standard issue white business shirt.

"I'm a standard maintenance robot. I wasn't told why I was sent here," says Dour Mike.

"We don't have you in the system," says the man, still looking Dour Mike up and down.

"Apologies, but I cannot speak to the reason why I am here, as I wasn't provided that information."

"Who was your previous owner?" asks the man.

"I cannot remember, as my memory seems to have been wiped before I was sent here. The first thing I remember is

191

powering on inside of the shipping container I was found in," says Dour Mike.

"Very odd. Well, we will just ship you back, along with the other cargo that mistakenly ends up here."

"Do you not have need of a maintenance robot?" asks Dour Mike.

"Of course we do, but since you aren't in our system, we cannot keep you. Protocol," says the man.

"Understandable. However, since I don't know who I belong to, or where I came from, I am in need of a job. I would like to request a job with you."

"A job?"

"Yes. I am apparently currently unemployed, and in need of a purpose. All robots have a purpose. I'm sure you will agree," says Dour Mike.

"Well, yes, I suppose so," says the man.

"And from the appearance of your office, you could use someone like me. I'm fully capable of moving office equipment, emptying trash receptacles, making coffee and tea, and cleaning bathrooms. Do you already have a maintenance robot that handles all of that work?"

"No. We have to do that ourselves."

"Then it seems like this is both of our lucky days, as you could use the help, and I could use a job."

The man stares at Dour Mike for several minutes, thinking about the implications of keeping him. The four other office workers glance over at Dour Mike off and on, and I can tell by their body language that they would all like to keep Dour Mike.

"Well, you'll need to prove yourself capable of helping. First, make us each a coffee based on how we like it, then go clean the restroom. Once you've done that, empty the garbage cans. If you can do all of that in the next fifteen minutes, and do it correctly, then you can have a job," says the man.

"At your service," says Dour Mike.

Instead of asking each of the office workers their coffee orders, he zips back and forth, looking at them closely, then quickly makes his way over to the coffee station. After a few minutes, he returns holding a tray, with five different steaming hot beverages on it. He carefully sets them down on each person's desk. Four of the five office workers smile, take sips, and admit that Dour Mike guessed their order correctly. The fifth one, however, seems nonplussed.

192

A middle-aged woman with red tousled hair and deep bags under her eyes speaks to Dour Mike, "you've gotten my order wrong."

"Respectfully, madam, I have not," responds Dour Mike.

She takes a sip from the cup. At first, she's stunned and blurts "this is delicious. But it isn't what I normally drink."

"No, madam, it is not. Your usual beverage of choice is coffee with two sugar cubes, but I made you an herbal tea instead. I can tell that the coffee has been affecting your ability to sleep. This late in the day, I recommend avoiding caffeine so that you can get a good night's sleep. I also picked out a tea for you that I thought you would enjoy based on what I could surmise of your personal tastes."

She takes a few more sips and eventually the frown turns into a smile.

"Good, well I'm off to clean the restroom," says Dour Mike.

We watch on the monitors as he zips through cleaning the restroom until it's spotless, collects up all the garbage bags and takes them to a large container just outside the building, then comes back inside and sterilizes his robot hands. It takes him nearly the full fifteen minutes to complete his tasks, with only three seconds to spare. He wheels up to the man he first spoke to.

"I have completed the tasks. May I have a job?" asks Dour Mike.

"On one condition, can you explain what your large phallic protrusion is?" says the man.

"Oh, this?" says Dour Mike, pointing to the dick shaped transmitter. "It's merely my recharger coupling. My battery life is several days, but I do require recharging. Consider electricity my payment for services rendered."

"Hmm, well then, you have met expectations. Since your duties are done for the moment, feel free to plug yourself into the power coupling in the supply closet. Your regular schedule will be to check every hour on the hour if anything needs to be taken care of. During times you are not needed, feel free to remain in the supply closet. Do not speak to employees unless spoken to, as we are very busy people. Understood?" says the man.

"Absolutely, sir."

We watch as Dour Mike wheels his way into the supply closet, closing the door behind him, and plunging himself into darkness. His infrared sensors come to life, and everything appears in black and white. He finds the power coupling and plugs his dick into it.

After a few seconds we hear him whisper, "they bought it, and more good news, I can access the entire security system from here, as they didn't isolate the security power grid from the main power grid."

Knob and I look at each other and smile then remember we hate each other and look back at the monitor.

A few minutes go by, and suddenly the receiver that Montgomery Israel gave us lights up. On one of the screens we see dozens of files downloading, with names like 'building1schematic', 'securitygrid15layout', and 'unicornbdsmpornvideo'. Apparently, Dour Mike is sending us everything they have in the system, whether we need it or not. Knob starts to reach out his finger to open the 'unicornbdsmpornvideo' file, but I slap his hand away.

"I really, really don't need that shit stuck in my head right now. Comprende?" I say.

"Yeah, sure," says Knob, clearly disappointed.

After about fifteen minutes the downloading is finished.

"Now we just need Nunya to look over the data," says Whip. "I'll have her review it in the conference room."

"Probably a good idea," says Knob.

It feels like it takes forever for Nunya and Whip to come up with a plan. I hate not being involved, but I hate the tension even more. I don't know why everything has to devolve into High School bullshit all the time, and why we can't just not fuck each other over. I guess people never really do evolve. We're all just slaves to our bodies, doing whatever idiotic thing it tells us to do. I also want to point out how many times 'volve' makes an appearance in this paragraph. You're welcome.

After about thirty of the most painfully irritating minutes of my life, Whip comes back with Nunya just behind him. I look over at her, but she's avoiding making eye contact with me.

"We've got a plan," starts Whip. "We're going to upload some maps and software to our PSDs, that way if all but one of us is out of commission, the last person left can still complete the mission. We know exactly where they're keeping him, which is in a high security bunker underground. There's a system of tunnels we'll need to sneak through, laid out like a labyrinth, set up with various booby traps and checkpoints."

"How about instead of going through the tunnels we just dig our way to him?" I ask.

"There's both vibration sensors and mines buried underground. Sure, you might be able to survive the mines, but they'll know we're coming, and we don't know what additional countermeasures they have," says Nunya.

"Well, the booby traps should be easy, but what's your plan for the checkpoints?" I ask

"We do the old prisoner transfer trick. We knock out a few guards, steal their uniforms, and Nunya will hack in and add us to the list of employees. Should be easy," says Whip.

"So, we're doing a dungeon crawl? Awesome!" I say.

"I mean, I guess you could think about it like that," says Whip.

"I've always wanted to do a dungeon crawl! A dungeon crawl within a prison break! Best day ever!" I say. Then I remember Nunya's betrayal and my mood quickly changes. I'm back to being dismal again. I wonder how long I'll feel this way, if time will make it better, or if I'll just have to keep distracting myself with increasingly insane missions to make the hurt go away. I guess it's good to know that my soul hasn't been completely destroyed, that I can have a brief moment of happiness.

44

"So where do we start?" I ask.

"That's the one thing we haven't figured out yet. We don't know what our entry point is. We need to shut down security in whatever area we land in, otherwise this whole thing may be over before it starts," says Whip.

"Do you think maybe Dour Mike already worked that out for us?" I ask.

"Oh, shit, yeah, maybe," says Nunya.

She brings up the display we were using to watch Dour Mike, and the little guy has typed out a message: "I figured it would take you guys a while to come up with a plan, so I set the five-minute window, where I'll be able to loop the security feeds, for a few hours from now. Planet time 08:00 PM is when you should fly down here. Come to the location I'm at to collect me. Everyone will have gone home for the evening."

"Sounds like we have our entry plan," says Knob.

Thankfully, there's enough time to use the bathroom, get changed, and get all my equipment together. I spend about half an hour doing last minute things, both to make sure I'm 100% ready for the mission, and to avoid Nunya. I realize I'm still hyper fixated on things with her, when I really need to get my head in the game. If I don't, it could get us caught, or worse.

About five minutes before go time, I make my way back to the bridge. Everyone's there, looking visibly concerned. I just act like I don't have a care in the world.

"Do we think one of us should stay behind with the ship?" asks Knob.

"My guess is we're gonna need all of our firepower on the ground," I say. "And which one of us would stay, anyway? We need Whip and Nunya for their intellect and abilities. You and I are the only two in the group who are kind of redundant, and we both have an easy to exploit weakness that the other one doesn't. The only way we both get taken out by the same thing is if a supervillain makes a super-suit with magical leather straps as weapons. What would they call him? Dr. Strappy? Lasso-man? The Noodler?"

"How about 'The Leatherman'?" asks Whip.

"Kinky. I like it," I reply. "So, unless that happens, we should be able to protect each other."

"What about Dour Mike?" asks Knob.

"Who was it that saved the day when the heroes had to slide down a garbage chute, and were nearly crushed to death? That'd be R2-D2. We'll need Dour Mike to tap into computer ports and disable security and things like that."

"Why do you keep bringing up the R2-D2 robot thing? And I thought Nunya can hack into anything," says Knob.

"I can, but I still need a way to interface with the system. There are outlets everywhere that Dour Mike can hack into, but there's not always terminal screens for me to access. Our best bet is to have Dour Mike with us," says Nunya.

"Shit. I just don't like leaving my ship parked in a strange neighborhood," says Knob.

"Well, it really isn't your ship, it's mine. Yours is being repaired back at Nunya's parent's ship shop. I paid for the damn thing. So, if it gets stolen, it's affecting my insurance, not yours," I say.

"True, but of the five of us on our team, two can't breathe in outer space. We still need to be able to leave Alphatraz once all of this is over, and we'll need to leave on a ship," says Knob.

"Actually, I had my lungs replaced as well, so I can probably survive in deep space," says Whip.

"You aren't impervious to temperatures though, like Dick and I are. The part of you that's still human will freeze and die, including your brain," says Knob.

"Oh, yeah, I forgot about that," says Whip.

"Anyway, the point is we go together, and we stay together. If anyone not named Knob isn't okay with that, tell me now," I say.

Both Nunya and Whip remain silent.

"Okay. Are we ready then?" I ask.

Nods.

Knob starts tapping away at the ship's console, and we begin our descent to planet Alphatraz.

45

As we fly down to Alphatraz, I stare out the glass of the cockpit, trying my best to memorize the layout of all the buildings below. I know we'll have access to maps on our PSDs, but sometimes technology fails and good old thinkery is required. It also helps distract me from everything else going on. I get anxious on missions, just like the next person, and this particular mission is going to lead to a terrible outcome, whether we fail or succeed. I'm basically kissing away my future to save Tiffany, because I'll be branded as a criminal once word gets out.

I wonder if I'll start doing criminal things after this, since I'll be known as one. Maybe it'll be fun. It always seemed like The Joker was having a good time when he went on one of his crime sprees. There's also a spectrum of criminality, where on the lower end you have Han Solo, who was a smuggler, but he still kind of did the right thing. Then on the other end you have The Emperor, who was a fascist monster who caused millions of deaths just so he could maintain control over the galaxy. Someone who didn't care about the people he governed and was only in it for himself.

Maybe being a criminal isn't for me. Maybe I'll just hole up somewhere, live off the fat of the land and all that. I could be a farmer. Till the soil, plant my seeds. That sounded a lot more sexual than I intended, but I kind of like that about me.

It doesn't take long to touch down. Thankfully, Knob is smart enough to park the ship in a ship parking lot so that it won't seem conspicuous or out of place. I follow the rest of the group out of the side bay door, bringing up the rear.

Nunya takes point, waving her hand for us to follow. For whatever reason I instinctually duck down, as we try to move quickly toward the building that Dour Mike is hiding in. I feel like if someone were to see our group right now they'd think we're up to no good, even though we're actually trying not to be spotted. Oh well, hopefully we don't miss our stealth checks.

As we reach the door to the office building Dour Mike is hiding out in, it makes a clicking and whirring sound. The door opens slightly. Nunya carefully pulls the door open and steps in, followed by the rest of us. Just as I step inside, Dour Mike comes wheeling in from the broom closet.

"Glad you got my message. Were you able to devise a plan based on the information I was able to send?" asks Dour Mike.

"We have most of a plan. Some will need to be improvised. But thanks to you, we were able to determine exactly where they're keeping Israel, and how to get there," says Nunya.

"Happy to be of service," says Dour Mike.

"Also, good job keeping your dick out of the toaster oven in the cargo ship. Proud of you, little buddy," I say. "There have been times where I wish I had that level of self-control when it comes to the ladies."

"It was possibly the most difficult thing I've ever done. Or have not done. I just humbly ask for one exactly like it once the mission is over," says Dour Mike.

"I tell you what, if we all survive this, I'll buy you three," I say.

"Triplets? Yippee!!!"

"This is all fine and good, but can we hurry it up a little? We're on a timetable," says Whip.

"Oh, shit, right," I say.

Nunya slips back out the door, looking at us expectantly. We quietly exit the office building, and again, I bring up the rear, making sure that someone is looking out for our backs. Nunya then turns around to address the group while we're following her. Over her shoulder, she says, "The entrance to the tunnel is about two klicks from here. It'll take us a little while to get there without being seen. Do your best to not draw attention. We'll need to stop along the way and get guard outfits."

"Wait, how far is a klick?" I ask.

"A klick is a kilometer," whispers Nunya.

I pause and think for a moment.

"How far is a kilometer?" I ask.

"Wait, what?"

"How far is a kilometer?"

"A little over half a mile," says Nunya.

"Then why didn't you say the entrance to the tunnel was about a mile away?" I ask.

"Dick, no one uses the Imperial system anymore!"

"They should, it's superior," I say.

"What? No, it isn't! The metric system is way more precise and easier to calculate," says Nunya.

"Not if you don't have a digital device to calculate measurements. Trying to calculate decimals when dividing things is a pain in the ass."

"Well, it's not like fractions are easy."

"They're way easier if you're trying to make a chair, or table, or build a house. You can do all the figuring out in your head."

"Dick, this really is the worst time you could pick for this argument. Can you just wait until after the mission to go down the measurement rabbit hole?" says Nunya.

"Yeah, fine, whatever," I mumble.

I know what you're thinking, I'm engaging in banter with Nunya, so maybe things will eventually get better. But since you're reading this, you should know I made my voice extra grumbly and mean so she knew that I still hated her. It's hard to convey that to a reader without specifically telling you.

Anyway, Nunya pulls out her PSD and starts typing away at it. She looks back at the group and says, "we're close to a checkpoint. We should be able to knock out the guards and take their uniforms. We need to be super quiet when we do this, and don't spill any blood. If the uniforms are caked with entrails, we won't be able to use them. Also, these guards probably have families who will miss them if they're dead, so don't kill them. Understood?"

"Understood," says Knob, Whip, and Dour Mike. I just shrug at her.

We continue sneaking between buildings, ducking under windows, avoiding security cameras, and generally just being rogues. Peeking around the corner of a tall brick building, we can now see the checkpoint. It's little more than a shack with windows. Inside are two guards, both looking like your average security mall cops. It's a bit disappointing, as there's nothing that would stop a vehicle or person from walking right by the checkpoint.

Using my super-vision, I see a big round button on the console in the shack. I also see the two guards watching a monitor together, but I can't tell what they're seeing. Unfortunately, I get a glimpse of their most recent meals moving through their stomach. Blech. The good news is there isn't anyone else in the general vicinity, just the two guards.

"Okay, we need to distract the guards somehow so we can knock them out," says Nunya.

The wheels inside my brain start turning. I tap Dour Mike on the shoulder and whisper into his ear. Or at least the sensor that lets him hear things. He looks up and smiles at me once he's heard the plan, then shakes his head in agreement.

"Don't worry, Dour Mike and I have this," I say.

"Wait, Dick, don't you think you should share the plan with the rest of us?" says Nunya.

"Nope."

As Dour Mike wheels around the corner toward the shack, I use my spy watch's laser to burn through the glass, disabling the large button inside. Next, I use the laser to melt the triggers on the two laser rifles slung up on the wall inside the shack. Just as I finish, Dour Mike reaches the shack. He's far enough away at the moment that we can't hear what he's saying, but he flails his arms around then points in our general direction.

"You guys might want to back up around the corner and get ready," I say.

Knob, Nunya, and Whip all pull back, giving ample room for an ambush. We don't have to wait long before Dour Mike comes peeling around the corner, blowing past us, deeper into the alley. A few seconds later the guards arrive with their blasters at-the-ready.

"Everyone put your hands up!" yells one of the guards, their blasters trained on us.

I nonchalantly walk over to them as they try to use their rifles on me. One of the two guards actually makes quiet pew-pew noises with his blaster as he tries firing, to no avail. The two confused guards freeze, not knowing what to do. I reach out and flick both of them on the forehead, knocking them unconscious.

"Wow, that uh, actually worked," said Knob. "Sorry I doubted you."

"I didn't doubt you, Dick," says Whip.

Nunya stays quiet.

"So yeah, the guard outfits will only fit Whip and Nunya, so you'll be the guards, and Knob and I will be your prisoners," I say.

"What about Dour Mike?" asks Knob.

"He can just be a robot. No one really worries about robots," I say.

"It's true. I can go just about anywhere because nobody suspects a robot. Most people just ignore us, assuming we're programmed to do something important that they don't really care about. I may as well be wallpaper for all the notice I receive," says Dour Mike.

We spend the next minute or so removing the guard uniforms, then Whip and Nunya put the guard clothes over the top of their mission outfits. Thankfully, both guards looked like they'd spent their fair share of time at Krispy Kreme (not a sponsor), so there was extra room to be filled anyway.

"What do we do with them?" asks Whip, pointing down to the guards who are still unconscious and are now stripped down to their skivvies.

"Well, do we have some rope?" I ask.

"Yeah, I always bring rope on every mission. Never know when you'll need it," says Nunya.

"Is it hempen rope?" I ask.

"Nope, I'm pretty sure it's just nylon. Why does it matter?" asks Nunya.

"Oh, no reason," I say. "Let's do a little Weekend at Bernie's trick, and make it look like the guards are conscious."

"Weekend at Bernie's?" questions Nunya.

"Yeah, it's a movie from Earth Uno. One of the finest! It's a story about a guy who's staying at his boss's beach mansion, when his boss dies. So, he and his friend make it look like the corpse is still alive using elaborate pulley systems," I say.

"Is it a horror movie?" asks Whip.

"No, it's a comedy," I say.

"A comedy? Dick, that's a pretty weird premise," says Knob.

"It won like 25 Academy Awards or something," I say. "Seriously, you guys should check it out."

"Hard pass," says Nunya. "But I think your plan makes sense. You can really only see the guards' heads when they're seated in the shack. If someone came up and inspected the shack closely, then sure. But it doesn't really look like a place vehicles and pedestrians must stop at; it just looks like they're here to alert everyone else if something looks suspicious. My guess is most people will just drive past without even giving it a look."

"Exactly," I say.

We spend the next few minutes tying up the guards, making sure that they're positioned as normally as possible in the shack. We also make sure that they can't let themselves free or signal anyone, which should buy us some time. Eventually, whoever has the next shift in the shack will find them, but hopefully that won't be for several more hours.

46

Nunya picks up some handcuffs kept in the guard station and tries to put them around Knob's and my wrists. It's difficult, because both of our arms are so huge, but eventually she's able to get them around us. The good news is even though they're actually secured, both Knob and I can break through them because they have no magical properties and aren't made of leather.

Man, that still seems dumb to me that Knob's weakness is leather. I mean, what happens if he gets into a fight with a cow? Does it just trample him and he's dead? And what happens if he has to use a saddle, or a guitar strap? It sure seems like a made-up weakness to me.

Anyway, we walk down the streets, trying to blend in with everything, so that when people see us passing by, they think we're just a prison transfer instead of some jabronies sneaking around. We actually do pass by a few guard stations on the way to the tunnel, and the guards inside look up briefly then go back to what they were doing. They don't care enough to stop us and ask where we're headed, who we are, or anything else.

After about ten minutes of walking, we finally reach the entrance of the tunnel. Two guards stand outside the tunnel, rifles slung over their shoulders at the ready. They notice us as soon as we're within about a hundred feet, and they aim their rifles directly at us as we approach. It says something that the security seems quite lax everywhere else, but here, the guards are acutely aware of everything that's going on.

"Halt! Who are you, and what are your orders?" asks one of the guards.

"Prisoner transfer to cell block D. Two high profile and dangerous prisoners, Dick Blowhard and Knob Johnson," says Nunya. "We need to get them underground as quickly as possible to minimize the chances of them breaking out."

"You cannot pass without the proper documentation. Let me look at my PSD to verify the transfer," says the guard who spoke.

"They won't show up on your PSD, as they've been working with some hackers recently who we're concerned are monitoring things on Alphatraz. We don't want to alert them to Blowhard and Johnson's location. I do, however, have a Presidential override

203

code that allows us unfettered access to all facilities. I'll beam that to your PSD now," says Nunya.

She slowly pulls out her PSD to avoid startling the guards, then starts tapping on the screen. After a few seconds the guard who'd been doing the speaking looks down at his PSD.

"Shit. Looks like they're legit. I've never seen this high level of security access before," says the guard to his buddy. They both seem to relax a bit, their shoulders dropping slightly, and they take their hands off their rifles. "How did you even get this kind of access?"

"Due to the dangerous nature of these individuals, the President himself has been involved with making sure they've been secured and transferred properly, as both were close personal friends of the President until recently," says Nunya.

"Well, wait, he's *that* Dick Blowhard? The guy all over the TV right now?" asks the second guard.

"Yeah, that's me," I say.

"I guess now would be a bad time to ask for an autograph, huh?" says the second guard.

"I'm heading into an underground bunker to spend the rest of my life as a prisoner, and you want my autograph? Yeah, maybe your timing isn't the best," I say. "Not only that, but my hands are bound. I'll tell you what, I'll sign anything you want if you let me out of these handcuffs."

"Ha! Nice try, but I don't think so," says the second guard. "I was hand-picked for this guard station because I don't fall for things like that."

"Yeah, you certainly seem like the brains of the operation," I say.

Nunya turns to me and glares, "prisoner, you're going to shut your mouth, or I'll shut it for you."

"Yeah, fine, sure," I mumble.

"So, what did they do?" asks the second guard.

"We aren't allowed to say. Need-to-know basis," says Nunya.

"Yeah, that tracks," says the first guard. "Anyway, you're free to go. I've alerted the other guards down the way that you're coming, so it'll be smooth sailing until you reach processing. Just make sure not to get too close to either side of the tunnel, as you'll set off the security measures inside. Stay in the middle and you'll be fine."

"Good to know," says Nunya.

"Fidete, sed verificate," says the first guard.

Nunya stands there looking puzzled for a second, but eventually responds "Fidete, sed verificate" back.

The first guard looks her up and down and his demeanor changes. He starts to move his hand back to his rifle, but in a flash, Whip punches the first guard, knocking him out, then the second guard, all before I can blink.

"Wait, what the hell was that?" I ask.

"He was going for his gun," says Whip.

"Yeah, I get that, but why was he suddenly going for his gun, since we had the Presidential access code?" I ask.

"Because either my Latin is terrible, or they have a two-part passphrase they use with each other to know the person they're talking to is legit. It's an analog way of improving security, and apparently it works, because we were just made," says Nunya.

"Well, how do we find out what the other half of the phrase is? Also, why aren't alarms going off after knocking out the guards?" I ask.

"To answer your second question, I don't know. I would think they'd have cameras and would alert everyone to our presence after attacking the guards. So, either they don't have cameras in this area, they aren't paying attention to them, or they know we're here, and they're just waiting for us to go down the tunnel where they think they can trap us. For your first question, I'm working on it," says Nunya.

She taps furiously on her PSD. After a few seconds she looks up at me. "The first phrase that the guard said meant 'trust, but verify' in Latin, and apparently, I should have responded 'excellentiam securitatis', which means 'excellence in security'."

"Well, at least we know for the next guards we come across, if they aren't shooting at us," I say.

"Let's assume they will," says Nunya. "We go in slow, keep an eye out, and Knob and Dick, don't hesitate to break your handcuffs and join the fight if need be."

"Roger," says Knob.

Nunya takes point again, Knob, Dour Mike and Whip just behind her, and me in back. As we move into the entrance of the tunnel, I spot a few cameras overhead. I also notice their little red lights aren't illuminated. That's weird. Maybe we're getting help from someone. Could be Israel, since he's already shown he can get messages out of Alphatraz and has some evil haxor skills. No one else knows we're down here, at least no one that would be able to help.

We do our best to stay toward the middle of the tunnel as the guard suggested. After the first hundred feet, we reach an unguarded set of metal bars reaching all the way to the ceiling. It must be remotely controlled from the inside, because we look around in the immediate area and can't find any controls. The bars glow a soft purple color. I motion to Nunya to undo my handcuffs, which she does. I reach out to touch the bars and my hands start burning immediately.

"Argh!" I blurt out.

"Shhhh!" whispers Nunya, very loudly.

"Sorry, but it's imbued with some kind of magic. I won't be able to break through," I whisper loudly back.

"You really shouldn't have tried anyway. I'm sure bending metal will make a lot of noise," says Nunya.

"So, what do you suggest, Mrs. Smarter-than-everyone-else?" I say sarcastically.

"We need a way to break through that's quiet. Do any of you have anything that could do that?"

We all stand there and think for a moment.

"I have laser beam eyes, but it'll probably make a high-pitched noise if I use them," says Whip.

"I could make sandwiches at it," says Knob.

"What?" asks Nunya.

"Sandwiches. The only equipment I still have is the instant food making machine, since I had to give up The Swiss Army Knife to save Dick."

"Now's not the time to be whining about your lack of Christmas gifts, Knob," says Whip.

"Oh, shit, I actually have something!" I say. I dig into my utility belt and pull out several vials. "Okay guys, stand back, you don't want to get any of this on you."

I carefully open the vials one at a time, pouring the contents onto the metal bars. They start to sizzle and smoke as the liquid melts through them. I nod my head over to Knob, who comes over and pulls on the bars, quietly removing them one at a time, until we have a hole that all of us can comfortably walk through.

"I'm guessing that was acid?" asks Nunya.

"Yeah, it came with the utility belt," I say.

"Dick, can you lift me over the hole? I don't want to get any acid on my wheel," says Dour Mike.

"Yeah, no problem, buddy," I say, lifting him up and over. Thankfully, although touching the bars briefly hurt, they didn't cause any real damage to my hands.

We continue down the tunnel, and I fumble to get the handcuffs back on, but eventually do. After another couple hundred feet we reach a corner, where the tunnel heads to the left. Nunya peeks around it, then turns to the group.

"There are two more guards, about fifty feet in, and both are wearing mech suits. Looks like they have guided missiles, laser beams, the whole thing," says Nunya.

"Are they wearing helmets or masks," I ask.

"They're wearing helmets that cover the top of their heads," says Nunya.

"Okay, I guess what I'm asking is if they have anything covering their mouths?"

"No."

"Okay, good. I think I have a solution," I say.

Digging into my utility belt again, I pull out a few small green balls. Each ball has a tiny button on them that I push, then as quickly as possible I huck them around the corner. After a few seconds we hear the guards hacking and coughing, then two dull thud sounds.

"Knockout gas?" asks Whip.

"Knockout gas," I respond.

We carefully make our way around the corner, just in case there's some other defenses we've missed, but all that we see are the two guards, unconscious, their mechs lying lifelessly on the ground.

"Good work," says Knob.

I just smile and nod at him.

Another hundred feet later and we reach a corner that heads to the right. Nunya peeks around the corner again, then turns back to us.

"Three automated machine gun turrets, unmanned, and my guess is they're seeking any sort of movement," says Nunya.

"Like in the movie Aliens?" I ask.

"Yeah, exactly like that," says Nunya.

"Wait, how the hell are guards supposed to come down here when there are unmanned machine gun turrets set to shoot anything that moves?" asks Whip.

"How the hell should I know? I don't work here," says Nunya.

"Maybe the guard badges let them pass safely, or maybe they radio to the other guards to disable them temporarily as they pass," says Knob.

"Well, no one's gonna turn them off for us if they don't think our voices are guard voices, and I don't think we want to risk the badge thing," says Nunya.

"Why not?" asks Knob. "I could just carry a badge, go around the corner, and if the guns go off, I'll be fine, and we'll know."

"Because, moron, the guns will be super loud and alert the guards we're here," says Nunya.

"Fine. But you don't have to call me a moron," says Knob.

"Perks of the job," says Nunya. She looks at Dour Mike, Whip and me expectantly.

"I could shoot them with my missile fingers, or again, I could use my eye beams, but they'll make some noise," says Whip.

"I'm less than helpful in this case, as I have no weapons, and without a panel for me to plug into I can't turn them off remotely," says Dour Mike.

I think for a moment.

"Yeah, I think I've got this one," I say.

I pull out three Dickarangs, slowly look around the corner, then throw them as hard as I can. Each one hits a sensor cluster on top of a turret, rendering all three useless.

Nunya shakes her head at me in disgust.

"What?" I ask.

"It's just super convenient that you happened to have exactly what we needed, when we needed it, to defeat the last three security measures," says Nunya.

"Yeah, pretty lucky, huh?" I say.

"It just seems like it was more than a coincidence. Like it was planned that way. Like breaking into Alphatraz is a bit too easy for us, and you're constantly getting to save the day," says Nunya.

"Wait, are you implying that I'm the one behind all of this?" I say, incredulously.

"It's just a little too convenient. Nothing ever goes this well," says Nunya.

"Nunya, you know me. When have I had the time to plan something like this out? And why would I? I don't want to break Israel out, and I certainly don't want my name tarnished, which is going to happen when we do break him out. What possible reason could I have for orchestrating all of this? I'm not even clever enough to come up with all of this," I say.

She stares at me hard, harder than I've ever seen her stare.

"It just seems too fucking easy for you. I hate that. It's some Pollyanna/Mary Sue bullshit," says Nunya.

"Are you talking about my tattoo of my mother's name?" I ask.

"What? No, I'm not talking about your fucking Mary Sue tattoo. A Mary Sue is a fictional character that's too powerful, and that all the other characters love, and nothing bad ever happens to them.

208

It's a trope used by writers who only write stories of personal wish fulfillment. Heroes are defined by the trials that they go through, the mud they crawl through. The horrible things they have to deal with. And so far, on this part of the mission, you haven't had to deal with much. Your memoir readers are going to hate this part," says Nunya.

"Hey, I can't help that I'm awesome, and I won't apologize for it. Also, fuck you Nunya, I've recently had my heart ripped out of my chest and was betrayed by the person I care about most in the universe, which is you. Yeah, maybe there isn't a literal hole in my chest where my heart used to be, but it sure fucking feels like it," I say.

Nunya gets real quiet and tears form at the corner of her eyes.

"Dick, I'm sorry. I fucked up. I already apologized. I don't know what else you want me to do," says Nunya.

"I want you to unfuck her. I want you to have never had sex with Nord. I want to be with her. I'm in love with her, and I won't ever get to be with her now. And I want you to be my best friend, who thinks the best of me, and doesn't fuck me over because you think the worst of me. You assumed I'd be a horrible friend to you, and you didn't give me the benefit of the doubt. Didn't give me a chance. After all the changes I've made to myself just so you'd be my friend, it didn't matter, you still see me as a piece of shit. I'm not a piece of shit, Nunya. I'm not someone you flush down the toilet. You're my best fucking friend, now start fucking acting like it!"

It takes a moment for Nunya to respond. "You're right. And I will. I won't automatically assume you're going to do something horrible. I'll give you the benefit of the doubt. You've earned that a long time ago. I should have trusted you. And I'm sorry."

I swallow hard. "We'll have to figure our shit out after all of this is said and done. But maybe I'll give you a chance to earn back our friendship. Things won't be the same between us, but you have the smallest chance right now. Don't fuck it up."

Nunya nods in understanding.

47

"Are we sure you actually disabled the sentry guns?" asks Knob.

"Like, a hundred percent?" I say.

"Preferably," says Knob.

"No. But you could walk around the corner and find out," I say.

"Why me?" asks Knob.

"Because the only weakness you have is leather, and as far as I know, leather bullets wouldn't do much damage. If they have magic bullets, which is more likely, I'm fucked. Whip is part human still, so theoretically he could die if he's shot, and we aren't going to risk either Nunya or Dour Mike," I say.

"So, it's me by default. Fine, I'll do it. Just wait here," says Knob.

He walks around the corner and the sentry guns start firing. Within seconds, Knob closes the distance to the guns, smashes them to bits, then comes back around the corner, smiling.

"I took care of it," says Knob.

"Yeah, that's great and all, but we've definitely been made," says Nunya.

"We need to proceed now like they know we're here, because they know we're here," says Whip.

"Well, what did you expect me to do?" says Knob, clearly annoyed.

"Exactly what you did. Not blaming you, Knob. It's just how things worked out," I say.

"Fine," says Knob, trying his best to calm down.

Nunya waves us to follow her around the corner, and we get back into formation, making our way toward the sentry guns.

"Oh, everyone, I see a security port I can plug into!" says Dour Mike.

He wheels ahead of us and sticks his large dick-like protrusion into the socket of a panel just a few feet behind the sentries. The electronic erection lights up when Dour Mike plugs it in and starts making whirring and clicking sounds.

"So, a silent alarm was tripped, which I've now shut off, and I've put out a notice that it was just a false alarm, and that everything is okay. I'm not sure if security is buying it though. I'm able to tap into a security camera not far from here, and the two guards at the station have their guns ready," says Dour Mike.

"Are they like the previous guards we dealt with?" I ask.

"Oh my, no. They're both large-chested beauties. In fact, they might not be security guards at all. Their uniforms look like they're the sexy version of a security guard uniform, without being real security guard uniforms. Way too tight to be comfortable. Something you'd see on Halloween."

"Sexy security guards? I got this!" I say.

"What do you mean, Dick?" asks Nunya.

"I'll sneak up to them and seduce them, so that you all can sneak right by," I say.

"Wait, why can't I do that?" asks Knob.

"Because I'm better at it than you are," I reply.

"Well, why not me? I'm even better at it than you are, Dick," says Nunya.

"Because I'm redundant. You already have Knob in case things get messy, but there's only one of you. One super-hacker. One leader. If you seduce them, our party loses a lot. If I seduce them, you're only down some firepower," I say.

"And you get your dick wet," says Nunya.

"Yeah, well, I think after all the bullshit that's gone down recently, I deserve it. Don't you?" I say.

"Sure, Dick. Alright, well, go fuck them, I guess," says Nunya.

"Cool. Hey, Dour Mike, can you loop the feed on the camera so that if someone else is looking at the next guard station, they'll just see the guards there?" I ask.

"Happy to oblige, sir," says Dour Mike. "It is done."

"Thanks," I say, as I take off all my clothes. I keep my watch on me just in case I need it in a pinch, but otherwise I'm naked as the day I was born. "Wish me luck."

"Good luck," says Whip, staring intently at my body.

"Eyes up here," I say to Whip, smirking at him.

"Oh, yeah, right," says Whip.

With that, I slowly walk down the corridor with the rest of the team hanging behind. It's a few hundred feet to the next guard station, and as we approach, it appears to just be a room off to the right side of the tunnel. Metal and glass carved into the rock, and sort of reminds me of the underground offices at Nunya's parent's dealership.

I put my right fist in the air, which is the universal symbol for 'halt', just before we reach the office's entrance. The rest of the gang stops. I peek around the corner and see two of the most beautiful women I've ever seen. Both have rainbow colored skin and hair, just like God did when I met her, shiny and shimmery and flawless. They have the most perfectly curvy bodies I've ever seen, as if Roger Corman and Russ Meyer got together and Weird Scienced two women into existence. Man, having to go through the rest of this horrible nightmare of a mission might end up being worth it.

I very slowly move around the corner to the door, my hands up in the air to signal that I come in peace. Both women quickly raise their guns up at me. I'm not afraid, and all I can do is stare at their bodacious breasts that are stretching their uniforms to the breaking point.

"Stop right there," says one of the two women, in a really sultry and seductive voice.

"Who are you?" asks the other one, sounding just as sexy.

"Who I am doesn't matter. What I'm here for is to treat you ladies to the best time you've ever had," I say.

They both smile at me sexily. "Oh, and how are you gonna do that?" asks the first guard.

"By taking you both, right here, right now, in ways that will blow your mind, and change your lives forever. You'll tell stories of this night until the end of your days, and no one will believe you because it'll be just that good. Tell me, have either of you had fifteen orgasms in a row before?"

They both start to giggle expectantly. "I haven't before, no," says the second guard. "Have you, Ember?"

"No, I haven't, Ember," says the first guard.

"Wait, you ladies are both named Ember? What are the odds? All the women that live on the planet I own are named Ember," I say.

"You own your own planet?" asks Ember number one.

"I certainly do," I say, proudly.

"If I wasn't wet before, I certainly am now," says Ember one.

"Me too. Alright, big boy, show us what you've got," says Ember two.

I move deeper into the office, as Ember one knocks everything off their shared desk, and Ember two rips both of their clothes off. They grab onto my arms, and I let them spin and drop me so that my back is now on the cold desk, and I'm staring up at the ceiling. Ember one climbs atop my engorged and massive meat jackhammer, while Ember two straddles my face. Both, thankfully, are turned away from the entrance to the office, and as Ember two pulls away from my face after her first orgasm, I see the rest of the gang scurry past the office and down the hall.

I grab Ember two's ass and pull her back down over my face, licking her like I'm in a pie eating contest, and my entire life's ambition is to earn a blue ribbon. She screams and struggles to pull away, because the intensity of her sensitivity hasn't died down yet, but I don't relent.

Ember one is really going to town on my love pole, gliding up and down it vigorously, like she's the plunger to some dynamite that won't explode that Wiley Coyote is trying to set off. Her tight lady bits make it really hard to control myself, but if I'm going to distract these guards for any length of time, I really need to keep my supergoo from erupting like Mt. Vesuvius. I start to think of other things like Spaceball, taxes, doing the dishes; pretty much anything to keep my mind off of the pleasure I'm experiencing.

After Ember two's fifth orgasm, I let her pull away from my face. She's gasping for air, and I think I made the poor thing hyperventilate. To give her a bit of a rest, but to keep up the distraction, I slide her ass higher up my face and glide my tongue up and down her tender emergency exit. She writhes sexily on top of me, enjoying the sensation of my mouth on her dirtiest hole. Dirty meaning naughty, because I can tell she keeps that thing clean.

Ember one moans loudly as she thrusts against my utility pole, gyrating her hips in circles as if my dick is a swizzle stick and she's the cocktail. I can feel her riding me like I'm a racehorse, she's the jockey, and it's only a few hundred yards to the finish line. She even starts making neighing noises and kicks the sides of my legs with her feet, as if she's using her spurs to get me to move faster. I oblige, and start thrusting upward at her, lifting her into the air with each thrust, as if I'm a bucking bronco, trying to knock her off. Ember one is obviously an experienced rider, and hangs onto my chest hair for dear life, never falling off my saddle horn.

After a few more seconds of thrusting, I hear Ember one scream, and the familiar feeling of warm wetness pouring down my shaft, onto my stomach and onto the desk. She lost control of herself so thoroughly that she squirted, coating my body in both her love goo and her hot clear fluid. It isn't the first time a woman has had that reaction to me, and I hope it won't be the last.

Ember one lets go of my chest hair as I stop thrusting against her. It takes her a moment to compose herself, then she very slowly and carefully lifts off from my love rocket, nearly having to stand to full height on the desk just to dismount it.

Ember two starts shoving her ass against my face forcefully, and I happily probe her with my tongue. I can tell she's frantically rubbing herself, building toward a climax. She screams, and suddenly it feels like someone dumped a can of warm, flat Mt. Dew on my forehead. Ember two takes a few deep breaths then dismounts my face, making sure to rub her ass against it for good measure, smearing as much goo around as she can.

Ember one and Ember two trade places, Ember two climbing on top of my Empire State Building like King Kong, and Ember one squishing her very messy love hole on my visage. I hear gun fire off in the distance, reminding me of why I'm bedding these two beauties. I can feel them both twist in the direction of the gunfire, so I raise Ember two into the air, pinning her between my body and the ceiling, while I go to town eating even more vigorously Ember one's glittery womanhood.

Neither decide to fight me, and both give up on any notion of investigating the gunfire. I spend the next ten minutes thrusting Ember two up and down with my hips while bringing Ember one to orgasm over, and over, and over. They scream and moan and quiver, until they both eventually pass out from sheer exhaustion and delight.

I very carefully place Ember one's unconscious body down on the table next to me, then lift Ember two off from my still firm tree trunk and place her on the desk, back down, where I was just lying.

Before I leave the room, I crush their rifles and damage their control panel, just to make sure they can't hurt us and can't alert anyone else to our presence once they come to. I start to wonder why they would station two insanely hot women here at this post, as it can't be a coincidence. Maybe their thought is if someone was escaping, they couldn't escape the beauty and sexuality of these two, buying time for backup to arrive.

I cover up their naked bodies with an emergency blanket I find with the first aid kit, then make my way back into the tunnel. I fly down the corridor to where I let my clothes and throw them on hastily, then hurry back to the gang to catch up with them.

As I reach the end of the long corridor, I find a large metal door that's been pried off its hinges, and about a half dozen unconscious guards lying on the ground. None of them appear to have been killed, thankfully, as the last thing we want is to end the life of some poor person just trying to keep bad guys from getting out.

I step into the doorway to find another corridor, only this one has cell after cell on either side, housing some of the worst criminals known to the galaxy. Many of them I put there myself, and

I make sure not to make eye contact so that they don't know it's me.

Looking down toward the end of the corridor, I see the rest of the gang, and I see someone I've never met before, but have seen countless times on TV: Montgomery Israel. It's weird, because at first glance you would never assume he was one of the smartest and most notorious people in the galaxy. He just looks like some bald middle-aged guy. He's fit, I'll give him that, but he just appears unexceptional.

In movies and TV shows, usually the villain has some sort of calling card. Usually it's an ableist stereotype, unfortunately, where the villain has a scar over their eye, or a patch of skin on their face that was burnt either with acid or fire. Or sometimes they walk with a limp or require a comfort animal like a fluffy cat that they stroke due to their anxiety. Sometimes they wear an eye patch, or have a hook for a hand, or some other equally offensive trope. Montgomery Israel is just some guy you wouldn't probably pick out of a lineup of six people if you had five guesses. He looks like a math teacher.

"Dick, did you take care of the guards?" asks Knob as I come strolling up.

"I did. Over, and over, and over again," I say.

I look over at Nunya, who is a few feet further back from Israel than the others. I can't imagine how much restraint it's taking her not to punch a hole clean through the fucker.

"I can't imagine how much restraint it's taking you not to punch a hole through Israel right now," I say to Nunya. She grinds her teeth, ignoring my comment completely. "Anyway, did you find out Tiffany's location?"

"No, he's refusing to tell us until we're all onboard our ship and off-planet," says Whip.

"Fine. Israel, if I pulled both of your arms off and started to beat you to death with them, would you give us Tiffany's location?" I ask.

"Just get me out of here, *Dick*, and I'll tell you where she is. No need for violence at this point," says Israel. I don't know why he had to put so much emphasis when he said my name. What a jerk.

I grab onto one of his arms, Knob grabs the other, and we start escorting him back the way we came in.

48

"I'm really looking forward to seeing each of you being hunted like vermin once it becomes common knowledge that you broke me out of jail," says Israel.

"You know, I've been wondering about that part, how you're going to let everyone know what we've done," I say.

"Oh, that's easy, but you'll have to find out for yourselves. If I told you now, you might do something idiotic to try to prevent it. I don't take chances with anything. So far, you've proven yourselves quite easy to outmaneuver. Giving away my secrets can only lower my chances for success," says Israel.

"Interesting. Most super villains tend to ramble on about their plans, bragging about how smart they are, what lengths they went to avoid detection, that sort of thing," I say, as we pass by the two hot unconscious guards.

"First, I'm not a villain, just someone who appreciates power and control. Control over time itself. It's not based on greed, just an intense desire to survive at all costs. As for the common trope of monologuing, I don't let my ego get in the way of the mission. Egotism is a character flaw that no truly exceptional person has," says Israel.

"So, you consider yourself a truly exceptional person?" I ask, as we pass by the automated sentry guns.

"Ah, there's the rub, for if I say that I am, I show that I have an ego, thus marking me a hypocrite, or at the very least self-deluded. And if I don't, I'm being disingenuous, because I'm acutely aware of my own intelligence," says Israel. "Instead, I choose to say nothing. I won't be goaded into simple-minded arguments."

"Oh, of course not. Your reputation precedes you. We know just how intelligent you are. And you're right, you've been a step ahead of us the entire way, to the point where you had to leave breadcrumbs for us to follow. I admit, if it hadn't been for your assistance, we may never have determined it was you behind the entire thing," I say.

"You think flattery will ingratiate you with me? I see through you, Mr. Blowhard," says Israel.

"It's Detective Blowhard," I reply.

"Not for much longer, I suspect. Surely, once you're outed as one of the people who freed the most dangerous person in the galaxy you'll be stripped of your detective's license," says Israel.

"For certain. But until then, I'm still Detective Blowhard to you, asshole," I say.

"It sounds like you're the one with the ego, Mr. Blowhard," says Israel.

"You know, as much as I like Tiffany, and the President, there's a possibility that my consideration for them won't outweigh my hatred for you anymore. I've been known to accidentally kill perps from time to time. Accidentally," I say.

"Your empty threats and false bravado have no effect on me, Mr. Blowhard," says Israel, as we pass by the two guards with their disabled mechs.

"Why do you think you know me so well?" I ask.

"Because I've been studying you ever since you and Nunya became friends. You try so very hard now to be a good guy just to impress someone who recently betrayed you. Someone who you hate, yet you still try to prove you're worthy of her admiration. Another weakness, shared by so many. You subjugate yourself to someone else's opinion of you, and how you can make them like you. It's so deliciously and deeply pathetic," says Israel.

"I mean, that's a fair assessment. I agree, it is rather pathetic, when you think about it. But don't worry, I don't care about what Nunya thinks of me anymore. I learned my lesson not to trust her," I say.

"I learned that lesson long ago, obviously," says Israel. "Well, I suppose that's an unexpected bonus that I hadn't planned for, breaking up your friendship with Nunya, further damaging her, further isolating her. My revenge so far has been quite sweet."

"As smart as you are, it's not the smartest to say things like that within earshot of the person who most wants to kill you in the galaxy. Nunya could do it easily. Neither Knob nor I can stop her," I say.

"I'm not afraid of her either," says Israel. "She's so concerned about doing the right thing now, and feels so much guilt for what happened to her crew, that she'll do anything to balance the scales, including putting aside her hatred of me to save someone she's never met. Another character flaw, another weakness; guilt. Guilt has no meaning to truly exceptional people."

We finally reach and pass through the purple glowing bars, which now seem to be glowing considerably dimmer. We must have damaged their magic when we first cut a hole in them.

217

"It's amazing with your inferior minds that you were able to form a successful plan to rescue me," says Israel.

I crush his arm by gripping it very tightly. I hear the snap of bone as Israel cries out in pain.

"Yes, you can hurt me, but I heal very quickly. Violence is the only language you are truly fluent in, Mr. Blowhard. Violence nearly always is a sign of mental weakness," says Israel, as we finally reach the main doorway.

"Well, you've been a lot of fun to converse with," I say.

As we step through the doorways, several hundred camera drones are waiting for us outside, as well as a service robot with a microphone.

"Let me do all of the talking, or Tiffany will be executed immediately," says Israel.

Through gritted teeth I mutter, "fine."

Israel walks in front of the robot with the mic and starts talking.

"I just wanted to publicly thank Nunya Business, Detective Dick Blowhard, Detective Knob Johnson, and Whip Noodbottom for releasing me early from jail, despite the public's preference to keep me there. They broke in, destroying millions in security equipment, and knocking out guards, just to free me from my bonds. I cannot thank them enough."

Israel turns and looks at Nunya. "If you would please do the honor of smashing the cameras, now that the transmission has been made. They don't need to know anything more than they already do."

Nunya spits and hits Israel right in the face. "Fine, I'll just imagine that all of the camera drones are you." Nunya spends the next twenty seconds ripping the drones apart, as well as destroying the microphone robot, which I thought about naming "Mike," even though we already have a robot friend named Dour Mike. Get it? Mike? Mic? Because mic is short for 'microphone' and it's a homophone of 'Mike'? Jokes are always better when you have to explain them.

"Now what, you sonofabitch?" says Nunya

"Now we fly off in your spaceship. Once we're in deep space, and we've rendezvoused with my ship, I'll let you know where Tiffany is," says Israel.

I notice that Israel didn't wipe the spit off his face. He does have a surprising amount of self-control. If only that included control over his murderous intentions and extreme selfishness.

"We may as well fly at this point. Subtlety is out the window," says Knob.

I pick up Israel, Knob picks up Whip, and Nunya picks up Dour Mike, and we fly as fast as we're able to, back to the ship. A few SAMs, or Surface-to-Air-Missiles, launch from the ground at us, but Whip uses his laser eyebeams to destroy them before getting close enough to hurt.

After a brief moment, we reach the ship. I drop Israel from high enough in the air that when he falls, he crumples to the ground, making a sickening cracking and smooshing sound as his limbs shatter. He cries out, and I enjoy watching him writhe in pain as his bones knit themselves back together.

"Unh, so very childish, Mr. Blowhard," says Israel.

"Yeah, well, I'm just a big kid at heart," I say.

Before he's completely back to what passes for normal, I pick him up and carry him onto the ship while the others follow. We all make our way to the bridge, and Knob fires up the engines.

"Where's the rendezvous location?" asks Knob.

"Make your way to planet Omar," says Israel.

Knob taps away at the control console. Lifting off, we encounter more anti-ship weapons being fired at us, but thankfully Knob uses his new array of countermeasures to counter the measures. Or something like that.

We pass through the atmosphere and make our way back to the space asshole, but it appears to be shut off. Using her superior hacking skills, Nunya takes control of the space asshole and changes the destination to the Corgi system where planet Omar resides. Our ship passes through uneventfully, and Nunya hacks the portal on the other side to prevent any ships from following us.

"So where is your ship?" asks Knob.

"It should be here any moment," says Israel.

True to his word, which doesn't mean anything, a large ship appears, about ten times the size of ours. Knob rolls our ship sideways to it so that it can begin the docking procedures with Israel's massive vessel. And by massive vessel I mean huge ship, and not his penis. I just really want to be clear on that point.

Anyway, we make our way back to the cargo bay, which has already opened to allow Israel to step aboard. Before he does, he turns to us.

"Well, it really has been fun," says Israel, smirking the smuggest smirk I've ever seen. God, I hate him.

"Okay, tell us where Tiffany is," says Nunya.

"Not until I'm safely onboard my ship and I've undocked from yours. I'll tell you over comms," says Israel.

"How can we trust you?" asks Whip.

"Oh, I don't expect you to, but you don't really have a choice, now do you? But I will tell you, because I'm excited to see your reaction when I reveal where I've stashed her."

Knob and I both lurch forward, but Nunya holds our arms, preventing us from pummeling Israel.

"Let him go. He'll tell us. It sounds like he'll get some sick glee out of it. So let him go," says Nunya.

With that, Israel steps aboard his ship. He stares at us as the portal closes between us. A loud clanging sound vibrates the ship slightly as Israel's ship pulls away from ours. We all race to the bridge and Knob pulls up the comm link. As soon as we do, our main ship power shuts off but leaves the comms up.

"Israel, you fucking sonofabitch!" yells Nunya.

"You didn't think I'd make it easy for you to rescue Tiffany, did you? In fact, you've made it impossible to rescue Tiffany in time through your own short-sightedness," says Israel, through the video display.

"Where the fuck is she?" yells Nunya.

"It should have been obvious to you. She's in a shielded facility on planet Chetney in the Tarragon Five system," says Israel.

"We scanned it, and there are no lifeforms there," says Nunya.

"That's exactly what I wanted you to think. I shielded her presence, so that when you found out where she was, and that you had been so very close to finding her, my revenge would be even sweeter. And since you destroyed the portal in your escape, it'll take you years flying at lightspeed to reach her. She'll be long dead before you ever get there," says Israel.

"You fucking asshole! You motherfucking asshole!" screams Nunya.

"And here, as a bonus, I'm sending you the coordinates of her exact location, so that you can retrieve her corpse, eventually. And just so you know I'm not lying, I'm also sending you a camera feed of the room she's locked in. She should be able to survive a few weeks given the amount of food, water and air I've provided. But only for a few weeks. And both you and the President can watch her slowly die, knowing there's nothing you can do to rescue her," says Israel.

A video feed of Tiffany, locked in a cell appears on the screen, alongside Israel's unbelievably smug face. Nunya turns to Dour Mike and just says the word "now".

Our ship's power suddenly returns, while the lights go off inside of Israel's. The comms are still open, and we can see the confusion on his face.

"What, what is happening?" yells Montgomery Israel, now panicking.

"What should have happened a long time ago. It's over for you. We're going to rescue Tiffany, but first, I'm going to come over there and kill you," says Nunya.

"Wha-wait, how the hell did you take control of my ship? And you can't save Tiffany now. The portal's destroyed," says Israel.

"No, it's not," I say. "On a hunch, I told Nunya to hack the space asshole instead of having Knob destroy it. We sent the sloths to your home world instead. My guess is they've probably obliterated it by now."

Israel's face goes rigid, but he uses his self-control, the thing he prizes most in the world, and calmly asks, "how did you take control of my ship, and take back control of yours? And what will you do now that you're infamous and hated across the galaxy? At least I have that modicum of revenge to keep me company as you kill me."

"Oh, your little transmission? Yeah, that never got out. I won't go into details, but we've secretly had help all along. The galaxy doesn't know what happened back on Alphatraz, and they never will. We've beaten you, completely and utterly. Your plans of revenge have all been thwarted, Israel. And now I'm going to come over there and tear you into little pieces," says Nunya.

The look on Israel's face is priceless.

49

I follow Nunya back to the cargo hold, where she puts on a deep space helmet, then taps away at her PSD. I can hear the two ships docking against each other again. The door opens, and Israel surprisingly isn't waiting for us in the doorway.

"Uh, hey Nunya, how are you going to get back aboard our ship if you have no way to dock with it? Maybe tearing his ship apart isn't the wisest idea," I say.

"Don't worry, I've got this," says Nunya

I watch her walk aboard Israel's spaceship, close the door behind her, and undock.

Needing to see the action going on, I run back to the bridge, and Knob already has Israel's spaceship's cameras all setup for us to watch.

"This is gonna be good!" says Whip.

We watch as Nunya searches the ship and eventually finds Israel cowering inside of a cupboard in his ship's galley. She holds him up in the air by the neck and carries him to the cargo bay of Israel's ship. We see her tap away at a console on the ship, and it slowly turns toward the nearby star for this system.

Knob decides to follow her. Once we get close enough to the star that it's hard to look out of the windows of the bridge, Nunya stops Israel's ship and Knob stops ours. We watch as Nunya spends the next few minutes trashing the inside of the ship by flinging Israel's body around. It's kind of like that scene in The Avengers, where Hulk smashes Loki like a ragdoll. I wish I were above such things as torturing someone, but in this case, I admittedly take some glee in seeing his body broken and torn and damaged.

When Nunya seems to have let out enough rage, she aims Israel's ship's cargo bay at the star, opens it, flies through it with Israel, and throws him straight at it. Thankfully, Knob has a way of aiming some of the scanners on our ship to keep track of Israel's body as it hurtles toward the brightly burning white dwarf.

While we wait for his imminent demise, Nunya goes back aboard Israel's ship, seals the bay door, then reattaches to our ship. We make our way back to the cargo hold just in time to see

222

Nunya coming aboard. She takes her helmet off then crumples to the ground.

Knob undocks from the other ship then returns to the bridge. A moment later he speaks over the intercom, "Good news. According to the sensors, Montgomery Israel's body has been completely and utterly annihilated by the star. It's over, Nunya."

Nunya starts to cry, as she curls into a fetal position on the ground, hugging her knees for comfort. I come over and put a hand on her and she starts to cry harder. I just wait there with her for a while, as she lets out all the pain and guilt, as both Whip and Dour Mike go back to the bridge.

50

After what feels like an hour, but was probably more like ten minutes, Nunya has cried her last tear over the pain that Montgomery Israel had caused her. I'm glad she was able to finish him off once and for all, so that the constant nagging feeling that she has to look over her shoulder all the time will be gone. I know what it's like to constantly be on edge, waiting for the other shoe to drop, while just trying to get through your daily routine. It sucks.

Nunya pushes herself up into a standing position and makes her way to the conference room. I decide to follow her, as it seems like she's ready to talk. We both sit down in chairs across from each other, and I just kind of take in everything that she's been through, and everything that she's done to outsmart the smartest man in the galaxy.

"So, how did you do it? How did you get us help?" I ask.

"You remember back to when I had sex with Dour Mike, and you all thought that was fucking weird?" asks Nunya.

"Yeah. It was fucking weird," I say.

"Well, I was giving him a message to pass along to Blhack Glass so that they could help us along the way," says Nunya.

"How the hell did you give him a message without Israel knowing about it? He had cameras all over you."

"I put my eyes right up to Dour Mikes sensors, so that only Dour Mike could see them, and blinked the message out in Morse Code while I fucked him."

"Whoa, holy shit, that's brilliant! How the fuck did you manage doing two things like that at once?" I ask.

"Pure talent. Don't get me wrong, there were some dramatic pauses here and there, but I was eventually able to give Dour Mike all the information he needed to get Blhack Glasses' help," says Nunya.

"Well, as much as I'm still angry at you, and still haven't forgiven you, I am proud of you for what you accomplished. I'm glad that this chapter of your life is over. And now that Montgomery Israel is dead, and you outsmarted him, I think you can consider yourself the smartest person in the galaxy."

"Thanks, Dick. I genuinely couldn't have done it without you and the others. I will say, not everything is 100% wrapped up in a bow yet. We still need to rescue Tiffany."

"My guess is that's already underway."

And if by some luck, magic, or just coincidence, we hear Knob's voice over the intercom, "we're here."

Nunya and I make our way back to the cargo hold where Knob, Whip and Dour Mike are waiting for us.

"Way to go, Nunya," says Knob.

"Brilliantly done," says Whip.

"Even I'm impressed, and I haven't been programmed to feel that emotion," says Dour Mike.

"Thanks. Let's go rescue Tiffany," says Nunya.

Knob opens the cargo door, and he's parked about fifty feet from a small building, maybe the size of a small grocery store. There are no guards outside waiting for us, and no sentry guns. There are also surprisingly no traps. Despite purporting to have little to no ego, Israel's egotism made him so certain that everything would go according to plan that he didn't need to set up any defenses or booby traps to keep us out. In fact, the only thing meeting us outside of the building is a door. An unlocked door that Nunya pulls open.

We follow behind her into the building, where there's only a small hallway, and a single cell, the one we'd seen in the video feed.

"Dick? Is that you Dick?" yells Tiffany, who starts to cry tears of relief.

"It is, dollface. Let us get you out of there. Do you know if there are any traps in here?" I ask, as I use my super-vision to make sure that we won't accidentally trigger any booby traps.

"No, not that I know of. Just the lock on the cell, as far as I know," says Tiffany.

I crush the lock with my hand, pull the door open wide, and Tiffany jumps into my arms, holding onto me like I'm her savior. She really lets the floodgates open as she starts sobbing and snot-crying in my arms.

"Thank you for saving me, thank you all for saving me. It's been a nightmare being trapped here. I just want to go home."

"That's our next stop. We'll make sure you get home safe," says Knob.

"Thank you. Who are all of you?" asks Tiffany.

"Whip Noodbottom, at your service," says Whip, shaking her hand.

"Nunya Business, miss," says Nunya.

"Um, I'm Dour Mike," says Dour Mike.

"And you already know Knob Johnson, here," I say.

"Actually, we've never met," says Tiffany.

"Wait, what the hell, Knob! You said you fucked Tiffany, her sisters, AND her mom!" I say.

"No, I didn't," says Knob, sheepishly.

"You totally fucking did! You said that you had nailed them, and you don't even know them?" I say.

"Fine, I'll admit it, I actually am a virgin," he says, even more sheepishly.

"Hah, told you so!" says Nunya, looking at Whip. He hands her a fistful of credits.

"Wait, you guys had a side bet that I wasn't in on? No goddamn fair!" I say.

"You have enough money, moron," says Nunya.

"It's about the thrill of the game, not the money itself," I reply. "And besides, you're super rich too!"

"Yeah, tell it to my destroyed bar," says Nunya.

"Insured destroyed bar," I say. "Anyway, let's get out of here, just in case maybe Montgomery Asshole had some sort of contingency plan waiting for us."

We hurry back to the ship, and just as we're about to board, nothing happens. We step inside, and no bomb goes off. No armada appears ready to kill us. I look around just to make sure, but we're safe. We're finally safe.

I look up into the sky after letting Tiffany down onto the ground so she can walk onto the ship on her own. Knob pauses next to me while the rest of the gang enters the ship.

"Is everything okay, Dick?" asks Knob.

"I don't know. It just feels like maybe we missed something, and that things worked out too well. I remember Nunya saying that readers will hate it if things are too easy for us in my memoirs. Maybe this was too easy. None of our team died valiantly, we didn't have a final battle with the bad guy. Things just sort of worked out," I say.

"Well, sometimes that happens in real life. I'm not normally an optimist, but maybe we just got a little lucky. We did outsmart Israel, anyway."

"Yeah, I hope you're right. But can we just be on the safe side, and go back to his ship and blow it up? Just to be sure?"

"We can totally do that," says Knob.

226

"Oh, and Knob, don't tell Nunya. Let's keep my paranoia just between us, okay?"

"Sure, no problem, Dick."

We hurry inside the ship. Knob heads toward the bridge while I quickly run to the conference room where Nunya, Tiffany, Whip and Dour Mike are all sitting down, patiently waiting. I run back to the bridge. "Okay, everyone is here, let's get this thing flying."

"Cool."

Lifting into the air, I feel the familiar rumble of the ship taking off. We make our way back to the space asshole then back to the Corgi system where we left Israel's ship.

"Shit," says Knob after tapping furiously at his touchscreen.

"Wait, what is it?" I ask.

"It's gone. Israel's ship is gone," says Knob. "I'm picking up zero on the sensors."

"Are there any lifeforms in the general vicinity?" I ask.

"No, no lifeforms that I can see, but that doesn't mean anything. He was able to hide Tiffany from us before, so he could be preventing us from seeing him now," says Knob.

"But I thought we watched Nunya launch him into the sun."

"We did. Or at least we thought it was him."

"Maybe it was a clone, or a copy of him," I say.

"I dunno. Could also be that the ship was programmed to automatically go back to his home planet once he was aboard. We don't know if Israel survived or not. Should we tell Nunya?" asks Knob.

I think for a moment. "No, not today. We don't know if he's still alive, and we don't have a way of finding him right now if he still is. Let Nunya have today. We'll talk about things tomorrow, okay?"

"Sure Dick. I think that's fair. Let her have the victory until we know if we're still up against her greatest nemesis."

"Thanks, Knob. Sometimes you're less terrible than usual. And sorry you're a virgin," I say.

"Yeah, well, maybe you could put in a good word with Tiffany. She's pretty hot," says Knob.

"Yes, she is, and yes, I will. She'll teach you the ropes, and I'll ask her to be gentle."

"Nah, she doesn't need to be gentle. I can handle it."

"You say that now, but just you wait."

We both chuckle.

51

We fly back to the Blue House after a video call with the President, letting him know that we have Tiffany, and she's safe and alive. He seems incredibly relieved and lets us know that there's a celebration planned for us when we get there.
We're all a bit grimy, so we take turns using the ship's shower to get cleaned up. I don't fit inside of it particularly well, and for the first time I regret the fact we don't have Knob's ship. My guess is that he'd retrofitted his shower so that he could fit inside of it, since we are roughly the same size.

I also wash my clothes, as they're even worse off than I am. I put on my tux, because it's my go-to for any party, even the casual ones. I do have a reputation to uphold, and you can never dress too well for a party.

Nunya decides to wear her armor, which always looks heroic and regal, as if she's an intergalactic warrior-queen with a cape and crown. Whip and Knob both change into tuxes. Knob ends up wearing his white tux, while Whip wears a dark blue tux with black detailing that totally reminds me of Duckie in Pretty in Pink. It looks good on him, thankfully, as I don't know of many people who could pull that look off.

After passing through the security bubbles, we stop to say hello to General Admission briefly, then follow security down a few corridors and into a large ballroom. The President, First Lady, and all of their daughters are there, as well as many other friends and family. Tiffany runs and launches herself at them, and they catch her in a warm dogpile-like embrace. Apparently, Tiffany is a flinger, launching herself at people she cares about.

Several moments of tears and hugs later and the President breaks away, heading toward us. He gives each of us a very firm hug, including Dour Mike. Once the embracing is done, we're each handed a swag bag by one of his assistants.

The President goes up on stage, grabs the mic and starts talking. "Thank you to the heroes who brought our beautiful daughter Tiffany back. Knob Johnson. Nunya Business. Whip Noodbottom, Dick Blowhard, and their little mechanical friend..."

"Dour Mike!" yells out Dour Mike.

"Yes, Dour Mike. Our family will be forever indebted to yours. Inside your swag bags you'll find vouchers for fifty million burgmorps each, along with a box of the galaxy's finest cigars, and a stress ball that will hopefully help you emotionally recover from the ordeal you went through rescuing our darling Tiffany," says the President. "Also, any crimes any of you may have ever committed have been automatically pardoned, and your records wiped clean. All taxes have been considered paid in full."

"Wait," I shout, "this swag bag doesn't have a free t-shirt in it!" The crowd laughs at my terrible joke.

"We'll see what we can do, Dick," says the President. "Anyway, please accept these gifts to show the gratitude we feel toward you. Let it be known that these heroes from this day forward will be known as "The Presidential Investigation and Security Service.""

"Wait, our new team acronym is 'P.I.S.S.'," says Nunya, quietly, to just our team.

"We'll workshop a new name," says Whip.

The crowd starts clapping for us.

We spend the next few hours eating cake, drinking champagne, and having a good time. Eventually, the party ends, and we're escorted back to our ship. As we all sit down in the conference room, we look at each other and bask for a moment in our accomplishments.

"So, what next?" asks Knob. "Are we going to keep the band together?"

"I dunno. Should we start our own detective agency?" I ask.

"I'd be down for that," says Whip.

"After I spend some time making love to the new toaster ovens that Dick promised me, I might be willing to do that," says Dour Mike.

"I don't know. I have my home to get back to. My bar to get back to. And I still need to fix things between me and my best friend," says Nunya.

"That will take some time for sure," I say. "But it might go quicker if we work together. Hey, if you aren't interested in starting up a detective agency then that's okay too. Maybe we can contract you out for special jobs that require your particular set of skills. Would you be okay with that?" I ask.

"We might be able to work something out," says Nunya.

"Also, I'm pretty sure that's the first time you've referred to me as your best friend. I mean, I knew you were mine, but I wasn't sure if I was yours," I say.

229

"Well, I haven't always treated you like one. Now that Israel is dead, I'll try to focus my emotional energy on being a better friend to you."

I just smile and nod at her.

52

A few months later, once the dust has settled, Whip, Knob, Dour Mike and I, after a long day of detecting, make our way across the street from our newly built office to the recently refurbished bar that had been previously destroyed in a hail of blaster fire. As we walk in, the bartender and owner Nunya Business greets us.

"The usual, gents?" she asks in a silly southern drawl.

"I reckon so, pardner," I say, doing my best cowboy impression.

We sit down at our usual table in the corner, and she brings us four whiskies and a can of V-8 Motor Oil for Dour Mike, garnished with a celery stalk and green olives. Nunya refers to it as a 'Bloody Car Crash'. Not the best visual when you're drinking, but it seemed appropriate.

"Do any of you want food?" she asks.

"I'd like to buy our team a stack of sliders," I say.

"And I'll buy us some wings," says Knob.

"And I'll buy us some cheese sticks," says Whip.

"And I'll buy us some… nice crunchy gears," says Dour Mike.

"Coming right up," says Nunya.

As soon as we get our food, and take a few bites, the door to the bar opens, and in walks a dozen or so heavily armed and armored unicorns. The leader of the group grunts, "Detective Dick Blowhard?"

"Oh shit, here we go again," I say.

Read Dick Blowhard's further adventures in the upcoming book

Dick Blowhard 3: With a Vengeance

About the Author

If you'd like to know more about T. M. and his other books,
check out http://www.tmbrenner.com.

You can also find him on BlueSky as @TMBrenner,
on Facebook as Author T. M. Brenner,
and on GoodReads as T. M. Brenner.